FORGED

BECKY BANKS

Ha'ikū
Press

Published by:

Maui, Hawai'i | Portland, Oregon
www.haiku-press.com

Cover design by James T. Egan of Bookfly Design

beckybanksbooks.com

4th edition

ISBN: 978-09882614-0-2 (paperback)

ISBN: 978-0-9882614-1-9 (e-book)

ASIN: B009SX8GA6

FORGE (V.)

1. To create form through fire and hammer; to beat into shape.
2. To imitate someone or something else.
3. To form or make, especially by concentrated effort: to forge a friendship through mutual trust.

VERSE IV

This book is dedicated to every human who has wondered: Where are they now? What if...

ONE

THE MEMORIES FLICKER BY LIKE THE FRAMES OF AN OLD FILM. Unfocused and dark at the edges. A punch to his gut, to his face. The wall behind him in the yellowing kitchen seems to punch him as well. It slams against his back and smacks his head to the tabletop as the fist from his father throws it there. He's seven.

By ten he learns to dodge the fists, to know when tension in the apartment would erupt. Eleven, he has one foot out the door, has found a second life, a best friend. Twelve, he has already left home to live with his aunt. Twelve slides into fifteen and fifteen into freedom.

Freedom? It was never free.

The memories of that final day came unbidden, as they always did—and slippery. That day he was twenty-seven and holding the phone to his ear, listening to a foreign sound. His father's sobs echoed over the line; they begged him home. To please come, it was his mother... These sobs, from the man who met every sobering morning with a toast of his golden can of Olympia and every sunset with his fist in his wife's face.

Could the son have known then? He'd always ask himself that. Was there any way to know what his father had in store for him when he returned home, for his mother, for the man who was his father? The scars on his skin and the wounds within that had yet even to scar told him not to go, but he had unfinished business with the old man. He'd go, and maybe this time it would be different.

Nate opened the door to the dark apartment he'd once called home. It was after work, the sun had gone down, his boots were slick with the rain he had just come in from. They slipped on the linoleum floor. A smell rose up and enshrouded his body like a cloak. It clung to his nose and at the back of his throat, a tangy, rusty tincture of blood. Warm, as if it were being pulsed from the veins of a being. Automatically he reached for the light behind him, his stomach clenching, his mind telling him no. *No. NO!*

That was when the memory got slick. Even now his mind recoiled, and the details of that night faded back into the black mist.

Eva, he thought to distract himself. *Where are you now, Eva?* Her name rolled around in his mouth softly, whispered to no one. An entirely different set of emotions consumed him as his parents faded away once more. She was seven when he was ten, and she was there for him every time he showed up with a black eye or a new burn. She'd shown him his first fast car, and later he taught her how to fix them, to make them go faster. At sixteen she rocked his world in a way he would never recover from.

The years had passed like lightning after that day, each one spent with Eva more mind blowing than the next. But as everything in his life tended to do, that too would come to an end.

The pain, now cathartic, motivated, consumed him. His dark past closed up shop and faded away, leaving him with his future. *His* future, where he was in control.

TWO

The rain hammered down on the windshield as Jenny and I made our way to our recently discovered import garage. I had been relieved to find a BMW mechanic that wasn't too drunk or too deaf to hear that I just wanted the oil changed, not a forty-minute hollering hand-gesture session about how he wanted to replace my brakes. I'd bought the ten year old German sedan used and she was perfect—aside from needing regular repairs, which was like Jenny's alpaca yarn, costing me a mint.

Though my car was going to reap the rewards and I would come to blissfully claim at least partial credit for the mechanic find, Jenny and her precious Peugeot were technically the sole heroes in the discovery. On Monday, I'd been in my office ostensibly reviewing the recent shoot for July's cover, but really wallowing in the current state of my life. I knocked the old-school desk light to motivate it to work and thought of the fashion rag—particularly the office—I'd left in New York City. That office had been wide and luxurious—plush gray carpeting and dark paneling, furniture handpicked from a sleek and modern designer catalog—and I'd bitten and clawed my way to that corner palace thirty-four floors into the Manhattan sky in just seven years. Now I felt like I was perpetually crouching low under the Portland, Oregon, cloud cover. My fourth-floor office's midcentury décor had nothing to do with design resurgence; rather, it simply hadn't been touched since *Mad Men*'s inspiration had been reality. On top of that, I had chosen this new life and had a magazine to run, which included advertisers and subscribers who didn't care what my current office looked like. In other words, I had made my own worn-out bed, and I was having to work hard just to sleep in it.

Jenny, my *Rose City Review* assistant and sometimes guest writer, came waltzing in that morning and flopped down on one of the chairs in the semicircle in the middle of the office. "You would not believe what I found," she said smugly.

"What's that?" I bit on Jenny's bait.

"So you know how I've been on this trek to find the best import repair shop in the city, right?"

"Please tell me that your ancient Peugeot has found one," I said with a laugh and returned to my work, editing pen in hand looking at the next issue's cover choices.

"I did...and they do all years of BMWs and the mechanics are H-O-T."

I glanced at her out of the corner of my eye. "So you asked one of them out with your oil change? Bold." I said then held up a cover option. "Does her skin tone seem abnormally red to you in this one?"

"No and no. I'll probably work up the gumption, though. This one guy is totally my type."

I gave her a distracted smile, the model on that cover was definitely too red.

"The head mechanic actually owns the place and he's not really hot per se, but he has that air about him that I thought would be perfect for you."

"Perfect for me, huh," I repeated. "And what's that?" I asked as I put down the cover art.

"Unavailable, uninterested, sort of dark—with a past, you know?

But I imagine that with him you sort of feel like you could take over the world."

I arched a brow at her. "Quite the brief first encounter." I looked back down. "If you're right, you just described *complex* to a T, my friend."

Jenny laughed, like a chiming bell tower, loud and ringing. "Yes! That's totally it. Anyway—didn't you say your door has a leak?"

I had dropped my car off the next afternoon, leaving the keys with their front desk woman, who wore something in the shade similar to safety orange and was the same age as my father, and not a single luscious or brooding mechanic was in sight. There were four work bays, from which noise screeched, and a parking lot full of average Euro cars, except for two. They were a little red family car and a black two-door monster. Though I was unsure of its heritage from a distance, however the black monster screamed: *fast*. Something I once knew a lot about.

Now, THROUGH THE SHEETING RAIN, FROM THE COMFORT OF the dry interior of Jenny's car, I saw the watery glow of my car idling, parking lights on, directly in front of us, beside the main office. I hoped the water seal on the rear door was indeed fixed; otherwise, my baby was now officially a fish bowl.

"Wanna borrow my umbrella?" Jenny asked.

"No, I'm good—I'll just run inside. I have to say"—my hand on the door handle—"I'm impressed already that they have the car running. I bet the heater's on too. "We'll see after I get the bill if I'm still appreciating the attention to detail. See you tomorrow and thanks for the ri—"

Jenny grabbed my arm. "Omigod."

"Wha-?" I said, leaning to the side, trying to see what had made her gasp but at that moment only my car and its exhaust and lights were visible through the sheet of water on the windshield. Then the wipers cleared away the water, and I noticed what had made her gasp.

He stood tall in slate-colored work pants and an open rough-hewn jacket with the company logo embroidered over his heart. Leaning against the building under the scalloped awning, he smoked a cigarette like it was the last one he'd ever have. His features were shadowed under the awning, but it could have been pitch-black and I'd still have known who he was. And he was looking straight into the car—and into my eyes.

"Lord..." I said like an oath under my breath.

"I know, right?" Jenny said, misinterpreting me.

"Wish me luck," I whispered to her and to no one and got out of the car.

Nathaniel Vellanova pushed away from the wall and in one smooth movement opened the massive umbrella that had been leaning next to him and strode toward me.

Behind me I heard Jenny reverse out the driveway, leaving me to my past.

THREE

Nathaniel Vellanova stubbed his cigarette out and closed the distance in a few strides, effortlessly getting up in my space, covering us both with the umbrella.

"Let's get this over with," he said, the hint of nicotine still on his breath. "This is your car, and this is the work order for the job that was done. Rear passenger door seal was leaking—it's fixed." He flicked the paper in his hand at me. "I did the work personally. There's no charge, and here are the names of two other mechanics in the area that I recommend for BMW owners."

I could feel warmth rise up in my cheeks, making me forget that it was raining and I should have been chilled.

My mouth opened and shut without my permission; my mind flooded with questions and observations. There was a change in the boy I knew—that was, he was a boy no longer. His strong Italian heritage was displayed in his high, wide cheekbones, firm jaw, and jet-black brows and lashes around chocolate-and-whiskey colored eyes. His long lashes had always made him a pretty boy, the kind who got his hair ruffled by old ladies, the kind little girls would befriend, thinking nothing of showing him what was under their dresses. Most unsettling were his eyes: When we were together many lifetimes ago, they communicated everything that his mind was thinking. Now, they were carefully in check, challenging even in their impenetrability, and yet I still couldn't find my voice—and that was a problem I rarely experienced.

I looked down at the paper in my hand, cold complete text detailing parts and labor, a total of zero at the bottom.

"I'm not sure what to say, Nate... Thank you... I—"

"Not interested in what you have to say, and I don't want your thanks. Good-bye, Eva." He turned, taking the umbrella with him, and wrenched open the front office door, tossing the collapsed umbrella to the side.

The rain drizzled cold and wet down my neck and slithered down my back. I stood alone and dazed in the parking lot as I recovered from colliding into my past. After years away from here, I had learned to successfully control my words, making them say courteous and rational things. But in my old world, Nate made me a very irrational person.

I walked. Wrenching open the front door, in imitation of the way Nate had, I crossed the linoleum floor, my two-piece business suit and hair dripping but my heels clicking satisfyingly, echoing against the sparsely decorated room.

"Ma'am!" said the woman behind the massive welcoming desk, startling me, her expression one of mild bewilderment.

I briefly registered her as the woman I'd dropped my car off with. Today her dark skin was adorned with jewels that matched her hot-pink nails and crisp blazer, which covered her ample bosom. It was immediately apparent that I'd just stepped into her territory. Nate could run the things in the shop, but she ran everyone who came through the front door.

Ignoring her, I strode for the closed door that I would bet my next paycheck led to Nate.

Despite her age and size, the older woman moved like lighting, shooting out from behind the desk, putting one hand up. Her pink nails were like a warning flare in my face. "Oh no, unh-uh. You are not going back there."

"I just need to speak to the owner."

"Who are you?"

"Does that matter?"

She raised her eyebrows at me. "The only time I've seen that man put his fist through the wall was when we first opened and someone stole half our shiny new equipment. He came right in, closed that door, and beat the tar out of that wall. Got three holes in it, and now? It's probably got ten. Who the hell are you and where the hell in his past did you come from because you don't look anything like the women he takes up with now." She placed her other hand on her wide hip.

I squinted. "Thanks? And that is where I came from, his past. Now if you'll excuse me, I have a couple things I'd like to say to him to bring him into the present."

"Well now, look who is handing out candy at the angry parade." She said, looking me up and down, "Don't give me your sass. If you go back there, where do you think that'll get you? Because I can tell, you got that look on you that says you're about to do something that you'll regret later."

"I doubt I'll regret it," I said, moving to the side.

She moved with me. "Not in my office." She nodded toward the front door behind me. "Go, while I still like you." She leaned, keeping part of her weight in front of me, to pull a card out of the holder. A pen came with it, and she scrawled something across the top of the card before handing it to me.

I looked down at the card. It was Nate's business card, and the woman had added in tidy handwriting what I guessed was Nate's personal cell phone number.

"What's this for?" I asked, and she used my distraction as time enough to put a hand at my back, ushering me to the door. "He's right in there; I don't need his number."

"Oh yes, you do. If this is still important in the morning, you can call him and talk about it."

She opened the door for me and effectively pushed me out.

"Give him a call in a day or two, and don't sit in that damn car waiting for him." She shut the door in my face, throwing the deadbolt and letting down the blinds.

FOUR

THE DREAM CAME TO HIM AGAIN.

He was ten, standing on the sidewalk under the tall fir trees that stood between the road and the apartment complex that he and his parents lived in. His pops getting drunk and busting up his mom. Some days he thought his mom's mouth was going to get her killed. She never seemed to know when to shut up, know when Pops was on a bender, know when it was better to let him sleep it off, not shake him awake to tell him what a lousy piece of shit he was. Or what she graduated to doing, leaving little hatch marks on his arm with the kitchen knife to remind him that he'd gotten so drunk she could do that and he'd not wake up.

Eva, three years his junior, ran up to him. All skin and bones, knobby knees and stick arms; Marvin's daughter. He felt his pulse quicken. She was a weird girl; she was like a guy, his best friend. Her nails were dirty with paint or grease; she had smudges on her face and arms, bruises on her shins from playing rough.

"Hey!" Eva yelled. "Where do you think you're going?" She skidded to a stop just in front of him.

"Home, dumb ass," he said nonsensically, since he was standing outside his apartment building. "Why don't you go play with dolls and leave me alone."

She cocked her head to one side and looked at him, as if she knew he didn't mean the words he'd spoken.

"I'm not a dumb ass—you're the dumb ass. You forgot to tell me you were leaving."

"I don't have to tell you shit."

"My dad says not to swear."

"Yeah well, still, I don't have to tell you anything."

"I know, but I meant to give you this before you left," she said, and in the dream everything became slow, his subconscious lingering. In his dream, he replayed those handful of seconds when her skinny arms wrapped around his waist in a hug. When she held tightly to him, squeezing him in his dirty white tank top and torn jeans, careless of who saw, careless if even he cared.

After a while he felt his hands come around her—the feeling so foreign to him but also so good. Happiness roared through his system, making him feel light-headed and something else that he'd not felt but a handful of times in his life up to then. It was the feeling of being loved—he would learn later.

She stepped back from him, looking up at him; Nate's voice cracked when he asked, "What the hell was that for?"

Her face screwed up tight. "Dummy. It's your birthday."

The dream faded as Nate woke slowly to the orange glow of the city lights pouring in through the floor-to-ceiling windows of his studio apartment atop an old refurbished brick flour mill.

He sat up and scrubbed his face and double-checked that he'd sent his date home already. His bed stood alone in the middle of the cavernous space. The developer sold it to him at half the cost when the housing bubble burst. It was considered unfinished, with no interior drywall covering the brick or ceiling lower than the one twenty feet above him and open to all the industrial HVAC. Not that Nate cared—the view was good and the apartment was in a central location, just down the street from the new nightclub he helped get off the ground, Festivál, and just over the bridge into the east side of the city was his garage. The hardwood floors still shone and the wide-screen against the far brick wall was well used, but the gourmet kitchen gleamed with unused appliances.

Nate lay there, not knowing what had pulled him from the dream or what had made him dream of her again.

Only, he did, of course. Seeing her again that day had him reburying her in his mind, only his subconscious was putting up a good fight against that.

His phone chirped. Reaching over, he grabbed his phone off the floor and slid his finger across the screen. Two unread e-mails. The first, which had probably woken him, was from European Forged Parts, and the second was from the district attorney's victim advocate department.

Fully awake now, heart hammering in his chest, Nate clicked the alert. It was simple text, an automatically generated electronic notif-ication that said one Butch R. Vellanova had been released on the third of the month. If there were questions, Nate could contact the issuing district attorney's office at the information below.

Nate felt his palms go slick. He knew Butch was coming up for parole and that good behavior and crowded prisons meant early release was possible, but he had also been told it was highly unlikely. And now the unlikely was done, and his father—the man who had sliced his mother to death—was out.

FIVE

JENNY FOUND ME THE NEXT MORNING WITH TWO LATTES AND something scandalous in a white paper bag that was showing grease stains already.

Even though I was seated at my computer—had been for a full two hours already—my brain was focused on one single thought: Nate.

"Please tell me one of those"—I pointed at the coffee cups—"is for me, and that bag is filled with doughnuts."

Jenny gave me a wicked grin. "Why, yes, it is! You look like you didn't get much sleep last night," she said, wiggling her eyebrows at me. "Care to spill the beans, you vixen?"

I gave an indelicate snort and took a sip of the hot beverage. The milky caffeine did wonders, and I let my eyes close to savor the heat in my hands and the energetic warmth settling into my belly. The day was a reflection of my mood. Through the moisture-tinged old windows behind me, the city was bathed in cloud cover while the rest of the nation was enjoying their summer. Sunshine and seasonable warmth, the early morning news said as it showed children everywhere but here playing in sprinklers.

"So?" Jenny pressed. "I only have a few minutes before I have to jump into an eight-thirty meeting."

"I know him," I said, looking at her. That, at least, was a place to start.

Jenny plopped down on a chair after depositing a doughnut on my desk, its soft body exhaling powder over everything. I touched my finger to my tongue and began cleaning up around it.

Jenny popped the lid from her coffee and blew on it before taking a sip. "What do you mean, you know him? As in, now you know him?" she asked with a smirk.

"As in, I *know* him."

"From New York?"

"No. Not New York. I know I said that I was originally from there."

"Yeah, Manhattan. Explains your shoes."

I paused for just a moment. "That's not true." I glanced under my desk at my very un-Portland platform peep toe heels. "Well, it does explain my shoes, but I didn't grow up in Manhattan or even New York State. I spent all my years after college there, but I wasn't raised there."

Jenny sat staring at me. "Uh, how many people know this?"

I waved my hand dismissively. "That doesn't matter. What I'm saying is that I lived in New York for a long time, long enough to basically forget where I was from. But I grew up here in Portland. I came back to stay with my father last year because he's sick. I know Nate from much earlier in my life," I said, feeling like my words were cramming at the back of my mouth.

"His name is Nate?" she asked, taking it all in stride. Very good stride, surprisingly.

"Yes, and I apologize for deceiving you Jenny," Thinking of the women I knew in Manhattan, I was expecting more scathing condescension at not being in on the full scoop.

Jenny just shrugged. "You have your reasons, I suppose. You're sort of a private person, Eva, and you're my boss. Seriously, Eva, it's not like you've done anything bad—so you've covered up that you were born and raised here. I'm sure you have your reasons."

I smiled at her, "Do you want a raise?"

"Can I have one?"

"No."

"Bitch," she mumbled into her coffee.

"Ha! I earned that." I said then, "After your meetings this morning let's talk over lunch. I'm taking an early day to take my dad to his chemo appointment this afternoon, but need to go over projects with you."

"Deal. Let's go to that spaghetti joint just down the street—I brought my knitting, and they have nice booths."

I paused as I reached for my coffee again, "Ah . . . Jenny, if you got any weirder you would *be* Portland."

SIX

OK, I was right in thinking that's really weird. How are you supposed to eat and not drop one of your stick things," I said to Jenny at lunch as I took a long pull on the robust homemade noodles, which were slathered in meat sauce and dusted with freshly grated Parmesan.

Jenny was working her needles like a knitting Olympian.

"Look, I only have a couple weeks before summer really starts here, and then I can't wear knitted anything."

"Yeah, but then you make booties and blankets for the neonatal units at the hospitals. Seriously, Jenny, how are you still single?"

"I thought that was obvious," she said, putting her needles aside to tackle the creamy Alfredo sauce that was smothering the wide egg noodles on her plate.

"Tell me what that tastes like," I said, pointing my fork at her plate. "Have we already featured this place?"

"Like a zillion times. But maybe should feature it in a PDX Eats e-mail?" She rolled her eyes heavenward in ecstasy over the bite of food in her mouth. "Sooo good!"

I agreed. And until I'd seen Nate at the mechanic's shop the day before, I had even managed to ignore the fact that Nate's aunt ran the joint with her husband—Mario's was that good a place.

As though reading my thoughts, Jenny butted in. "Tell me why you guys broke up."

"And how is it that you knew we were together?"

"I'm a mind reader," she said and sucked up a stray noodle. "Give me a break, Eva—I might be ugly, but I'm not stupid."

"When you say stuff like that, I seriously doubt your IQ. You're not ugly—and I'll kill anyone who begs to differ. Just try." I pointed my fork at her.

"Fine, whatever. I had some time after the meeting to do some Google stalking and found out his full name. And other stuff."

I choked on my spaghetti. Then just stared at her. When I knew Nate, he was far from a good boy, and a simple Google search would tell you just about everything, since his name was on a lot of documents that were public record.

"I saw that you guys went to the same high school. He graduated a couple years before you."

I felt a sliver of relief.

"Then, it looks like six or seven years after you graduated high school, he jumped off the deep end?"

"It was six, and yes, he did."

"Is that when you guys broke up?" she said, homing in on the target like a heat-seeking missile.

"Yes."

"Eva," she said soothingly, "you can't blame yourself if he flipped out; that's his deal."

"I don't blame myself; it's just that the situation isn't that simple. Though life isn't that simple. Anyway, this," I said, pointing my fork at my marinara, "is delicious."

Jenny was undeterred. "OK, well, either way, you guys broke up. If that's an excuse for a guy to jump off the deep end, my cousin Margaret should be in jail for manslaughter for life." She shoveled another forkful of noodles into her mouth. "Seriously."

"Yes, but it wasn't cut-and-dried like that." I couldn't change subjects on that note. "We were best friends, and that's how I loved him. It got complicated. He wanted...he wanted something I couldn't give him then."

Jenny had the fork halfway to her mouth again. "Go on."

I shook my head. "We had a falling out when I went to start my internship at *Vogue*." I put my fork down to wipe my damp palms on my pants.

Jenny just watched me, her fork still midair.

"Excuse me," I said, feeling a little sick. I had the sudden urge to stick my head under cold running water.

In the restaurant bathroom, I ran cold water over my hands and patted my face. I stared at the woman in the mirror. Dark, nearly black, hair pulled into a bun at the nape of her neck. She was a driven, and unapologetic businesswoman—who was about to have a category four meltdown in a restaurant bathroom.

"You're fine," I said to the reflection. "It's nothing you can't handle so suck it up, Rodgers." And took a couple deep breaths and reminded myself that the past was that, past. That nothing I did now could reconcile that. I gathered my wits, dried my face, adjusted my makeup and clothes, and headed back out.

"Aiyee! I thought that was you!" a woman's voice squealed as I stepped out of the bathroom. Her voice carried in that back hallway, which connected the bathrooms, kitchen, and dining room. In the next moment I found myself being embraced by her, then held out at arm's length.

"Flora," I said and smiled at her. "Glad to see you." I lied for the first time to Nate's aunt and godmother.

"Come," she said, leading me out the restaurant's backdoor.

SEVEN

FLORA LEANED AGAINST THE OUTSIDE WALL OF MARIO'S AND LIT a cigarette as we made small talk. She took a long drag. The constant breeze carried the smoke away. Her auburn-red hair, scrunched in wild curls reminiscent of 1984, was as vibrant as it had been when I saw her last, six years before. She clicked her index fingernail against her thumbnail as if dislodging something there, something I remembered that she did right before launching into a story. And memory proved right.

"He's a good boy—you know." She gave the cigarette a flick before resting her elbow on her hip, her other hand cradling it. "Always was."

It was an old argument. Was Nate a good boy or bad? The cops said bad. Flora said good. I'd lost the right to vote. I just gave her a placating smile and tried not to look at my watch as I too leaned against the cinderblock wall.

"I don't think you know that," she said, as if I'd responded in the negative. "I knew when he came to us that he was good, just messed with..." she said, taking another drag, letting the implications of Nate's childhood abuse be said in her silence. "I don't think I ever told you the story of when he first came to us. You know, we had him for only two weeks when it happened."

It took me a moment before I realized I didn't know which Nate story she was about to start.

"The boys had all gone out, Lou was at the restaurant, and Nathaniel and I had just gotten back from the grocery store. I told him to go to the bathroom and wash up. We were going to have a snack—a treat for just him and me. Chocolate chip cookies—he'd picked them out. Mother Mary, it took him a long time to choose which box of cookies he wanted. Like it was the first time anyone had asked him that," she said, smiling at that memory. "Well, I was in the kitchen, had my head in the refrigerator, when he started screaming." She closed her eyes then and took a deep breath. "Screaming, and crying, and something else; it sounded like something was getting torn to death—something plastic. I ran to the living room doorway and stopped—right there, dead in my tracks. Nathaniel had grabbed one of the sofa cushions and was taking to it like it was the devil itself. Little fists beating it, pulling on it, screaming, like from here," she said, gesturing to her middle. "It tore my heart in two. But I just watched him—I held myself back—he'd never cried until then, and I knew, just knew, that it was coming. So I let it go. Until," she said, holding up one well-manicured finger, "I figured out what he was doing. All our furniture was like his mama's—you know, the kind with plastic on the cushions to protect the fabric? He was trying to get it off. Attacking the plastic," she said, taking a deep thoughtful drag on her cigarette. She removed a bit of tobacco from the tip of her tongue before continuing. "It represented her. And that apartment, all those memories. So we tore all that plastic off, right then and there. The last day I ever saw that stuff—and the first day of a goddamn dirty house. But I tell you what, we threw it all in the trash and ate cookies. Never had another outburst like that again."

She was silent as she finished the rest of her cigarette, letting what she said sink in.

"Smart boy, that one. Owns a fancy automotive shop on the east side—doing real well, now. You seen him since you've come back?" she asked as she stubbed out the butt in a bucket of kitty litter and then tossed it into an open Dumpster.

I smiled at her, not wanting to lie again. I said, "Not really."

"Not really," she repeated, her keen eyes seeing more that I wanted to share, "What does that mean?"

"Just that I've been busy with work . . . And things."

"You should go see him. I think he'd like to see you. It's been so long and you two were always together."

"Yes. Well, I don't think he wants to see me."

"Pshh, how do you know if you don't go to see him though, eh? Unless, you did?" She said and eyed me closely.

"I, well, let's just say it's a hunch." I said thinking of earlier, then, "I really should be going. I left my coworker at the table."

Flora hugged me again and gave me a double cheeked kiss before we promised to keep in touch and see each other more soon.

The story she'd told was new and added to the mountain of guilt that I had recently tried re-submerging. I felt uncharacteristically cold and wanted desperately to flee.

I found Jenny and left shortly with to-go boxes in hand.

EIGHT

THE CHEMO ROOM WAS BUSY, NURSES TAKING VITALS OR
hooking newcomers up to the various chemical cocktails. The liquids
hung in clear sacks from metal rods at every station. It was a large
room. White linoleum flooring, bright fluorescent lights. Monet
lookalikes on the wall trying to make the space bright and cheerful
when in fact every person not in uniform, young and old, was
plugged into death juice. All these people were taking themselves to
the brink of death so that they could live.

My father had once been a strong man, liked fast cars and loose
women—then he met my mom, so the story goes. He retained his
affinity for cars, but after that, he only loved one woman. My
mother got sick when I was very young and died before I could
really know her. Dad raised me as though I were a boy—I was in
the body shop every day he was. I learned about cars, learned to
love them as much as he did, and learned how to freehand a
pinstripe down the side of a '57 Chevy pickup by the time I was
sixteen. I saved my pennies and drove Dad's second wife—the '57
Chevy—in every neighborhood parade. Until the year I did a
burnout to show off for a group of boys (yes, Nate was in the group),

and my Chevy rights were revoked. After college, my career took first place over everything else, until Dad called with the news that he had cancer. I shuffled things around at work, and when the opportunity to run a magazine in Portland came up, I landed it because I had to. I told myself that I landed it because that was the logical next step in my life. Come home and settle down—don't think, just move.

Each time I took him to his chemo sessions, I wondered, now that I'd come home and done my "settling," what was next? My father was the only family I had left and, though he was still strong enough, still walking upright, even if with a cane since starting chemo, he still had cancer. Luckily it was the cancer that has a 90 percent cure rate, but it was cancer nonetheless, requiring him to get his arm stuck and death dripped into him for hours.

"So, what do you want to watch, Dad?" I asked after he settled in and the personal LCD screen was pulled forward.

"Nah, I want to talk to you. Haven't seen you in a while."

"Dad. We live together. I see you every day; what are you talking about?"

"Something's up, something's different."

I looked at him. He looked great since I dress him every time we leave for chemo. He says he hates it, but he has more of a strut in his step. Today's swank smoking sweater in harbor gray over a baby-blue shirt with snazzy slacks and leather loafers—you'd never know he didn't own a multimillion-dollar home in the West Hills. Of course, at that very moment, his sweater was pulled off and a shirtsleeve was rolled up to allow for the IV, and he was giving me a pleading look.

"Fine," I said, slipping into the upholstered chair next to him.

"Work troubles?"

"I wish. Those I can handle."

"Man troubles?"

"Not really," I said, stretching my legs out, trying out the full comfort of the flower-printed visitor's chair. "I saw Nate the other day."

"Ah, Nate," he said knowingly. "He's come a long way, you know."

"Apparently."

"Where'd you see him?" he asked, ignoring my snark.

"One of my coworkers...Jenny—do you remember Jenny?"

"Yes, I'm not senile, you know. Cute girl. Knits a lot."

I focused on the arm of the chair, picking off miniature fuzz balls and flicking them to the floor with laser-like precision, while I told him how I'd come to reconnect with poor, misunderstood Nate.

"And?" my dad prodded.

"And it went over like a lead balloon. He fixed my car for free, gave me the name of two other mechanics for future reference, and sent me packing."

We were silent for a while, my father taking in everything I'd said. He knew our history, knew Nate's history, intimately, since early on he'd always been Nate's first phone call from jail.

"You'll pick that chair apart if you keep at it like you are."

I stopped picking and splayed my hands on the armrests.

"I saw him the other day too."

"Really?" I asked, looking over at him.

"Yeah, well, I guess now that I think about it, it wasn't the other day, must have been last year sometime." I smiled at my dad's view of time now that he was retired. "He had gotten a load of his stuff stolen and gave me a call. He knew how to take care of things but was a little hazy on the details of how to go about it without breaking the law. I helped him with the police reporting and things." Dad paused, then chuckled. "Asked me how I used to keep *him* out of my really expensive stuff. I told him he has to give robbers a little something—you keep everything under lock and key, they'll keep trying until they get what they want. So you have to write a police report once a year—what does it matter as long as you don't lose it all? Which is what had happened to him."

"Oh," I said. "Doesn't he have an alarm or something? I hope he had insurance."

"Hadn't gotten installed yet. He had insurance, but it didn't matter—all his stuff got returned to him after a couple days. I swear, that kid's got great karma. Or whatever you call it."

I snorted in disgust. "Karma, sure. He knew who jacked his sh—"

"Language."

"Who stole his *things*, and they found their way back home so that kneecaps were kept intact."

"He's not like that anymore, Eva Lynn." My father said, using my middle name purposefully. "And I believe his days of trying to forget you are over."

"That's great, just super. Let's not talk about him. Let's talk about you, Dad. So, what's new on television?"

"Ha-ha, don't take a stab at me, daughter, just because you still haven't faced your past and forgiven yourself."

"Seriously?" I stood. "I'll be in the car."

"Eva Lynn Rodgers, don't you leave here mad."

I gave him a false toothy grin. "I'm not mad; I'm so happy. See? Call me when you're done."

Dad harrumphed and straightened in his chair. "I'm fixing up the Chevy so when I'm done with all this, I can take her for a ride. I'm thinking of starting up another shop—no one does paint work like we used to do—nothing real big, just enough to offset social security checks, you know?"

I sat back down again. "A new business? Dad, I'm sure there is someone in the city that can do the work we used to do," I said, pulling out my phone to search for one. "And what's with the Chevy? It was running not too long ago."

This launched us into a two-hour debate on what was really wrong with the Chevy and why it really wouldn't run. He answered all my suggestions with: "She's more complex than that."

Right.

"You know, Dad," I said as we merged onto the freeway after the chemo appointment, the sedan pulling easily into traffic, her German motor silently roaring us effortlessly home in quiet leathery comfort, "if you moved the Chevy into a climate-controlled storage facility, I could keep this car in the garage, and she wouldn't be in the shop so much."

"Eva Lynn, this car is that. A car. It takes you to point A and to point B. You should be able to leave it outside."

"Oh-ho! And this from the man who married a '57 Chevy—you want to talk about 'just cars,'" I said, making air quotes.

"Hands on the wheel! We're going seventy!"

"Sorry," I said, looking heavenward for a second. "Dad, seriously, though, have you thought about the fact that having her in climate-controlled storage would keep her running?"

I heard him grumble, "You know, you can move out anytime you want; I don't need you at the house. Marta comes by every day every other week and, in between, well, I'm more than happy to work on the Chevy, or I'm sure Chuck and I could dream up something to do."

"Oh god, you and Chuck...Yeah, like knock over a convenience store. I'm sure that's on his bucket list. I can see the headlines now: Sixty-Year-Old Men Arrested in Convenience-Store Burglary after Telling Cashier to Have a Nice Day at Gun Point."

We cruised onto the off-ramp and made our way through the neighborhood, Dad trying to convince me that Chuck and he were not troublemakers. I was sure the Chevy was going to be a new project for the two of them, one that I would have to oversee since Chuck thought nothing of keeping my father up for hours regardless of things called *chemo* and *cancer*. Gear heads, the lot of them.

"And another thing: I'll not have a German sleeping under our roof," Dad said plainly.

For a second I thought he was talking about Chuck, but then I realized we'd jumped backward in the conversation to my BMW living in his garage. "Whatever. This thing is much more reliable than that piece of crap," I said, smiling and nodding up the driveway at the closed garage door, behind which I knew the Chevy silently lurked.

"Language!" Dad hollered.

Just as I put my car into park, it died.

"Eva Lynn, what have I told you about turning off the car before you put the gear into park?"

A sinking feeling went through me. I reached forward and turned off the ignition.

"Oh." Dad looked at me and then to the key again. Then in all seriousness: "Try it again."

"Yeah, I know, Dad." I turned the ignition and nothing happened; it was as if the battery connection had just ceased. "Dang it..." I hissed.

"Stay calm, Eva Lynn. It's just a car."

I gave my dad a look before getting out of the car—he was one to talk. I popped the hood, and tried not to think that my baby had just come back from my ex's shop. It had better be a loose wire in the engine compartment. I pulled the safety hood latch through the grille; the hydraulic lid lifted. The terminals were fine, no hanging wires, no loose connections.

"What is it, Eva?" Dad said as he came around the front, leaning on his cane.

I just stared into the compartment. All the visible wires still looked solidly on.

"Oh, come inside, Eva; we'll deal with it tomorrow. And who knows—these German cars are known to fix their own issues overnight. Just let it sit for a while." He reached for my arm, but I was using it to slam the hood closed.

I put my hands on my hips, feeling my annoyance morph into frustration. *Tricky*, my mind supplied. *How'd he do it?*

When we had gotten to the rocky part of our time together Nate would find out of the way fuses and portions of my car's wiring harness to sabotage in an effort to get me to stay with him. A dead car and a missed final exam that cost me an entire college course brought up old angry feelings.

"It's cold out here; come inside, Eva. Stop looking like that—you look like you're going to kill that car."

"Not the car," I said, relieving my father of my purse and grabbing my cell from its depths.

"Eva...never mind. I'm going to go inside."

"OK, I'll be just a minute...Start tanking water and watching your movie. I'll be in to cook dinner, OK?"

"Yeah, yeah," he said, waving a hand over his head, dismissing me and my car. He'd be fine today—it was three days from now, Saturday, which was when this treatment would hit him. It was worst three days from the drip. This had to be fixed by then.

"Yeah, hi, Speedy Towing?"

NINE

ALRIGHTY, MA'AM, HERE WE GO," THE TOW-TRUCK DRIVER SAID as we pulled into the parking lot of Portland's European Pro Auto and reversed my shiny ride in front of the open bay doors. It was after five, and though the front office was dark, it looked as if the mechanics crew was still there.

"Yup. Here we go." I opened my purse and pulled out my emergency hundred-dollar bill. "I know this is covered by insurance, but this is personal insurance—no matter what happens, you unload my car. You got that?"

Gap-mouthed, he looked at the hundred and then back to me. "What you specktin' here?"

I looked at him and lied like hell. "My ex-husband owns this shop, and he thinks he can mess with me and my car—but now that we're here, we're going to make him fix my car, and I'm not leaving until he does. And you're going to help me make sure his cheating, lying ass does that. Right?"

"He has a gun?"

"Nope."

"Good, 'cause I do," he said and wrenched his tubby body out of the cab.

"Uh-oh," I said then swore under my breath before exiting the cab behind him.

Sliding down from the idling truck, I saw one of the mechanics, hands on hips, standing in an open bay and watching my car being lowered. He was chuckling.

I heard an interior door slam, echoing out from the garage. A moment later, Nate strode out, pointing toward the tow-truck driver. "Stop right there, buddy."

The driver no doubt remembered the hundred in his pocket, because he played deaf and continued to let her down.

"I don't think so, Nate." I gathered every ounce of moxie I had and went up against the Italian.

"I don't goddamn believe this. What part of our conversation yesterday did you not understand?"

"I don't know—the part where you have shoddy workmanship, and now she's dead as a doornail. I think that's a pretty big reason that I should bring the car back," I said, feeling my eyes narrow to slits. "Is that why you didn't let me pay, Nate? Too guilt-ridden over purposefully sabotaging my car? You know, though that if I found out you broke it I'd hunt you down and make you fix it. Kind of works against your preference to not see me again. Now, you're going to fix it proper-like so I won't shade your doorstep again. Got it?"

Nate's mouth went into a firm line, and his eyes sparked.

His arm shot out, pointing to the driver, never taking his eyes off of me. "Put. That fucking car. Back on. That fucking truck."

The driver was bent down unhooking her from the tow truck and looked over his shoulder at me. I shook my head at him.

"Sorry, sir—lady's orders."

Nate snarled, turning on the driver, "What'd she pay you? No, nix that, I don't care what she paid you. Whatever it is, I'll triple it—just put this car back up on the bed and get it the fuck out of here."

"Nate, don't be a child, you broke my car. Now you're going to fix it," I said, impressed with my steely voice. It belied my jackhammering heart and liquefying insides.

Nate took a moment and slowly turned back to me. "Don't tell me what I'm going do. I didn't fuck it up; it's a luxury sedan babe—you should have bought a Honda if you didn't want it to break when you park it outside."

I wanted to tell him to shove his rationale up his ass but refrained. I still got a wolfish grin from him, as I'm sure that thought ran clear across my face. I rephrased the thought. "Then explain to me why, almost immediately after leaving my angry ex's, it dies? Not sputters and dies, but as soon as the gear shift hits park, it goes kaput?"

The tow truck suddenly roared to life, and the truck driver gave a cursory wave before escaping.

Nate gave him an Italian hand gesture before looking back at me. "How much did you pay him?"

"More than I'm going to pay you."

Nate's head tilted slightly. "A blow job?"

It was like a slap in the face, and he knew it. I sucked in air and closed my eyes, saying softly, "Watch your mouth." I opened my eyes and gave him a stare equal to the one he was trying to bury me with. Felt the heat of his comment flash all the way up to my hairline.

He just looked away at my dead car. "I just want to know how low the new Eva would stoop to get what she wants."

As he walked toward my car, I let out the breath I hadn't realized I'd been holding. Nate ran his fingers over his mouth while he studied the car.

"Anthony," he said to the man who'd been laughing earlier, "get Greg. We'll need to push this up on the lift in bay four." Nate wrenched open the driver's side door and pulled the hood latch. I slowly closed the distance, very aware of the fragility of our truce. "I assume you checked the battery terminals?" he asked, and glanced to the rear of the car where the battery was oddly located. "Or did you let them corrode?" he asked looking back.

"Sure, I let them corrode and then replaced them with soda cans.

That's OK, right? Oh, and I did all that since you saw it yesterday." I responded with equal sarcasm.

Arms spread over the engine compartment, Nate peered in and around the small-block V8. I noticed for the first time that he wasn't in his workmen's gear; instead he wore jeans, a hoodie, and the workingman's jacket he had on yesterday with black boots. A knit cap was folded in half and shoved into his back pocket. *Some things never change,* I thought.

Nate grunted as Anthony and Greg came close but stood their distance, as if at any moment we would break into a fistfight and they were ready to lay money down. They certainly looked like they were starting the betting with whether or not we would fight.

I turned to them. "I don't bite—despite what's he told you. My name's Eva, by the way." I held out my hand to each of them.

"Despite what she says, she does bite," Nate said and then added to me, "Keys?" His face was impassive again, his palm a steady horizontal.

"Here," I said, slapping them into his hand. The small skin-to-skin contact was like a memory snap: being naked with him in the back of more than one car on some back road or the random parking lot, those very palms gliding over my summer-heated skin, memorizing my curves. The breath of his voice in my ear whispering that he loved me, that I was the only woman he ever loved or would love. And my voice completely gone, my mouth simply biting into his shoulder, riding into blissful ecstasy.

Nate had slammed the hood down and was at the driver's door watching me for just a moment before sliding into the driver's seat and pointing to the hood. "Push."

Glad for the distraction, I helped push my car up onto the lift rails, and then it was the end of the workday for Anthony and Greg. I was sure they exchanged money before getting into their cars and heading out. Anthony stopped in front of the bay that Nate and I stood in and rolled down his passenger window. "Eh, boss! You coming out tonight or what?"

"Maybe," he said stonily and then added, "See you in the morning."

Anthony chuckled as he powered up the window and drove off.

"Is he always that jovial?" I asked.

"Yeah." Nate was under the car poking and prodding. "Mmmph," he grunted and ducked out from under the car before lowering it. He walked to the back of the bay, where seemingly millions of tools hung on the walls and overflowed trays on shelves and filled wheeled carts in organized chaos. Nate disappeared into the madness and came back with a handheld device that he pointed at the car.

"What's that?" I asked, thinking it was probably a problem-code reader for the car's computer. Something we did not have in my father's shop growing up, since he considered such technological devices as black magic.

It's a good thing I wasn't dying to know because I would have died—Nate was silent as codes ran over the screen. He hit a button, then another, then swore under his breath.

He turned around and looked at me and folded his arms across his chest. "Let's first get something straight: I didn't fuck up your car."

"What'd you find?"

"Admit it," he said, his voice low and controlled as he slid into the driver's side.

"So you want me to lie to you before you give me the diagnosis?"

"Let's be rational," he said and then added, "You can still do that, right?"

"You're definitely in the Asshole of the Year running right now— keep it up."

"I'll put it with all my other trophies. Eva, I want you to admit that you faked a dead car just to see me again."

His words caught me off guard and I laughed. "What? You're kidding, right?"

He just smiled bitterly and turned the key. As if touched by magic, the car started.

That made the smile slip right off my face. "It started," was all I could manage.

"Exactly," Nate said condescendingly. "Now you can get the fu —" he barely managed before the car died once more.

The smile slipped right back onto my face.

He just narrowed his eyes at me and then looked at the dash. Nate was silent for a very long time. I stayed silent, immobile, and hopeful as hell.

Finally, he looked up. "Bad luck, shall I call you a tow?"

"You can't be serious."

"As a heart attack. Who was your mechanic before you brought her here?" he asked, climbing out of the car and pulling out his cell phone.

"Nate. It's already here; why can't you just do the work? It's not like I'm asking you to do it for free," I pleaded.

"You don't get it, do you, Eva? I don't want you here, I don't want to see your face, I don't want to touch your car, and I certainly don't want a fucking dime from you." His words were angry but quietly and calmly delivered. "So, which tow service do you want? Maybe your Speedy Tow will come back for you—seemed like you two had something going."

I looked down at the floor and then out the door of the open garage—my control was slipping. A few more minutes and I'd be on my knees begging. "Nate," I said, looking back at him as he looked at me, his eyes guarded. "Tom and Marvin, the guys who I used to—"

At this, Nate smirked. "Deaf and Drunk? If I gave a shit, I'd feel sorry for you, babe."

I closed my eyes and counted to five. "Tom and Marvin don't take new work after Wednesday since they don't work weekends—and because they're crazy—"

"I'm sure they would make an exception for you; just flash them a couple Bennys." He was looking back down at his phone. "Here we go—Speedy Tow. What was that guy's name? John?"

"I don't know, Nate—please." I held my palms up in surrender.

"You don't know his name? What, you can't read nametags? I would have thought they taught you that in college," he jabbed. This was bringing him small bits of joy.

"Please. I have no choice. Dad's truck is shot right now, and I need reliable wheels. Please work with me."

Nate's face illuminated with a wicked grin, and he got in my face. "You should have thought of that, babe, before you kicked me in the nuts and walked out of my life. Didn't your pops teach you to never burn a bridge? You never know when you're gonna need it, Eva, and this one's nuked."

"This isn't about us right now, Nate—"

"It's not? Why you need your wheels so bad? Hot date tomorrow night? Some exec that you need to impress so you can use him as a stepping stool to your next gig? Sorry, I feel bad for the guy already, and I'm not going to help you bury someone else."

I looked up so I wouldn't have to look at his face. "It's not like that. I was lucky today that Dad and I were at the house when she died. I can't have an unreliable car by the time—"

"If only I gave a shit, Eva," he said, hit a button on his cell, and put the phone to his ear.

I looked back at him and said pointedly what he needed to hear. "It's my dad."

"What about him? This isn't his car—wouldn't be caught dead driving a German car. This is just about your ego— Yeah hi, I need a tow," he said into the phone.

I kept talking to Nate. "He's got cancer and just had a chemo session today. Saturday it's going to hit him like a ton of bricks, and I can't have this car randomly going dead..." I trailed off, seeing that Nate had heard me. Had probably stopped thinking, now was just staring at me. I could hear the towing dispatcher on the line, her voice tinny and repetitive with her "Hello?" The phone gapped from his ear slightly before he simply brought it down and ended the call.

"Are you fucking serious?" he asked, challenging me.

I looked him in the eye. "What'd you say just now? Oh yeah. Like a heart attack."

Nate stared as if he were still determining whether or not I was telling the truth.

"He was diagnosed at the end of last year, I moved back, and we started chemo earlier this year. We've only got a few more treatments, and then he's done...for now."

Nate wiped a hand over his face. "What kind of cancer?" he asked and took several steps back and leaned against the doorway of the bay.

"He calls it Lance Armstrong cancer—it's testicular."

"Shit..." He made a face out the door, then looked back to me. "I can get started on it tomorrow, but you won't have it for Saturday. I've got to figure out what's causing it—could be anything from fuel pump to wiring harness." He sighed, cursed, then said, "I'm doing this for him, not *you*."

I just nodded. Thinking that he couldn't be any clearer in that regard.

He continued, "I've got to lock up—my ride's at the far end there."

I walked out of the garage in the direction he pointed. I took my time crossing the small employee parking area. Big pine trees, appearing fluffy from a distance, bordered the side street; the pavement was a shiny black from the earlier rain, and if the sky was any indication, it'd rain again soon. I was alone in the lot save for my thoughts of how I felt, standing there at Nate's business. The place he owned and ran. Me, needing *his* help. I loathed needing help from others, and it was even harder when the person I was asking it from was a rightfully bitter man.

The familiarity of him ate at my stomach lining. Being in his presence for more than a few moments was waking up a part of me that I'd iced numb and forgotten about. One that was ruled by emotion.

Hearing his booted feet on the pavement behind me, I shuttered my thoughts. I rolled work into my mind, the stories I had to edit the next day, the guy in the mailroom whom I had to put pressure on HR to fire for sexually harassing our electronic communications person, and the never-ceasing chaos that characterized print time.

I turned to face Nate, who was pulling his cap down over his head and zipping up his jacket against the chill as he closed the distance.

It was then that I realized the black, god-like car I'd seen yesterday in his lot was still sitting there. Its red DBS badge on its rear end now visible to me. And Nate was walking toward it.

"DBS, huh? I thought Aston Martin was a rich man's car," I said, taking in its low black contours that said it was a curve demon.

"It's just a car, babe."

"Right," I mumbled. "And please don't call me babe."

"Fine," he said, looking over the top of the car as he rounded it to the driver's side, "how's bitch?"

"You are such a child, Nate."

He stopped with a hand on the door handle. "Don't forget who's pulling the favor here."

"This isn't a favor you're doing for me; it's called a service, and despite what I said earlier, I'll expect a bill at the end."

Nate let go of the handle. "Babe," he said again, "you don't call the shots here, not on this property, not in my life. I'm doing this, and then I'm going to tell your pops to get you another fucking car because I'm not going to be your mechanic. Are you clear on that?"

I felt my lip lift into a snarl. "Crystal. I'm not here because I'm loving it, Nate; I'm here because my other choices are zero." And I'd get a new car when I damn well felt like it. And I'd pay for it.

"Rent a car, rent a BMW. You just see your options at zero—your way or the highway right, Eva?"

"All my parking permits, especially for the hospital, are associated with and stickered on that car." I wanted to add that it was the principle of the matter—that he broke my car and now he needed to fix it—but we'd already been over that.

"On that point, that parking permits are such a big deal, let's just agree to disagree."

I just shook my head. And opened the passenger door to that leathery new-car smell and paused.

I'd lusted for shoes, I'd lusted for six-figure paychecks, but there was something primal and *satisfying* about beautiful, fast cars. The way your heart clenches when you see one, and the giddiness that bubbles up from inside as you easily take corners at twice the speed limit.

Looking at it, really *looking* at it, I realized that Nate's car was the child of a panther who had mated with God: low, sleek, and having every intention of breaking speed limits wherever she went. In comfort and style.

A half-laugh came from Nate, and I saw him watching me. "Some shit never changes. Does zero to sixty in four seconds. Now get in and stop getting a woody."

As I settled into the taut leather passenger seat, Nate brought the beast to life. I said jokingly, high on feeling the surge of pure mechanical power, "Can I drive?"

The corners of his mouth curved up as he shifted into reverse. He slid his palm over the back of my seat and looked behind as he moved us out of the spot. "Sure." He actually sounded sincere.

"Really?"

Nate braked gently, bringing the car to a stop; his face was close to mine. His arm came over the headrest and lighted across my shoulders, warm and heavy as his thumb stroked the nape of my neck in gentle circles. The effect that old move had on me...That simple act with his thumb had been something that he'd done a million times if he'd done it once, the prelude to his wide hand taking up residence at the back of my head and pulling my face to his lips. Those lips, which were now just inches from mine...

But his eyes were like ice.

"Over my fucking dead body," he said and pulled us away.

TEN

NATE'S MIND WAS SPINNING.

Martin has cancer.

Eva's sitting right next to me.

She's right about this car.

Shit.

"Where's your place? Or do you want me to take you to your pops's place?" Nate asked as he pulled up to the light at the corner of his shop and the main boulevard.

"I'm living with dad at his place." Eva leaned her head against her hand, which was against the window frame.

He stole a look at her while pretending to look at traffic. Her hair, which was wavy black-brown and long when it wasn't pulled back tight into the twist thing at the nape of her neck. Those freckles on her nose and cheeks, the flecked green eyes that changed colors, telling him when he was in deep shit or was going to be a lucky man. She was blessedly curved in all the right places, curvier now, if memory served him, all he'd have to do is just...

"Green light," she said.

"Yeah," he said, shifting into first and easing onto the gas.

"He's going to be fine, you know."

Martin's got cancer.

He cursed again softly as he took the urban highway at a good clip.

"They say it's 90 percent curable."

He looked over at her again—she was still watching the world go by outside her window, her face hidden from his view.

He reminded himself how much he hated her, hated the grip she once had on him, the way she ended things with him. He was cured of her disease, but just two fucking hours with her and he was starting to feel things stir that he was sure he'd killed.

The thought of Martin having cancer was mind numbing and that scared him.

Better scared than fucked, he reminded himself. He had to dump her on another mechanic; he'd go crazy if he saw her again and again, and he'd already done crazy.

"What kind of work do you do?" he asked, thinking about Martin, focusing on him. *Focus.*

Her hand fell out of the open window as she turned to look at him. "Why?"

"Just wondering."

She was silent for a while, and Nate just waited, feeling the heat of her gaze on the side of his face. He slowed for a red light as she answered.

"I'm the editor-in-chief for *Rose City Review*."

Nate whistled. "Wow, that take up a bunch of your time?"

"It's a full-time job, if that's what you're asking."

"Long hours?"

"Come publishing time, yeah," she said, and then added, "You're fishing—get to the point."

"Who's taking care of your dad while you're at work?"

Eva took up looking out the window again. "Why? Are you volunteering?"

"So you don't have anyone looking after Martin while you're at work and he's home after chemo?"

"We have a nurse who comes in daily to check on him."

Nate looked over at her after taking off again down the road from the green light, and Eva was looking right at him.

"Thanks," she said and looked away.

That hit him sideways. "For what?"

"For not taking your anger at me out on him, for caring about him despite your urge to bury me under a cement truck."

The side street that her father's house was on came up, and he cut across the light traffic. He pulled in front of the cream-colored ranch-style house that was just as familiar to him as it had ever been. The low-cut lawn with minimal hedging and the wide garage that he knew held the old man's favorite thing in the world.

"He was there for me, Eva. I have a good memory of that. And it's not a cement truck," he said, turning off the motor. "I never wished you dead. Sent to the South Pole? Every goddamn day."

ELEVEN

As soon as we walked in the house, a party erupted. Chuck was there watching sports with Dad and upon seeing Nate, they started their yells of welcome.

"Good to see you, Nate!"

"Nate! My god—how are you? I was just talking with Eva about you."

"Chuck, how you been, old man? Martin, looking good."

The elephants in the room were completely forgotten and, for a moment, there was relief. The living room was probably the same since Nate had seen it last. Dad's old recliner was in the corner, pictures of the family hung on the walls: faded color photos of my mother and my dad at their wedding; me and the Chevy. Pieces of art, both homemade and bought, mingled with the photos. The hallway to bedrooms and the guest bath and the door to the garage were ahead of us.

The likely only new thing since Nate's last visit was a big screen I'd gotten Dad for Christmas. Now, the sports network competed with the men's boisterous conversation. I veered to my left, away from the chaos and into the kitchen.

The kitchen was my sanctuary in this house. It was the one thing that I was allowed to remodel after I moved in. All the cabinetry was new; gleaming hardwoods; polished stone countertops with stainless pulls. Dad complained about the eat-at island bar: "What do we need a bar for? It's not like we have people over." He said that and then sat in his chair and turned on the TV, and I installed it anyway.

I dropped my purse on one of the bar stools and set to work. I didn't have the heart to tell my father then that while he may not have a need for a bar, I—now that I lived at home again—needed an ample one.

I had planned takeout for dinner, but considering what had happened and was still happening—specifically, with the tall Italian in my father's living room—I thought I could use a bigger distraction and a longer prep time with a chopping knife.

Sometime later, after emptying the fridge and freezer, I had pots simmering and a chicken roasting in the oven, my third glass of wine in my hand. I closed my cookbook and flipped through the mail, setting to the simple task of sorting it as the familiar sounds of a sports announcer emanated from the TV in the other room, the men having gone silent. Life was for the moment as blissful as it could have been, the kind of domestic quaintness that I edited stories about. Ones that you secretly dream of and that had me sighing—it was a feeling that I could live in forever. The only caveat was that I had to have three glasses of wine to blur reality.

Mail sorted, I headed back to my gravy and gave it a stir and checked the vegetables; the chicken would be nearly done. Polishing off the last of my glass, I looked at it forlornly and set it down to the side of the stove.

"Smells good," Nate's voice came from behind me. Instead of stiffening at the sound, I found it oddly comforting, its low pitch so unique and familiar to my sluggish wine-addled mind. I smiled.

Nate moved in close behind me, and when I didn't retreat, he reached around me to take the spoon out of its holder and into the gravy. I would have to have been in a coma to not have noticed the warmth of his body behind mine, to not have felt the brush of his jacket on my back as he brought the spoon to his mouth. And in a complete lapse in judgment, I relaxed back into him.

Like two spoons in a drawer, we fit right next to each other, just as we always had, as if we'd been made for each other. Nate was a whole head taller than me, even when I was in my low heels, broader in the shoulders, and incredibly warm, sturdy—and responsive. He slid an arm around my middle as he leaned forward, putting the spoon back in the pan.

"Mmm," I felt his voice rumble in his chest then felt his body move, but the world around us stopped. The air held its breath as our two worlds melded together once more, softly, gently, as they had a decade past. His thoughts had been mine and mine his—nothing was unknown to each other, and when we came together, it was as easy as breathing.

His breath now came warm on my neck, as if he were breathing me in. The spoon dropped into the pot and slipped under the gravy. Nate's expert thumb lifted the hem of my shirt and he slipped his wide palm under it, making undeniable skin-to-skin contact with my belly. His touch, however, was like ice water to the brain, shocking and sobering.

My breath made a noise on its inhale, and Nate stiffened.

His hand slowly moved away from me, the realization of what had just happened dawning.

"Fuck," Nate said softly, taking a step back.

Reality flooded in, cold and unforgiving. I took a deep breath and pulled the spoon from the gravy, tapped it on the edge of the pan, and dropped it on the spoon holder. Sucking on my burnt fingers, I walked away to the patio door, undid the latch, and stepped out into the crisp evening air. Sliding the door closed behind me, I stepped to the side of the house, leaned against the fence, and very gently lost it.

· · ·

SOME TIME LATER I HEARD THE ASTON PURR TO LIFE, signaling Nate's departure. I looked up into the now cold and darkened sky and, wiping my eyes dry, took another deep and cleansing breath. The clarity brought with it the realization that the chicken was still in the oven, and the stove was on. I was back in the kitchen in seconds, only to find that someone had turned everything to warm. Walking into the living room, I found the old men were passed out and snoring.

TWELVE

Tonight Nate needed loud and distracting, he needed the thump and pulse of life and bodies to distract him.

Anthony was where he said he would be on the second floor, where Festivál's balcony was open to the dancers below. It was mostly women tonight, Nate saw. That was good—he had one in mind he wanted to forget all about and had a feeling that he just might be able to in the arms of another. Sarah? Rachel? Or would it be Veronica?

Nate nodded to Anthony and Mikey as he unbuttoned his black suit coat and sat on the edge of the white couch. The upper floors were VIP and ladies only; everything was dark and swirling and pulsing with light. The low glass coffee table was already outfitted with his iced club soda. Everyone knew he didn't drink—couldn't—not after his father.

"So what's with the lucky red shirt coming out?" asked Mikey. One of the smartest people Nate knew with computers and anything that had to be plugged in but dumb as a doormat when it came to social interaction. And it was that that made Nate Mikey's best friend. The first words to him had been, "Dude, the chicks come to

you like bees to honey—let's be friends; I'm Mike Spetterfield."
Mikey'd been around ever since. Though he didn't do well with the
ladies even with Nate's advice.

"Because I'm in need of some luck tonight." Nate raised his glass
in a toast. Remembering one piece of business, Nate pulled out his
phone and sent Anthony's phone Martin's address. "Anthony, need
you to run a car over to this address tonight."

Anthony checked his phone, then put it away and took a sip of
his drink. "Yeah, sure. Any kind in particular? You need this
clean?"

Nate looked over at him. "Yes, I want this legal. When have I ever
asked for it not to be?"

Anthony smiled. "Never, but I just keep waiting." Snakeskin
boots poked from underneath his designer jeans. He reclined back
against the semicircular couch, his arms across the top.

Nate shook his head before taking a sip of his drink before
adding, "Talk to the dealership—see if we can borrow the 6 Series
and give her—the client," he corrected himself, "my 330ci." He
would probably regret her sitting in that car for a couple days leaving
her scent behind, but that could be fixed. "When you pick it up from
the client, detail the shit out of it."

"Got it. Anything else?" he said with a smirk.

"No," he said and stood, walking to the balcony, resting his
elbows on the railing, and looking down to the dance floor.

Mikey joined him, downing his cocktail.

Nate nodded to the tumbler. "Going on a bender or drowning
your sorrows?"

Mikey grinned at him, sweeping his arm wide to take in the floor
of shimmying women. "Liquid courage, bro. I hear you have a particular lady friend that lit a fire under you today."

"Don't believe everything you hear."

"Eff that, dude. Anthony told me you went ballistic all over her,
and she didn't even flinch. Look man, I'm good with numbers—that's
my schtick—but you, you're good with people, and I've never seen

you lose your cool with the ladies. Something tells me she might be your base integer."

"My what?"

"You know, the foundation, the base, of your mathematical framework."

Nate couldn't help himself. He smiled and shook his head at Mikey. "Yeah, she might have been once, Mikey, once a long time ago."

"What happened?"

"I don't want to talk about it."

Mikey nodded. "Yeah, I get it. But maybe I can learn from your mistake?"

Nate knew Mikey wasn't purposefully being an insensitive asshole; he didn't have the filters for polite society like others did. He was straightforward. Nate liked that about him.

"What makes you think I was the one who fucked up?"

Mikey shrugged. "Men usually are, right?"

Nate nodded. "You know, you're right, Mikey. But this time it wasn't. She walked out when I needed her. She said a lot of things that made me believe we'd be together forever, that she loved me. Then one summer she left to go be somebody important and to do that, she had to shake me out of her life. So, she flipped me the bird and walked the fuck right out. That was almost ten goddamn years ago. Then, this week, she walked right back in."

"What did she say when you told her how you felt?"

Nate raised an eyebrow at his friend and looked over at him. "I was too busy yelling at her to tell her that."

"Seems unlike you. I've heard that love makes people irrational."

Nate scoffed. "Yeah, irrational is one way to put it. Fucking nuts is more like it."

"So, you still love her?"

Nate watched the heads bob in the sea of people below him as he thought about that. Mikey had no idea how loaded that question was. He was a black-and-white kind of guy, yes or no, one or zero. Nate was cursed with seeing the shades of gray and the emotional impact of it all. Did he still love Eva?

The bodies jostled and gyrated in time with the thundering dance music. It shook your soul and asked you only to move in time with it. Not to ask questions about how you feel, if you could even still feel anything in a heart so burned it smoldered black. He didn't have an answer for Mikey. This was a part of his life he was hoping would be over soon.

He was saved from answering by the regular troop of girls who frequented the VIP section of Festival.

Mikey pushed off the rail, looking from the girls to Nate to the girls again.

"Damn, dude, what do I say to them?"

Nate cuffed him on the shoulder. "Introduce yourself and tell them what you make in a year. Then keep your mouth shut." That would at least get Mikey a phone number, maybe more.

Nate spotted Veronica in the middle of the approaching pack and gave her a nod. Veronica. He was sure that wasn't the name she had been born with, but he didn't care—they all had only first names. Her black hair came to a point at her jawline, and she was wearing a black second-skin thing that was supposed to be a dress, but he bet if she just thought about bending over, he'd see Venus.

And that was just fine.

Keeping eye contact with him, she pressed against him as the girls swished by, cooing their hellos.

"Hi, Nate."

"Nate, looking good, baby."

"Mmm, hi," the one in red purred as she dragged a nail down his arm.

Nate was more than a little disturbed to find that he saw—and felt—Veronica's body but felt nothing inside. Rather, he thought of what Eva would look like, natural curves filling the black dress like God herself. That little thought, that millisecond of imagery of her long, dark hair curving under her breasts and moving like water down her back, made him think about her body against him earlier. She had been in jeans and a regular damn sweater, but he'd felt his chest squeeze and his breath catch when his hand grazed the naked skin of her belly. The reaction was instant in his slacks, too.

Veronica slid her hands into the back pockets of his pants. "Mmm, where did you just go? Are you thinking ahead again?" She looked up at him through her lashes and bit her lower lip that was plumped and painted red.

He gave her a crooked smile. "I was." He bent to her ear. "Have I shown you my place before?"

She moaned. "Mmm, yes, but I've only seen your bed. Care to show me something different tonight?"

THIRTEEN

Two glasses was always my max; three, with the start of a fourth? That was the cause of a real headache. I couldn't sleep, and Dad was well into REM in his room, the snoring a familiar sign of his sleepy bliss. I took a couple Advil from the medicine cabinet in the guest bath and padded into the kitchen for a glass of water. Standing in front of the sink, I watched as an unknown silver BMW pulled into my father's driveway; then a little red car parked in front of the house. Anthony, dressed to the nines, got out of the BMW and ran up to the front porch. I heard the mailbox open and close, and then Anthony bounded back down the steps and into the waiting red car. My ride for tomorrow had arrived. A small bit of gratitude at Nate's gesture bloomed in my gut.

The next morning I dressed for a long day; as sure as it would rain, it would be a long one. We were going to print soon.

Dad was already in the kitchen with an orange juice poured and bread in the toaster, going through the morning paper.

"Morning, Dad," I said as I breezed in, giving him a peck on the head.

"Morning," he said solemnly.

I buttered the toast that had popped up and plopped it onto a plate. "You feeling all right?" I pushed two more fresh slices down.

"Mmmph."

"Marta's going to be here in a little bit, and you're fully stocked with queasy pops, so things should go OK today. Did you tank water yesterday or were you too busy yakking with Chuck?"

"Looks like you've got a shiny new ride"—he winced—"out there."

"You OK, Dad?"

He nodded. "Just the nausea, hitting me quick this time."

"Well, lay off the orange juice, then," I said and opened the fridge. "Here, we've got some apple juice instead." I poured him a glass and downed the orange juice, put the glass in the sink.

"Mmmph."

"Dad," I said as I polished up my toast and wrapped it in a paper towel to go, "take the antinausea pills if it gets too bad, if the queasy pops don't help." I looked at my watch and then back at him just as the doorbell rang.

I kissed him on the head again and let in Marta, the in-home nurse, and filled her in on what was up. I had a feeling that I'd be bringing work home—the bad news was starting fast for Dad this time around.

I headed out and slid into the immaculate German coupe, throwing my giant black leather sack purse onto the seat next to me, and had a moment. Something was nibbling at my memory. It was the spice of a cologne so subtle that it was barely noticeable over the car's leather smell. In a rush of memory, it came to me: This wasn't just any rental—this was one of Nate's personal cars, and I would think of him the entire drive to work and back. I balanced my toast on my purse and reversed out the drive and thought about how beautiful the strawberry jam would look splattered on the gray interior if I accidentally took a corner too fast. In the end, my hunger overrode my spite and I ate my toast without spilling any jam, but I made a mess with the crumbs.

FOURTEEN

Work was chaos: last-minute stories flying around, and the front-page image files corrupted. By the time Jenny was at my office door frazzled over the state of a freelancer's story, it was only noon, and I realized my distracted thoughts were not helping my dad, nor could I get any real work done continuing to put out others' fires. I left Jenny the privacy of my office to sort through the article and went home.

I called Marta when I was on my way, so she was waiting for me when I arrived. She was in mauve scrubs, and her black hair streaked with gray was pulled back into a Marta-bun at the back of her head.

"He's asleep," she told me, gathering up her purse. "I had to give him the antinausea pills. Anyway, when he wakes, he'll need to eat but should continue to rest."

I set up shop on the dining room table. Laptop out and papers scattered around me, I immersed myself in my work, the task of editing an article word by word and shifting paragraphs around to improve flow, and when that one was done, I'd move onto the next. Every story had to see my virtual Editor's Pen of Doom, but as I'd advised more than one disgruntled writer, take your heart out of it, and it'll bleed less.

Several hours passed before my father stirred, and when he did, I made him soup and brought it to him. He ate in silence with me trying to keep chipper, entertaining him with my day and the nonsense that I had to edit out of stories. After eating, he had another nausea pill and lay back down and turned on the TV, and I went back to my work.

It was dark out by the time I came up for air again and looked at my watch, midnight. Dad was still asleep in his chair. *The meds and chemo must be hell on him this time,* I thought. I turned off the TV and shook his shoulder. "Dad, time to go to bed."

"Mmmm...mmmph," he replied, his eyes fluttering open then closing again.

"Dad, you can't sleep in your chair, no matter how far it reclines —come on, up." I put an arm under his shoulders, attempting to give him a boost.

"Mmmph!" He rolled over onto his side. "Leave me alone."

I stood over him, glaring at his backside. "Fine, but if you have a backache tomorrow, I don't want to hear about it." I turned off all the lights and tossed a spare blanket from the couch over him.

Back at my computer, I stared at the glowing screen for a while before I realized where I was in all the work. I pulled up my e-mail and typed Jenny a quick update on the stories and inquired after her ghostwriting.

She pinged me immediately, saying she continued to find factual errors that made her question the validity of all of the research the author had done.

Restless, tired of working, and anxious about what seemed to be a mess of a job I'd gotten myself into, I went to the fridge and grabbed some grapes and the filtered-water pitcher. At the sink, I rinsed the grapes and filled my glass. I stood looking out the window at the pitch-black night, illuminated only by front porches and the lone streetlight. I took a sip of water and let the day's events wash over me.

There was still so much work to do, and it looked like this production round was going to be no different than the last. I'd thought that at a smaller magazine it would be proportionately easier. Instead, keeping the struggling magazine afloat and doing the majority of the editing was overwhelming. I was reminded of stressful nights in school, when I took my car to the drive along the river and pretended to break land-speed records. I was craving that again. My gaze drifted to the silver coupe parked on the street and I thought about it being Nate's car—that alone meant it would be fun to drive at the redline. I looked over at my dad and knew that my escape wouldn't be tonight; he was in such a fragile state that I wanted to swaddle him in bubble wrap.

I heard him mumble something from his chair. Setting my water glass down i padded over to him. I felt his forehead it was cool to the touch, but something was bothering him in his sleep.

"Dad," I said softly, brushing his hair off his forehead as if he were a child, "it's OK, Dad. You're fine."

He settled down as I returned to the large living room windows that overlooked the lawn. Just beyond our cul-de-sac, on the nearest side street, a large truck with a flatbed trailer sat parked. I watched the truck for a moment before snapping the curtains shut. I double-checked the front and patio doors to make sure they were locked before settling down again at my station at the dining room table.

As soon as I sat, my father screamed, ""Betty!"

My pen fell with a clatter as my stomach dropped.

"Dad," I said, rushing to his side. "Dad, it's me, Eva. Are you OK?"

He looked around him, wild-eyed and frenzied but still in his chair. "Betty, she's gone," he said.

"Dad—" I started, not knowing what was happening to him but thinking I should tell him first that Mom wasn't there. "Dad, Mom's not here; you're here with me. Mom's been gone for many, many years now."

Dad just looked straight at me. "Why didn't you do anything!"

"Dad...I was four when mom died; she's not here. Dad, do you know where you are?"

"No! Not your mother—the car! Betty is the car!"

"Dad, you're not making sense. What car?"

He struggled to put down the footrest, making the chair wiggle and wobble. "The '57 Chevy, Eva Lynn! Someone is taking it!" he said with such conviction that I almost believed he had watched it walk away.

"When did they take it, Dad?" I asked, despite its absurdity, and helped him put the chair right.

"Just now—they've got it now!" he said and, getting to his feet, pushed me aside and went down the hall to his room.

"Dad, just calm down. No one has the truck; it's in the garage. I would have heard the garage door open," I said, following him then stopped at the short hall that lead to the garage. "Come here, Dad, and look for yourself." I walked past the washer and dryer and opened the door to the garage.

The Chevy, which my father called by my mother's name, was gone. Everything else was there. The fifties-era garage was immaculate, with shelving on the bare wood and supports, tools in toolboxes and floor jacks and engine winches. All of these things were plainly visible in the low glowing light of the street and porch lights through the open garage door. In the distance on the flatbed I had seen earlier was my father's truck.

"Dad . . ." I said and slammed the door and went swiftly back into the house. "Do *not* go outside! You are in no condition to—" I broke off as I heard the front door unlock and the faint whistling sound it made as it opened; then the screen door slammed. "Dad!" I shouted and broke into a run.

I got to the screen door and whipped it open to find my father wavering on the front lawn, an old revolver in hand, pointing it at the far street.

"Get back here you bastards!" he said before pulling the trigger.

The gunshot exploded into the night air as I raced down the

stairs. The truck with my father's Chevy was pulling away. My father shot again and broke into a hobbling run across the lawn.

I yelled over the gunshots, "Stop! Dad!" The grass was cold and prickly under my bare feet as I came up behind him and grabbed his gun arm and pointed it to the ground.

"Nooo!" my father wailed. "Let me—Oh..." he said.

In the next instant, my father crumpled.

"Dad—" I said grabbing him to me. I fell to the ground with him and as I laid him onto his back said, "Dad? Daddy?" I gently slapped his face as his complexion paled. Panic started to grip my insides and I more forcefully, slapped his face.

I looked up wildly for help and saw my neighbor step out onto her porch clutching her robe to her.

"Mrs. Murray! Call 9-1-1, quickly, please!" I screamed, barely noticing her other hand was already to her ear.

"Dad. Daddy," I said, again looking down at my father. His eyes had rolled up into the back of his head, and the silence of his wrist, then his neck—I pressed my fingers against him repeatedly—said he was dead.

Everything was happening so fast. Too fast.

Truck gone?

Revolver in my father's hand?

And now he was collapsed on the ground. My mind went blank then suddenly sharply focused.

As soon as I had realized that I could add *death* to the list of things I could control, I'd taken CPR classes. Then refreshed them once my father was in chemo. Following that blindly, I administered chest compressions, feeling his ribs give way and then fill with air as I breathed air into his lungs.

An eternity passed.

"Come on, Daddy," I whispered.

I made deals with the devil and with God, anyone who would listen; I bargained my life for his. He was all I had left in this life.

I was barely aware of the flashing red and white of the fire truck and ambulance when they arrived. In one moment, I was breathing for my father, and in the next, a hand on my shoulder was shoving me aside. A breathing bag went on his face and a defibrillator to his chest. The latter went off the instant the bag left his face. It was a rhythmic dance of life, and in the end my father decided that living was more important and returned from wherever he had gone.

As fast as he came back to me, he was taken again. This time two medics swept him up into the waiting ambulance and prevented me from following. I stood in all the chaos feeling like I'd been cleaved, one part gone.

"Ma'am?" came the voice of one of the firefighters who'd detained me. "We're going to need some information."

I told him what my father's name was, that he was currently a chemo patient. This caused a flurry of radioing to the ambulance paramedics, and as my mind waded through the trauma, it gave another directive: *Go*.

"I'm going to have to leave now. Tell the police, when he collapsed, my father was running after the people who stole his truck." I ran inside the house, retrieved my purse and keys, locked the front door out of habit, despite the garage door being wide open, and went to the loaner BMW in the driveway.

"Ma'am! Wait just one moment, the police will need your statement—"

"No," I said, and I left.

The drive to the hospital went by in a blur—when I got to the parking lot, I did not remember how I'd gotten there. I was walking across the parking lot; I was asking the ER nurse where Martin Rodgers had been taken. I was walking to the ICU; then I was asking at the nurse's station about my father. I was told to wait in the waiting room and someone would be with me. I did. And I was waiting. And I was waiting until I was crawling out of my skin.

Back at the nurse's station, I asked what was happening with my father and learned he was in surgery. Yes, they knew he was a chemo patient, and I was asked to have a seat again—the surgeon would be out to talk to me soon.

I pushed back through the double doors that separated the sterile-looking halls of the nurse's station from the waiting room where cheerful colors were everywhere. I wanted to light all those cheerful colors on fire and throw them out the window. Turning around, I walked right back to the nurse's station. "How long do you think the surgery will take?" I asked, sounding like a junkie needing to know when she could have her fix. My voice wavered and cracked.

The nurse glanced at her computer screen with more attitude than I wanted. "He's just gone in, *ma'am*. So, he'll be an hour, or maybe two."

"What kind of surgery is he getting? What are they doing to him?"

"Have a seat back in the waiting room. The doctor will come out when he's done to talk to you," she said and pointed at the waiting room behind me.

Ignoring her finger, I persisted. "Can't you tell me anything about why he's in surgery? He's in chemo. Surgery could kill him." I could hear my voice rising, and it felt good.

"I'm sure the surgeons contacted your father's oncologist to get the OK for surgery. Now please *sit*; there's no more for you to do."

"'You're sure'?" I repeated the nurse's statement. "Not, *you've verified*? So I'm to take your guess on this, just have faith that everyone has done due diligence?" She just stared at me, so I continued, "I take that as a no. How about you hand me the phone, so I can call his oncologist myself." I held out my hand.

Her stare shifted to my hand. "There is a phone for family members. In. The. Waiting. Room." She pointed again behind me.

I hissed, "Listen, bitch, hand me that fucking phone or lose your fucking finger."

Before she could respond, I felt a wide hand on my back and saw a cell phone slide in front of me across the counter. "Use my fucking phone."

FIFTEEN

THE BLACK CAR CUT THROUGH THE RAIN LIKE A KNIFE, A KNIFE going close to a hundred miles an hour. The freeways were clear at this time of night, and Nate's mind was focused. The call had come in as he was elbow deep in Eva's 540i's wiring harness.

"Fuck," he'd said as an immediate answer to the ringing phone, his voice echoing back to him from inside the engine compartment. Once he had his cell phone out of his back pocket, his second answer wasn't much better: "This had better be good, Donny." The caller ID had told him his cousin, a cop, to boot, was calling.

"Well, I was just calling to say that to you. What the hell are you thinking, doing those kinds of speeds in the city?"

"What the fuck are you talking about?" Nate asked as he headed to the sink, stripping off his black mechanic's latex gloves.

"Don't mess with me. I just saw you fly over the 405 like your ass was on fire. I'll let it go this time, Nate, as long as everything's OK—someone you know at OHSU?"

"Donny, you're seeing shit. I'm at the shop tonight—come on by; we'll have doughnuts."

"You still own the silver 330ci?"

Nate dried his hands as he stepped into his office. "Yeah, Donny, me and just a few thousand other people—"

Donny rattled off a license plate number.

Nate felt a chill slither down his spine. "When'd you see it?"

"I just caught up to it in the ER parking lot."

"Eva's got my car." Nate ended the call just as he heard his cousin say,

"*The* Eva?"

And broke into a run for his car in the far bay.

Now, without missing a beat and still glaring at the nurse, Eva snatched the phone he was offering her. "Someday your father will die in your arms," she pointed the phone at the nurse, "and then will you know what I'm going through right now. And you know what? You'll wish that someone would have just given you a damn phone." She turned on her heel, slamming through the waiting room doors.

Martin died in her arms? *Nate's stomach clenched.*

He followed her and took the chair next to her. She handed him his phone back after fishing her own out of her purse.

"You have your phone with—"

"Don't ask." She said as Nate tucked his cell away and just watched. Watched as her hands shook while she tapped through her phone contacts, watched as her other hand kneaded her grass-and-mud-stained pants.

Questions piled up in his mind, yet he kept quiet.

Her eyes, dark-green now, lasered onto the far wall as she held the phone to her ear, waiting for someone to answer.

"Yeah, hi, this is Eva Rodgers. Yes, he's apparently still in surgery —so you did authorize the surgery? What is he getting surgery for? I'm getting stonewalled by the nurses here in the ICU."

At her statement a shred of relief went through him.

The phone shook harder as she got the confirmation she needed and was having a hard time turning it off. Nate reached forward and took the phone. As he turned it off, he saw the caller ID as Zimmerman, Portland Clinic Oncologist. He handed the phone back to Eva.

"Wanna tell me what's going on?"

SIXTEEN

Nate looked at me like he'd wait forever for my answer. Which was good, since I could feel the adrenaline bleeding out of me, making me shake, my voice quiver, and giving me the distinct urge to vomit, all at once.

I crossed my arms. "My dad's in surgery. Why are you here?" I asked.

"Donny called."

"Your cousin?"

"My car was spotted doing a buck-twenty on the 405. What happened, Eva?"

I stood, suddenly unable to sit still any longer. Nate was asking me the one thing I was trying like hell to ignore, asking me to think about what I couldn't. The shaking continued, a bone-rattling shake that starts in your core and moves out toward your skin, setting every-thing a-jitter.

I looked at him apologetically; I couldn't give him what he needed. I was having a hard time just forming words. "I'm this close to losing it," I said, holding my thumb and index finger close together.

"Eva..." Nate looked at me for a long moment, his face a mix of emotion, anguish being the last before he stood and gently pulled me in against him, wrapping his arms tight around me.

I felt my breath give out as I clutched him for dear life, an unlikely sanctuary in all the chaos. Nate's fingers snaked through my hair, his strength holding me up, letting me give way. The emotional blocker I'd constructed to get me to the hospital fell away, and the memory of my father falling dead into my arms hit me like a ton of bricks. I heard a woman's racking sobs echo in the small room. My chest heaved, tears ran down my cheeks, and leaked out my nose. I buried my face deeper into Nate's jacket, breathing him in, pulling every ounce of him to me. Breathing in my old safeguard.

Nate shifted and pulled me onto his lap as he sat back onto the chair behind him. With my head still buried in his shoulder, I felt him grip my thigh and tug me in even closer, and then he held me still.

"You're scaring the shit out of me." I felt his head dip toward my ear. "Jesus Christ, Eva, tell me what happened."

I nodded and tried taking a deep breath, only to have it catch in my throat.

"It's OK," he whispered into my hair.

I took another shuddering breath and attempted to dry the black streaks of mascara, resulting, no doubt, in a deeply haunted look. I kept my head down, my forehead resting on his chest, my face covered by his open jacket, unwilling to fully face the world just yet.

"Dad's Chevy was stolen from the house tonight," I said, my voice sounding far away and nasally.

I heard him grunt. "Stolen? As in, jacked-from-your-dad's-garage stolen?"

"Yes."

Nate angled me back just a bit to see my face. "Details, babe," he said softly, "I need details."

I looked back at him. His eyes had gone dark around the edges—

he was just as haunted as I was, if not more because of his lack of knowledge of what had happened.

"I'm not sure myself. Everything is such a blur. I know that Dad's Chevy was stolen out of the garage, and they were able to load it on their truck without making a sound." I just shook my head. "Dad had a gun. He was outside running after them and shooting when he... when he—"

"It's OK, babe." He pushed a lock of my hair from my face. "It's OK."

"Died. Right there." I gestured toward my feet. "He fell dead at my feet."

Pain, raw pain, registered on Nate's face; his ministrations ceased, and he became like stone. I could barely hear his next words: "Then how is he in surgery?"

"Ambulance," I said by way of explanation. "Brought him back, and now I don't know what's happening."

"Zimmerman?" he asked. "What did he say when you talked with him?"

Zimmerman, I'd forgotten. "Right. Heart attack, and something about a stint or a splint," I said, trying to think hard and not coming up with anything. It was as if I'd hung up on the doctor after hello. "I can't remember," I said, becoming frustrated.

"It's OK," Nate said, pulling me in against him again.

"No, I should remember."

"Babe. Let it go, your pops is in surgery, the doc will be out to talk with you, and we can ask questions then. Zimmerman is your pops's cancer guy?"

"Yeah," I said absently. "Actually, I think I remember now: He said that he gave the go-ahead for the surgery, something about percentages of blockages. And that he'd be fine." I scoffed, "'Fine'— what does that mean, anyway? My doc says I'm doing fine when I see him, and then Zimmerman just said it about my dad, and he'd just had a heart attack, died, been brought back to life, and admitted to surgery to give him a stint. So what does *fine* even mean?"

I felt Nate chuckle. "You sound like Flora. She says shit like that all the time." He added, "It means just that—he's fine. If he's not fine he's—"

"Dead," I finished for him.

"Right. So fine is good."

I took a deep breath. "Fine's good."

We were quiet a while, each of us in private ruminations.

Nate spoke aloud again first. "What the hell is Martin still doing with a gun?"

"What do you mean, still?"

"He always had one at the shop."

I leaned back and looked at him. "When we were kids?"

"You didn't know?"

"No," I said, taken aback, "I guess that was not something that a girl was supposed to know about."

"You mean not like learning how to paint cars, fix them, and teach you how to drive like a bat out of hell?"

A smile touched my lips. "Yeah, not like all that girly stuff."

"It was just an old 9mm that jammed every third bullet." He added softly, "He taught me how to shoot it after the old man left bruises. That Martin could see," Nate amended.

Nate had come in, a bruise blooming on his cheek, black-and-blue finger marks on his right forearm. "I remember that day," I said solemnly. "That was the first time Dad had you spend the night at our place."

Nate smirked. "Yeah, he pretty quickly realized he should take Flora up on her offer to take me in."

"After he caught you in my bedroom, and you confessed to liking the way I smelled."

"I never said that. I said you were pretty—"

"You were smelling my sheets, I heard."

"I was napping."

"Facedown on my bed?"

This brought a grin to his face. "Maybe."

Thankful for the diversion, I added, "Actually, I think what really did you in with him was the report from school when you got caught kissing Lucy deMarchello in the bathroom—in the girls' bathroom."

"Not my fault. She called me in there and told me to hold still," he said, shifting my weight on his lap.

I thought of getting off of him then. I was a grown woman after all and didn't need to be mollycoddled but it was as if he were a rare earth magnet and I, a thoroughly abused piece of tattered metal, was inextricably attached to him.

I laughed softly. "If I hadn't known Lucy, I'd say you were lying. But knowing Lucy, I'd say you're lucky you got out with just a smooch."

There was a long pause as Nate looked at me, his gaze traveling from my mouth to my eyes. Then something beyond me caught his attention. "You've got to be fucking kidding me," he said under his breath.

I turned to follow his gaze and saw a man in a long tan coat and black wool cap with two others dressed in cop uniforms walk into the room and head in our direction.

"Ms. Rodgers?" the older man asked. He was middle-aged and looked tired and overworked. The two officers behind him looked to have seen the chair behind a desk or the seat of a cruiser for a little too long.

"I'm Detective T. H. Shelby, and these are officers Mitchell and Ableton. May we have a word with you, Ms. Rodgers?" he asked, the corner of his mouth quirking up in a possible smile.

"Yes," I said and stood. I started toward the hallway but didn't get far before I heard Detective Shelby say, "Evening, Mr. Vellanova."

"Shelby."

In the hall, I leaned back against the wall and had a sudden urge to hit my head against it.

The police joined me, and I saw over their shoulders that Nate was leaning against the doorway, his eyes on me. He'd get answers to all his questions too, no doubt, by the time the officers were done with me.

"Mitchell—go to the nurse's station and see about getting Ms. Rodgers a pair of shoes."

I looked down. Sure enough, I was barefoot. Shelby addressed me. "Ma'am, can you tell us what happened tonight?"

"Thanks," I said as Officer Mitchell returned with hospital booties. I slipped them on and looked at Shelby as he repeated his question.

His stare was carefully unbiased and looked to be genuinely curious.

I swallowed hard and thought of the night as a story, as one of the stories that one of my writers would tell me—except I decided this was a fictional story. At that point, in my mind, that's what the night felt like.

"Well, to be to the point about it...Someone stole my father's car, and he ran outside and shot at them as they were putting it on the back of their truck. I ran to my father to get him to stop shooting, and that's when he collapsed. I gave him CPR; the ambulance came, fire trucks too; and now we're here," I said without emotion.

"I see."

We proceeded to narrow the night down by the minute, every move questioned. Where was I, what was I doing, and what kind of handgun did my father own? Would I recognize it if I saw it? What kind of vehicle was the one stolen from my father, and what kind of vehicle was the one that had carried it away?

The set of doors at the other end of the hallway opened, and a man in light-green surgical garb from head to toe approached.

"We're done here," I said to Detective Shelby and walked toward the surgeon.

"Are you Eva Rodgers?"

"Yes."

"Let's have a seat, shall we?" he said, walking past me and into the ICU waiting room.

I took up my place in my old chair, and the surgeon squatted down in front of me.

"Your dad's fine," he said and waited for that to sink in.

I closed my eyes as relief flooded through me. "Thank god." I took a moment to revel in that before I realized his face had said there was more. "But?" I asked, opening my eyes.

He nodded. "But since he's on chemo, and he's got a reduced white-blood-cell count, and since we've just cut him open, making him vulnerable to infection, he'll need to be in isolation. You can come with me to see him, and your husband too"—he nodded at Nate over by the door—"but no one else."

I ignored the husband comment.

We left and Nate was right behind me, taking up the position of pretend husband, his fingertips gently pressed against my lower back as we walked.

Down one hallway then another until we finally came to a floor that had glass walls and sliding glass doors to the rooms.

My father wore a hospital gown with a blue paisley pattern, and a white heavy blanket pulled up under his arms; his eyes were closed, and he appeared to be sleeping peacefully despite the fact that equipment was in his arms and nose and clipped to his fingers. Should he so much as think about dying, they would know.

My hand went to the glass wall—I wanted desperately to touch him and make sure his skin was warm, that his breath was coming easily. I didn't want to see that from the computer screen; I wanted to feel it against my cheek as I kissed his own more hollow one and feel the scruff of his gray beard beginning to show. I needed to know undoubtedly, pressed against my own pulse, that he still lived.

"Your father sustained three fractured ribs, likely from the CPR he received. The heart attack that he experienced caused a small portion of his heart to die, about 5 percent. This is not too big of a deal in a man his age, as he was already slowing down; a twenty-five-year-old athlete would feel the difference in 5 percent.

"The reason that we needed to do surgery is that your father has severe arterial plaque buildup; he's lost 90 percent of blood flow in his right coronary artery—we had no choice but to do an emergency surgery to insert a stent. We consulted with your father's oncologist." He looked from my father to me and added, "Mr. Rodgers was lucid enough to tell us his name and that his daughter would be here." He smiled. "He thinks very highly of you."

His last comment made my heart clench and lower lip tremble.

"When will she be able to talk with him?" Nate asked, thinking much more clearly than me.

"We'll start pulling his breathing tube out in about another hour or so, then dialing back the sedatives around noon. Go home, get some rest and food, and come back. He'll be ready to see you when you do."

I gave Dad one more glass-wall hand press before turning away. Nate walked in silence next to me; we got to the parking lot before either of us spoke.

"Leave the car here; I'll take you back to my place—it's close, just around the corner. In case your dad..." He trailed off. "That and your place isn't safe."

I simply nodded.

The night passed by my window dark and silent; my brain—tomb quiet.

At his place Nate ratcheted back the iron screen to his lift. The building's entire top floor was his, but I barely noticed its interior. I headed straight for the bathroom, which was easily the size of my father's living room. It included a Jacuzzi tub, shower, double sinks, toilet, and linen storage with heated towel racks.

Shutting the door behind me, I sat on the edge of the tub looking into the mirror. *OK now*, I thought, *go ahead and really break down.*

A mascara-smudged face looked back at me in silence. I didn't have anything left.

I could hear Nate talking with someone on the phone. I stripped and took a blindingly hot shower. Sometime later, when the water had begun to cool out of the taps, I turned it off and stepped out. I slowly dried my body then hair before I looked down at my pants crumpled on the floor. They were torn and soiled, they'd shared in my evening's drama, and I never wanted to see them again. But I had to a little longer, so I stepped back into them.

As I left the bathroom, Nate was sitting on the corner of his bed watching me, a black V-neck shirt in his hand. "Here," he said and stood, handing it to me. "You can change out here—I need to take a piss. Anthony will be here within the hour with some of your stuff from the house. I told him to lock up and make sure the garage is secure before he leaves."

"OK. Right."

I changed into the oversized shirt in seconds, glad to be rid of the clothes I was wearing. I simply dumped them in the kitchen trash and went to the bank of windows to look out over the city. My mind was carefully blank once more, but my heart had become heavier.

I heard Nate walk out of the bathroom and come to a slow stop some distance behind me. My body hoped he would be closer, that feeling of being held tight by him would be worth the mental turmoil later.

"You need to sleep. I've got some stuff in the fridge if you're hungry."

"No," I said, taking a breath, not sure what I was saying no to, to myself or to him.

He seemed to hear that. "No what?"

"I just meant no, that I didn't eat." I was suddenly very tired.

He gestured to the bed as he headed toward the elevator. "Bed is yours; I'll be sleeping on the couch. But I'm going out first anyway."

"OK," I said and I looked at the rumpled bed. "Are the sheets clean?"

There was a pause and I realized how that must have sounded. Before I could apologize, he said, "I always change the sheets after fucking a chick. So yeah, they're fresh."

Something sparked within me. "Why are you doing this?"

"Doing what, Eva?" he said his hand on the elevator's gate, holding it open.

I splayed my hands. "All this. Why are you taking care of me, when it seems so obvious," I said, thinking of the right word, "the contempt you have for me?"

"Because," he said and paused as he stepped into the elevator, "your dad would want me to."

The elevator descended and I was alone once more.

SEVENTEEN

Nate felt the lie roll off his tongue: "Because your dad would want me to." The truth was, it was more than what Martin would want. Now he needed a cigarette, because Eva was in his bed, in his shirt, in his garage, and in his whole goddamn life, and he didn't know how much longer he could keep himself from not wanting more from her.

Lips to the cigarette, he drew in a long, deep, smoky breath on the sidewalk outside the front door to his building. Scarcely lighted, the exterior was something out of a mobster movie, dimly lit just beyond the train tracks.

Nate smoked his cigarette to the butt, putting it out on the bottom of his boot before tossing it away, and dug out another; at least this addiction he could handle.

When his pack was considerably lighter Anthony pulled up. He got out and tossed Nate two sets of keys and then set a bag for Eva next to him. Nate recognized one set as his 330ci keys.

"Your car's parked out back. My sister volunteered. I think she's hoping to get in good with you."

Nate thought of the larger and much older sister of Anthony and all her kick-ass cooking and smiled. "Tell her thanks but, she knows the way to my heart."

"Yeah? You wanna eat enchiladas and carne asada for a month, you sure?" Anthony asked, laughter in his voice.

"Yes. Yes, I do. So, how'd the rest go?"

Anthony shrugged and tucked his hands in the pockets of his damned sequined designer jeans. "Nothing much—cops got that black dust shit everywhere, even in the house." He smiled, noticing as Nate shook his pack letting the one cigarette rattle around before slipping it into his jacket pocket. "She upstairs?"

"Yeah," he said with finality; there would be no probing that subject. "What about the garage door?"

"That other key set? That's her new keys—changed all the locks and ratcheted down the garage door, old piece of shit that thing is. Cops got pissed we were changing everything out—I told them to take it up with Shelby, like you said. I got a guy coming over tomorrow to install a new garage door."

Nate just nodded, pocketing the keys.

"And the other thing?" Anthony reminded Nate.

"Yeah, what'd you get?"

"Nothing yet, but I got five guys out on the freeways, the 5 north and south, 84, 217, and 205. No way they'd go rural with it; sounded like the truck's too big for it." He paused, looking a little confused. "You know why they had a truck and trailer and not a tow truck? I mean, what the heck do they want with that thing? Not like it's anything special, right?"

"Hell if I know," Nate said, then reiterated, "Hell if I know."

He pulled from his jacket pocket an envelope he'd put together while Eva was in the bathroom. "Here, make sure they get paid for their time."

Anthony stuffed it into his back pocket. "And tomorrow, you in?"

"Yeah, I gotta get that 540 out of the shop and back to Eva. It's backing us up."

"You want me to work on it, so you can do the new ones?"

"No one touches that car but me."

EIGHTEEN

THE SOUND WOKE NATE FROM HIS HALFHEARTED SLUMBER ON the couch. Rubbing his face and all the grogginess from his mind, he waited until he heard it again.

A low keening sent chills up his arms. Sitting up, Nate looked over at the bed to Eva—probably having a bad dream. No shit that she would have one, after last night. Nate stood, kneed the couch cushions straight, and padded into the kitchen. At the tap, he filled a glass with water and watched the bed as he drank.

Eva, facedown in his shirt, was tangled in his sheets, the top blanket kicked off to one side, an arm and leg visible. Her outer hand clutched and released the pillow as if she were struggling with something, or someone.

Nate debated waking her up as she twisted again and her moan became a sob. Resigned to quiet her down for his own sake, he padded over to the bed.

Nate put his knee on the edge and leaned over to shake her shoulder. Eva, hand in a fist, rolled away from him, knocking the glass from his hand.

"Shit!" he said as he lunged for the slopping glass. But not before

Eva, still thrashing, hit it with her knee, sending it to the opposite side of the king-size bed.

"Goddamnit," Nate murmured as he climbed over Eva to retrieve the glass. As he reached out, Eva turned again, and her knee struck Nate on the inside of his thigh.

Nate left the water glass and grasped Eva. "Wake the fuck up," he said to her, his heart hammering at the near miss to his groin.

Eva emitted a strained groan as her whole body tightened like a bowstring. Readying for round two, he pinned her bodily to the mattress and stretched one arm out, picking up the now-empty water glass and putting it on the side table. Glass out of the way, lest there be actual bloodshed, Nate looked down at Eva, expecting her to be wide awake.

Nate's breath caught. Her lips were softly separated now, as if she had woken only from her nightmare and not from sleep itself. Her hair was strewn in a wild dark mess across the sheets.

Roll off of her, *he told himself.*

Just roll off her.

Nate felt his pulse quicken.

The feel of her, despite *everything*, was bliss.

"Wake up," he choked, managing to slide his leg out from between hers.

As Nate lifted his weight off of her, Eva's eyes snapped opened and she inhaled sharply. "Dad."

Nate said under his breath, "Definitely *not* your pops."

In a rush, I sat up and wavered, looking around the darkened space. "Where..." Then saw Nate next to me and remembered. "My dad—"

"Is alive," he finished.

My heart was still trip-hammering in my chest from the nightmare in which he'd permanently died. I shook my head against the nightmare and groaned. "He died."

"You're pops is in ICU—"

"I know," I said weakly, then, "I know," more firmly. "Only it was so real, god, that was so real..." I said still feeling the fog of the dream. I looked over at Nate and was startled to find him closer than anticipated. With no shirt on.

"It wasn't real," he said softly, and uncharacteristically brushed a lock of my hair back over my shoulder.

I looked into Nate's face in the darkened room, his firm shadowed jawline and eyes intense, missed nothing. His hand caressed up my arm and cupped the side of my cheek, wiping an errant tear as the remnants of my nightmare fizzled away like ice on the hood of a car on a midsummer's day.

His hand slid up into my hair and guided my face to his lips.

Someone groaned as the feeling of smoke and fire filled my insides with its breath-stealing heat. Nate's mouth slid open, and my lips, still confused on what exactly was happening, simply gave him the right of way—the right to taste, to remember. Memories unbidden stirred within me. I remembered distinctly the way his skin smelled, crisp and earthy—like a man who bore sweat and exertion for a living. My lips remembered every word he'd ever uttered to me. The whispers in the dark, the silent *I love yous* when his eyes met mine, the confessions that only my ears heard. The childhood hurt he showed to no one but me, and it was only me who knew what his mother and father had done to him. His lips spoke of patience; his hands, capable and confident, reached out for me.

I gripped his naked waist and pulled myself in against him as his grip at the back of my head tightened. Crushing my mouth to his in lustful hunger just as emotion bloomed in my chest.

Nate deepened the kiss, pulling another groan from me just as he severed the connection.

"Damn," he said and, breathing heavily, looked down at the sheets.

"Oh." I said light-headed and, following his gaze to the mattress, asked, "Why are the sheets wet?"

His dark gaze came slowly back to mine, the smoldering in them shifted.

"I didn't...? You didn't...?"

Nate simply looked at me, looking as if he'd like to say something, but nothing would come out. My heart raced as he leaned forward again only to have it slow in disappointment as he picked up an empty water glass off the side table behind me.

"You knocked this out of my hand when I tried to wake you from your nightmare," he said, slipping off the bed and walking to the kitchen put it in the sink. He wiped a hand over his face. "What are you doing?"

"I . . ." I managed, touching my fingers to my lips then looked back to him, "was that question for me or you?"

Nate just shook his head and stalked to the elevator, where he pulled his jacket from the hook and slipped on shoes. "Fix the sheets before you leave," he said and descended out of sight.

NINETEEN

Oh my god, Eva," Jenny said the next morning when I called her, "I'm so sorry. What do you need me to do?"

"Thanks, Jenny. I've got those files on the shared drive, so you can access my edits; I'd just opened Cathy's article when it happened, so I haven't edited it yet." I briefed Jenny about what to expect from the art department for the cover graphic and what was due at the end of the day. "If my dad is doing good, I'll swing by later today. If not, I'll see you Monday, Jenny," I said and ended the call, trying not to think about that latter possibility.

I grabbed my things and gave Nate a mental thanks for getting the 330ci from the hospital to his place. At the nearest café, I ordered coffee and gave in to the fragrant doughnuts sitting in the glass pastry case next to the register. I arrived at the hospital right before visiting hours started.

Dad was awake but looked like he'd gone three rounds with a prize fighter and then run a mile.

"Hi, handsome," I said, putting the sack of fragrant, fatty baked goods on the rolling table by his bed and bent, kissing him. "How are you this morning?"

He smiled weakly and tried to speak, only no sound came out. A massive container of water with a straw like one would get in a super-size Big Gulp was on his nightstand.

Holding it to his lips, I watched as my dad strained to take a sip, then tried again. "Good," he finally croaked. A few sips more, and his voice came fully back. "Tired is all."

"Just tired, huh? No pain?" I said, unearthing the doughnuts from their bag.

"Leg hurts where they went in with the probe thingy, but the doc says that's normal."

"Ah," I said and handed him a doughnut, of which he took a tentative bite.

"I'm not sure I'm supposed to have one of these after a heart attack."

"You are most definitely not," I said and polished one off—and then felt immediately sick as the sugary fat hit my empty, nervous belly. "But that is your reward for coming back to life. And it's the last one you'll ever have. So enjoy." Thinking better of the coffee I'd just taken a couple sips of, I poured the rest down the drain in the room's bathroom sink.

"Well, when you put it that way..." I heard him say and when I left the bathroom, I found him licking powder from his fingers.

I sucked down some of Dad's water, and we sat together in companionable silence, just looking at each other. I felt myself smile at him, and he squeezed my hand in understanding. He'd died, come back, and now lived, but he still battled the cancer. Every moment from then on was precious.

"So," I said softly, breaking the silence, "any ideas on who stole your truck?"

"Mmmph. Nate asked me that same damn question earlier."

His visitor and his change in attitude took me by surprise. "Nate? He was here today? Are you sure? Visiting hours just started." Then I realized, if all that stood between Nate and a little rule like visiting hours were nurses, he'd be able to charm his way to success every time.

"Well, I'm no fool, he was here—looked like he just rolled out of bed and tossed on his jacket."

I nodded, thinking, *that was exactly what he did.* "What'd you tell him?"

"I was out of it—you ask *him* if you want to know that."

I leaned back in the chair, watching him. "Are you in any pain, Dad?"

"No," he said curtly to the ceiling.

"OK, then, seeing as I'm here and Nate isn't, how about you tell me? I doubt you were that out of it."

Dad leveled his gaze at me. "You two are circling each other like two dogs—just bite each other and get it over with, Eva Lynn."

"What?"

"Now, Eva, that boy was your first love, and damn it if you weren't his—"

I stood abruptly and went to the window, folding my arms over my chest. "Sure, but Dad, I'm not having this conversation with you. And I sure as hell wasn't Nate's first," I added.

"I didn't say you were his first; I said you were the first woman he's ever loved, probably the only. And you should do something about it before one of you kills yourself going three hundred miles an hour in the opposite direction."

I was quiet for a moment and decided to switch tactics. I turned around and said flatly guessing, "Drugs."

"What?" my dad replied, derailed from his original thought line.

"Is that what you were hiding in the truck?"

His eyebrows shot up. "Drugs? You think they stole my truck because I had drugs in it?"

"Well then, what am I supposed to think? Who the hell comes to the house in the middle of the night when we're both there, breaks into the garage, and hauls away the truck?"

The incessant beeping of one of the machines hooked up to Dad increased its tempo as though to match my voice's rising ire.

"Eva Lynn, how could you—"

"Or, maybe you got a loan on the truck and refused to pay it back, so that was actually a repo service? Dad, did you shoot at people trying to repossess the truck because you defaulted on the loan?"

"How dare you—"

"No, Dad, how dare you," I hissed. "After all that's happened: the chemo appointments, and despite your nasty temper when you're feeling down, I help you out and bite my tongue when you need to lash out, and then someone steals your truck—you shoot at them with a gun I didn't know you had, and then fall dead on me. Dad—I brought you back to life. You scared the ever-living life out of me and I pumped your damn heart and body back into this world. And after all of that, you can't answer one simple question? Instead you feed me some crap about love and Nate and what I should do with him. What the hell, Dad? Who stole your truck?"

The door slid open and two nurses rushed in, the first going to Dad and the other to me. Of course—the machines would have sounded an alarm.

"Ma'am, I'm going to have to ask you to leave now," said the one nurse as she gently got a hold on my arm and steered me out.

"Fine," I said and snatched up my purse, shaking her off as I did so. "I'm done here anyway." Then I added between gritted teeth to my dad, who was giving me a filthy look, "I love you, and I'll come by later."

"Don't bother!" he hollered as the glass door shut behind me.

The nurse and I walked along in silence to the elevator. As we waited for it to arrive, she said, "I'm sure this goes without saying: When you come back later, try not to stir up such a fuss, OK?"

A sound came out of me, sort of like a choking snort. "Yes, *I'll* be sure to not kick up a fuss."

"Mind you, if there are fewer episodes like this, he'll be fit to go home in just a couple days. Keep it up and we'll keep him forever, if you know what I mean."

I sighed.

"Thanks for the reality check," I said over my shoulder as I stepped into the elevator.

"Bye," the nurse said in a falsely cheerful voice and waved as the elevator doors shut.

TWENTY

NOT IN ANY MOOD TO GO HOME AND HAVING NOWHERE ELSE TO go, I headed in to work. As soon as I stepped into my office, I was immediately swamped, and completely grateful for it. It turned out that no one had respected Jenny as the acting editor-in-chief in my absence.

"I dunno, Eva, I can't seem to get anybody to give me their updated stories, and the art department said that they are waiting for your go-ahead before they finalize the cover page. Then one of our advertisers called because they wanted to update their ad before it goes to press, but they're not ready with their new artwork and want us to help, and art is slammed with the cover-page changes since Karen's out sick and I still have to finish writing that damn story! Oh, and how's your dad?"

"Fine," I lied as the feeling of a dark cloud moved over me. The department was made up of four individuals, Karen being the director, but even in her absence, a single image with updates should take just one person no more than an hour to do. And that was if they were trying to do it drunk.

"Who'd you give the cover art changes to?"

Jenny was leery at my change in disposition, "It's fine, Eva—"

"Never mind, I know who it is." I said and I stalked out of the room toward the art department.

I heard her call from behind me, "I'm sure it's on its way Eva, there's no reason to go down there in person!"

Thirty minutes later, I was back in my office, a piece of ire sufficiently gone. And it took only thirty seconds after that for word to spread to Jenny and bring her white faced into my office.

"Sorry," she said meekly, "didn't mean to make you go on a rampage."

"Actually," I said, sliding in front of my computer, "it was quite therapeutic. I should threaten to fire people more often."

"OK," Jenny said, drawing out the word, and then quietly went back to her desk.

At my desk I worked through lunch reviewing last-minute story and ad changes. Halfway through the afternoon, an e-mail from IMG, the magazine's parent company, came through. IMG's newest investor would be in town the next day and would need showing around the office and (this wasn't mentioned, but implied) one night's worth of entertainment and ass kissing before he jet-setted to the next magazine headquarters.

I growled at the screen, "I don't have time for this crap,"

Jenny came bounding in. "Did you hear the news?"

"Which news, Jenny?" I asked wearily.

"The *investor*," she said as if he were James Bond.

"Jenny, hands off the money." I hit the reply button on my e-mail, sending my confirmation that the team and I would be happy to show the investor around and, as a side note, we were in full swing trying to get the July issue out the door—i.e., we didn't have much time to spare.

Sliding my gaze from my computer screen to Jenny, I had a

wicked thought, "Actually, you can take him around, what do you say? Show him all your hot knitting spots?"

"Ha-ha," she said dryly. "But really? Can I show him around?"

"Absolutely. But just don't get fresh, this guy is an investor, probably twice your age and married with grandchildren."

"Umm, Eva? He's in his early thirties and has just taken over his father's role in all the family's investments," she said a mite too dreamily.

"Seriously Jenny, I just got the e-mail—please tell me you didn't Google stalk him already."

"No," she said indignantly. "I just heard about him."

"From whom?"

"Just about everybody..."

"Right. Well, you're definitely in charge of taking him out."

"Really? Excellent! Where should I take him?" she asked full of bubble.

"Just grab a couple of the department heads and go out for cocktails somewhere."

"OK! But, where though? And don't say knitting spots because I know that's not his brand of kink—"

She stopped, something caught her attention, and looking to her right, out my office window into the office area said, "Oh, gotta go," and beelined out my door.

"What in the world..." I murmured and rolled in my chair around the corner of my desk and leaned back, looking out my office window, which faced the main hallway to the elevators.

Halfway expecting a fuming art-department employee, I was surprised to see Nate striding purposefully toward my office. A quick glance at cubeville said that more than one person had noticed him: several female staffers and one male were standing to watch his progress.

Immediately I checked my cell phone—there were no messages from the hospital. None on my desk phone either.

I stood as he walked in and closed the door behind himself.

"Is everything OK?" I asked cautiously.

"Peachy," he said in a snarl, as if he had been working a mood all day.

That instantly got my back up. "How can I help you, then?" I asked cooly and walked around my desk. I leaned back against it, thanking the good lord that I'd faced down more than my fair share of complicated situations. Still, images of our kiss the prior night slipped into my mind, conjuring up feelings, which led my mind to stutter stepping. My past was now standing in the midst of the life I single-handedly built for myself. And built such that the two would never meet.

I realized this situation was more than complicated—it was doomsday.

Nate looked me up and down. "I'm not here to buy a goddamn subscription." He pulled two sets of keys out of his jeans pocket, tossed them onto the desk behind me. Conveniently getting into my space for a few short moments as he did so.

I gave the keys a cursory glance—house and car. My beautiful car.

Nate put his palm out. "My car keys?"

"Right," I said and fished out the 330ci's keys from my purse and handed them over. "Thanks. I could have come by to get them."

"And have you on my property again? I don't think so." He pulled out what I quickly saw was an invoice—a curiously two-page invoice. "It was the wiring harness—corroded; keep it out of puddles large enough to hit the floorboards. And the second page is for rekeying your house and a new garage door that was installed this morning, also a new security system. The manual for the alarm is on your counter."

Once again the invoice totaled out to zero. "Nate, tha—"

He put a hand up. "I'm not done yet. Last night was a one-off, I'm not gonna be your fucking boyfriend, your fucking mechanic, or come running when you need someone. I'm doing this for your pops." He kept going, seemingly building steam. "Under no circumstances are you to come onto my property—don't call me, don't stop by, no shit,

Eva. I'm done looking at your mug and having you in my space. Got that?"

"Yeah, I got that," I said, my voice monotone with anger. "Thanks for stopping by and making sure you fed it to me in my office where I have glass windows looking out to my staff—feel safer with witnesses?"

"You bet your sweet ass. Now you know how it feels to have your ex walk into your work life and fuck things up for you." He gave me a grin that was far from friendly.

"Really? *I* messed things up for *you* these past few days? I don't buy that." I held up my index finger. "One, I'm still not convinced you didn't wreck my car's wiring in the first place—"

"I'll show you the corroded wiring—"

"And two," I interrupted, holding up two fingers in case he'd become dense, "I went to you for a legitimate business reason. And it's obvious that's not why you're here, as you delicately put it not just a few moments ago."

Nate's eyes went dark as he leaned in. "You're right I'm not here for your services."

I walked smartly to the windows that looked into the inner offices and snapped the old dusty miniblinds shut, then went on to the door and flipped the lock. Privacy gained, I turned on him.

"I hear your words, Nate. Loud and clear: Get out of your life. But what I don't understand is why last night you were there, right when I needed you the most; right when my world crumbled under me, you caught me. Despite *everything*."

Nate's eye ticked. "I didn't come here to—"

"Listen," I said with force. "I'm sorry. So, so, so sorry, Nate, for not being there for you all those years ago, that the way we left things made me cold to you. I wanted to leave Portland behind me. I had to go be someone, and the internship at *Vogue* was my ticket out. I should have called my dad more than once a year. I should have been there for you. I shouldn't have been embarrassed because of where I came from and who I fell in love with—who I am still in love with."

Nate flinched as if slapped. "Don't say another goddamn word."

My hands had started to shake. I clutched them together and took a stabilizing breath. "Tough crap. Now you know." I felt light-headed and tamped down a nervous laugh. "Now I know. Nearly losing my dad last night was a wake-up call. I suppose the one I've been needing for a while. What happens if I lose him? What do I have? My job?" I snorted.

Nate's face was frozen in a snarl, though no sound came from him. He stared at me as if he were watching a train wreck and couldn't look away.

"I'd have nothing," I continued breathlessly. "That's what I would have. I've just started to ask myself who in my life do I care about? And how have I been treating them? Have I been telling them that I love them and showing them? Because having you come to me last night was like a lifeline when I thought I had lost everything... Everything, Nate—I thought I'd lost it all."

My words rang true in the air and speaking them felt like going to confession, letting all that had been buried for so long come to the surface and be aired out between us. It felt cathartic.

Nate blew out a breath and stiffly walked to the bank of windows looking out over the city. He stood for a moment and then put a stabilizing arm up on the window frame. "Jesus fucking Christ." I heard him say, as his other hand pinched the bridge of his nose.

Nate's voice was muffled behind his hand, but I heard him say, "I wasn't ready for that."

I was silent for a moment and then said softly, "Nate. It's OK if you can't forgive me—I can understand if you can't go back to where we were. I'm not asking for that. I'm just telling you how I feel, truly, and I won't keep my feelings from you or from my dad."

"Eva, I hear your words. And, yeah, you're too fucking late. Seven goddamn years too late. I'm not going to run to you whenever you need me; you might think you can just walk back into my life, but I don't want you here"—he seemed to be struggling with his words, but he finished—"in my life."

"I see."

I could see a snide comment forming in his mouth, and that knowledge must have shown on my face, because the words never came, and his own angry face softened slightly. He looked back out the window for a moment and said, "Butch is out," before turning back.

"Oh. What? How?"

"So you did know."

I'd been baited. I closed my eyes and sat on the edge of an arm chair before I fell down from emotional exhaustion. "Yes. And no. Nate, I didn't know that right away. I heard—"

Nate held up his palm. "I don't want to hear your shit."

Nate's gaze was piercing as he took me in, looked right into me, to the very heart of me. With my confession I was naked, flayed, and vulnerable as hell.

The room was quiet except for the thrumming of my pulse in my ears. I opened my mouth to fill the silence but closed it again. I had no excuses, deserved none. This was the one thing I'd never forgive myself for. Nate's gaze was chilling; I could almost watch the slow shuttering, him becoming an emotionless shell.

In a quiet and eerily calm voice he said, "He was released early by twenty-five years. Keep an eye out. No late nights in this place." He pulled his cap out of his back pocket and walked out my door. I just watched him go.

I sat still on the arm of the rickety armchair in the middle of my office. I watched his back as he strode toward the elevators, making the trip past all the cubes and, to my dismay, Jessie from the art department, who was coming my way. I watched as she made eyes at him, letting her curves sway. Nate being the man he was, I expected his head to turn, but he never broke stride or looked back at her.

Jessie sauntered in. "Your cover art is done. And I quit."

I just looked at her. "You want a box?"

TWENTY-ONE

In the elevator, Nate didn't even notice the girl until she spoke to him, he was so wrapped up in his own internal dialogue. Eva still loved him. Her words circled in his head like rats on a wheel.

Fuck that. She was just playing with him. What happened when she left again?

But what if she never left? What if she was for real about loving him? His brain shut that thought down. He'd never be used by Eva Rodgers again. Fuck her pretty face, fuck her talk about love, fuck her. Right? *Fuck.*

He wanted her, felt that needing pull in his gut. It was like the breakup had never happened when he looked at her now.

He needed a cigarette.

Was someone talking to him?

Nate looked over at the girl in the elevator with him. She'd asked him something...

"Peugeot, right?" he said to her.

"Wow." She seemed genuinely impressed. "Good memory. I'm Jenny."

"You've been in a couple times," he said and shook her hand. "Nice to meet you, Jenny. Nate."

"Yeah," she said and smiled, showing two dimples. "I sort of know who you are." She blushed.

Nate wasn't sure what the blush was about—had he fixed her car *and* slept with her? *Shit.* "You know Eva?"

Her mouth opened to reply, then closed, then opened again. "Actually, I know you because we met when you worked on my car. But, yes, I also know Eva—she's my boss."

Nate smiled, but it didn't reach his eyes. "Everything OK with your car?"

"Well, no," she said, still smiling, "but sort of goes with the territory, right?"

"Yeah, you don't buy the '77 Peugeot because you want reliability. I have this discussion a lot with my clients: Euro cars, sexy as fuck but reliable as the goddamn weatherman."

Jenny flinched at his language. He cleared his throat as though to clean his mouth out.

"So true," she said and looked like she wanted to say something more as the door chimed, and the polished steel doors slid open to the lobby.

"Yeah?" Nate said encouragingly as he stepped out and held the door for her. "Coming with? Looks like you got something on your mind."

"Yeah, well it's not really about my car, though..."

Nate's stomach did a flip as his mind—before he could shut it down—hoped it was about Eva.

The lobby was all soaring glass windows and marble floors and columns with massive lush plantings. Nate stepped to the side with Jenny next to one of the leafy pots. And just waited.

Jenny looked around awkwardly, then said in a rush, "We have a guy coming to town, an investor, and he's young and I volunteered to take him out because Eva can't with her dad and all. So, I need to know where to take him because I'm not real sure because I'm not a guy and I like to knit and he's used to high-end things and, well, you're a guy, and I hear you get around a lot—oh, er, get *out* a lot—and I thought I'd ask you—"

Nate gave a low chuckle at her fumble. "For the record, I get around a lot, *and* I get out a lot, Peugeot."

She flushed at his sudden nickname for her.

He pulled out his phone. "What's your number? I'll send you the contact info for the two places I'd recommend. Let me know when you'll be there and I'll take care of you and your exec—trust me, it'll be a night he won't forget."

Jenny's mouth opened and shut again.

"Just your number, and I promise that's all I'll send you," he said, this time giving her a genuine smile.

"I—yeah," she said and rattled off her number. "Wow, that's really nice of you."

Before Nate could help himself he said, "You work closely with Eva?"

"Yeah, she's my editor-in-chief, er, boss. I'm her assistant."

Nate nodded. "Outside of work, you guys hang out?"

"Yeah, I'd like to think we're friends. I was the one to introduce her to your shop."

"Yeah, she told you I'm her ex, right?"

"Ah, yeah."

"She tell you about us?" God, he couldn't stop.

"Little bit," she said slowly, cautiously. "I think she feels that she messed up. She didn't say why, or how, since she really doesn't like to talk about it. Guilt, I think."

Nate grunted a response and pretended to still be entering info in his phone, buying time. "Guilty, huh? Interesting."

"I have a lot of vicarious experience with relationships because I have a whole bunch of sisters and cousins, and I read a lot—" She pinched her lips together. "Never mind. Thanks," she said, pointing to his phone, "for the suggestions."

"Peugeot," he said, pinning her to the spot with his eyes, "spit it out."

God, he wanted to know, to hear confirmation from this girl who was her friend.

He watched as Jenny took a deep breath while staring back at him as a deer in oncoming traffic would.

"Jeez, I can see why you get what you want all the time."

He liked Peugeot. "Not every time."

Jenny rolled her eyes at him, finding her gumption. "Go upstairs right this minute and tell her."

"Tell her what?"

"That you love her."

Then something occurred to Nate. "Could you hear us?" He felt a little cold trickle down his back at the very thought of anyone, *anyone*, else hearing them in Eva's office a few minutes before.

"My cube is right outside her door. I'm the only one who could hear, and I only heard Eva."

"Fuck," Nate said, looking around as he ran a hand through his hair. Then he looked down at her. "Well, shit. See you around, Peugeot—let me know when you hit the clubs." He saluted her good-bye with his cell and stalked from the building.

TWENTY-TWO

AFTER JESSIE LEFT, I DROPPED BACK BEHIND MY COMPUTER TO find a follow up e-mail that our young exec would be landing in an hour and that we were expected to get him.

"Son of a..." I knocked on the wood paneling when the thought that this day couldn't get any worse slipped into my mind.

Too many hours later, after giving Kenneth Wellington III a tour of the *Rose City Review* offices and situating him in the most expensive penthouse suite (feeling like we had investors just to be able to afford our investors) in downtown Portland, apparently the same suite Mick Jagger and friends ripped to shreds in the eighties, I stopped by the hospital.

My father was sleeping, low flickering light of the television illuminating the space and playing shadows across his face. I dropped my gear in one of the stuffed guest chairs and plopped myself into the other.

Several hours later I woke to my neck aching and my mouth dry.

"Snore like a freight train in a tunnel, child," Dad said, spooning applesauce into his mouth.

The lights were blaring overhead, and the news was on too loud.

"Jeez," I said, scrubbing my face. "How long was I out for?"

"Couple hours since I woke up."

"Jeez," I said again and stood. I slugged back half of Dad's jug of water.

"You come to harass me again?"

"No," I said from the bathroom as I refilled his water container. "I just came to see how you were doing." I sat back down.

We were quiet again.

"So," I broached, "how was your day?"

He gestured around him. "Fine, just fine, Eva Lynn."

"Ah," I said. "My day? Thanks for asking, Dad. Well, someone quit, and we have a new investor surprise visiting. Worst part? I couldn't give a crap. Oh, and I told Nate I loved him," I mumbled the last part.

"You what?" my father said, his head whipping around to look at me, spoon midair.

"I asked if you knew why someone would want to steal your truck."

"No, you didn't. Eva Lynn, I might be deaf, but I'm not—"

"Why would someone steal your truck?"

He narrowed his eyes at me.

"I tell you what, you tell me who you think stole your truck, and I'll tell you what I told Nate."

Another long pause. "Fine, you first." He said.

I tried not to smile. Then told him the whole conversation, right through the parts where he told me it was too late and that Butch was out of jail. Dad's response to that last bit was not at all what I expected.

"Butch paid me a visit the other day."

I kept my voice calm as my hands clutched together in my lap. A cold-blooded killer stood on my father's front porch and chatted with him? "At the house?"

"Yes."

I waited for the rest. When he offered none, I said, "Thanks for telling me, Dad, I'll let the officer in charge of your case know so Butch can go back behind bars."

Dad made a frustrated face and waved his spoon back and forth in the air. "No, no. No police. It's gone. So be it; we have to move on now." He tucked into his applesauce again with vehemence.

"Dad," I said patiently, "move on? What did he say to you?"

The machines started to beep faster, and I stayed as quiet as my father.

The silence lengthened.

"Did Nathaniel tell you that he saw him?"

"No," I said.

"Oh," he said and relaxed back onto his pillows on his inclined bed. "Butch is looking for Nate."

Oh god. I closed my eyes.

"He came by the house looking for Nate's address, said he needed to see his son. All he had left in life, or some crap like that. I told him that I didn't know and he should beat it or I'd call the police. He did leave right away, but he wasn't happy about it."

"Then he came back and stole your Chevy," I supplied.

"Maybe," he said.

"Dad, I'll have to tell Detective Shelby about this."

"No, Eva Lynn, we're even, he and I. And it's a better trade. We have Nate, he has my truck, so be it."

"Dad...he's been released from prison early on good behavior. The police need to know that he contacted you and you felt threatened. Help them build a case to put him back behind bars. He needs to be behind bars."

"Eva Lynn Rodgers, if the police go to question him, he could come back and take something more valuable from me. He could take you. No, let it be, Eva; we're even, and he knows it."

"But Dad, this goes against every grain in my body—this is not right. This is why he's dangerous—he's temperamental, irrational. And probably drinking again, which will make it all the worse. My goodness Dad, when Nate finds out, he'll hunt him down. Do you want that? We have the law in place for things like this. Please—"

"And what happens, Eva, when you are at work someday, and Marta's not there, and I'm day three past the latest chemo? You want to come home to my body hacked to pieces?"

The retort was so childish that I wanted to laugh in response, but the image he painted silenced that laugh. "That was a low blow."

"No police. He and I are square. He'll sell her and with any luck, he'll get enough money to be so piss drunk he won't think about Nate until he dies."

I just shook my head. "Fine," I said. "No police for now."

The conversation was officially over when Dad's doctor came in to check on him before heading home for the night. He checked his vitals, checked his chart and all the special notes scribbled there before flipping it shut and slipping it back into the pocket at the end of the bed.

"All right, Mr. Rodgers," he said with a smile, "looks like you are healing up nicely. It looks like you'll be ready to go Sunday. Monday at the very latest. How's the food?"

I rolled up to Dad's place and put the car in park. The house felt weird, even from outside; the grass was trampled; the new garage door gleamed too white in the headlights. Making my way to the house, I watched the street and everywhere around me. The thought of Butch being out of jail and having jacked my father's truck as payment for Nate creeped me out. Inside I disarmed the new security system with the code Nate had given me—note to self: change that, tomorrow—and then rearmed the perimeter. It was going to be a long night.

TWENTY-THREE

The rain poured down around Nate as he got out from his 330ci and ducked into Mario's.

"Ayeee!" his aunt Flora squealed, coming around the counter to kiss him. "There he is, little Nathaniel."

The deli was empty, but the attached restaurant was bustling, Nate could see, as waiters moved back and forth through the swinging door to his right.

Despite Flora's lack of height, she still managed to grab Nate's face and give each cheek a loud kiss. "It's been too long. How are you? And don't say fine!" she said, shaking a finger at him before heading back behind the counter to grab the order he'd called in.

Nate smiled. "Good," he said instead.

"Speak in sentences! You do know how, right?" she teased.

"How are you and Lou?"

She turned to look at him, her eyebrows raised, over-processed auburn hair wilder than ever. "Fine!"

She dropped two bags on the counter in front of him, suddenly very serious. "You heard?"

Nate knew what she was talking about. Her stepbrother being let out of jail twenty-five years early would be weighing heavily on her mind. The noise from the dining room and the hiss and clank of the kitchen behind the deli filled the air between them.

"Yeah. I got the alert. You heard from him?"

She shook her head. "Not a peep, thank Mary." She looked heavenward and then crossed herself.

"Right," Nate said. "How much I owe you?" He pulled out his wallet.

His aunt snorted. "What's this? Your uncle and I are never able to pay at your shop, and now you come here thinking you can pay here? Put it away." She stabbed the air. "Your money's no good here."

"Flora..." He pulled a couple twenties from his wallet.

"*Aiya!* What happened to Mama? You too old now? And if you don't put away that wallet, I'll choke you with it, got it? Now, did you know that Eva's back in town?"

Nate wiped a hand over his face. "Really?"

"Oh," she said quietly, "I see."

"What? See what?" Nate said, gesturing around him.

"You back together with her, then?"

Nate looked around him some more. "Where are you getting this? No, we're not back together."

"So you've seen her?"

Nate saw Lou, a round and stern man, make his way through the kitchen to the server window behind his wife. "Eh, Nate! How are you?" He leaned into the chest-high ledge, a spatula in hand.

Nate nodded at him. "Lou, good. You?"

"Good, good as well."

Nate picked up his bags. "Good seeing both of you," he said as he made a hasty retreat.

"Good! Good! All you men ever say: good. Or fine! What does that mean?" he heard his aunt saying behind him.

Lou's response escaped the door swinging shut behind Nate: "Just what it says, Flora—good!"

Back at his place Nate dropped the bags onto the counter and checked his phone: Anthony and Mikey were out, wondering where the hell he was. Veronica was "waiting" at Festivál with her crew.

Flicking on the flat screen, he found a game and sat down with the food and dug in. The NBA playoffs in the final throes—he probably had money on the game he was watching but couldn't remember.

Polishing off the rest of his lasagna, Nate scraped the bottom of the to-go box, pulling the extra cheese off. His phone trilled as he dropped the box and fork into the sink. The unlisted number on the caller ID screen gave him pause—*where is Butch right now, anyway?*—and the fact that he paused made him angry. "Vellanova," he spat.

"Good evening, Nathaniel. This is Detective Shelby."

That it was. His was a voice Nate would never forget. "Shelby."

"You busy tonight?"

Nate looked around his empty apartment. "Depends. What do you want?" He grabbed a glass next to the sink and filled it.

"Butch Vellanova."

"Who's that?" Nate said as he slammed the tap off, his heart hammering and his mind running through the possibilities, all horrible and violent, of what his father could have done now.

"He's still dead to you?"

"What do you want, Shelby?"

"Your cousin Donny over in traffic said you weren't busy tonight" —Flora, Donny, bigmouths, all of them—"and I'd like to talk to you about Martin Rodgers and talk to you about your father." His voice was steady and firm.

"And if I say no?" Nate said as he switched off his flat screen.

"Well, I can come by your place now."

Nate slipped his coat on. Despite Shelby being a cop, he wasn't a bad guy, and he wouldn't have called if he didn't have something important to say. "You know where Shugga Brown's is?"

"Sure do."

"Meet you there."

Shugga Brown's was an always-crowded jazz club serving up down-home Southern food and a renowned music calendar.

Nate walked in to raucous horns filling the small, heavily draped restaurant. Despite the darkened club being standing-room-only, Nate could get a table, and he did, on the far side of the room in the very back where the stage was barely visible and the sound reverberated less.

Soon Nate spotted Shelby making his way over. "Nice seats— who'd you have to take out at the kneecaps for these?" the older man asked, taking his time with his coat and hanging it on the back of his chair.

Shelby always reminded Nate of Morgan Freeman, with his slow and deliberate style, a hard-ass at his core.

"Cut the shit, Shelby, what'd the old man do?"

"For one, he's out of prison. Did you know that?" he said as he got himself situated in his chair.

"Yeah, what else?"

"Oh, OK." He thanked the waiter who brought waters to their table and the next one, who took his drink order. "So, how are you doing with that?"

Nate blew out a breath, looked around the room, and then sat forward, one elbow resting on the table. He felt like he was in lockup again and stuck playing word games with his lawyer. "Jesus, Shelby, spit it out. What'd the old man do?"

"Nothing. He's at a halfway house, and we've got his post-prison supervisor on speed dial but, Nate, this has got to hit you hard."

Nate shook his head and sat back. A social call? Maybe he'd been wrong about Shelby's OK factor. "What are you? A goddamn therapist? What halfway house did you say that was?"

"I didn't."

"I've got a couple things to ask him."

"Mmm-hmm. I'm sure you do."

"What? You worried I'm gonna do more than just talk with him?" Nate turned his water glass around and around slowly.

"Are you?"

Nate eventually looked away to the trio jamming on stage. "Who knows. Right now, I'm just trying not to think about it. That's all I do these days, try not to think about shit."

"I hear you, son, but be sure you don't bottle it all up inside and let 'er rip like you did in your twenties. You have too much at stake now."

Nate gave him a look. "Thanks for the pep talk, Pops. You heard anything on the Martin Rodgers thing?"

Shelby nodded. "That's the thing, Nate. I'm getting tripped up on the coincidences in timing on the whole thing, which happened at your ex's father's place just days after Butch was released."

Nate just looked at him, then shook his head. "I thought of that, but it doesn't make sense that he'd take it. What would he do with it? It's not important enough. If anything, he'd take Eva."

Shelby raised his brows. "You really think your old man is still capable of something like that?"

"I'd have to see him to be sure, but an asshole like that? Prison won't have changed him. At least it won't have made him into a better man."

"OK. But I still don't believe in coincidences, Nate. I have to explore the option that it was Butch who stole Martin's truck. Though right now we have no evidence that he has been anywhere near Martin's place, and when I spoke with Martin yesterday he was...let's just say he was uncooperative."

Martin was probably hella uncooperative. Just like his daughter could be.

Shelby continued. "You heard anything that could help?"

"No. But I haven't pressed Martin, and I haven't talked to Eva—won't talk to Eva," he corrected. Then kicked himself. Shelby would want to know why.

As if on cue: "Why?"

Nate just stared at Shelby. He knew why.

Shelby stared back.

"Why do you think?" he said. "Or you having a hard time remembering things now that you're sixty?"

"Fifty. And I remember vividly every arrest I make, including all three of yours. You know, Nate, no one's good at running from problems; we always do better facing them head-on."

"Except for this one. Just drop it. You need me to talk to Martin?"

Shelby watched him for a moment. "She married?"

"Nope."

"She not into boys? She always was a little tomboyish as a kid, right?"

"You need me to talk to Martin?" he repeated.

"Yeah. And I don't suppose I have to ask you to put the word out on his truck too."

"Already did—had some guys take a look at the freeways right after and found nothing."

Shelby took the information down and was silent. His drink came, which added bourbon to the information he was digesting. "So it's in town."

"The truck? Nah, too risky. Just missed it, and it's halfway to Mexico by now."

"OK," Shelby said, sounding unconvinced, "I'll talk to Eva Rodgers again."

Nate looked away from Shelby as he said her name.

"You want me to pass along anything to her?" Shelby asked. "Seeing as you're not talking to her. You know, it's kinda hard to have a relationship with a woman without talking to her."

Nate slid his eyes back to the older man. "Keep it up. I'm feeling a joyride coming on."

All this got was a hoot of laughter from Shelby. "Someday, Nate, you'll understand."

TWENTY-FOUR

My cell went off at six a.m., not long enough after I'd fallen asleep in my clothes, my laptop and papers pushed to the far side of the bed, and too long before my coffee meeting with Detective Shelby, which I'd agreed to just to get him out of my hair when he'd called during the issue's final push the night before. Groggily, I grabbed for the offending thing off my nightstand.

"Hello?" I asked it, rather sharply.

"Ms. Rodgers?"

"This is she," I said, sitting up, alarmed by Dr. Zimmerman's voice on the other line.

"Good morning, Ms. Rodgers, this is Dr. Zimm—"

"I know who this is—is my dad OK?"

"Yes, but he is going through a bit of difficulty, and that's why I called."

"But I just saw him last night."

"It started this morning. Your father has had an adverse reaction to one of the chemotherapy drugs. It's causing him to hiccup quite badly. We've got him on an antipsychotic that is helping until this passes."

This took me a moment. "Wait. He's never had hiccups before—did something change in his treatments? But besides that, did you say you have him on antipsychotic drugs? Like, neuroinhibitors for hiccups? Isn't that a little much? Drinking water, holding his breath didn't work?"

There was dead space on the line.

"Hello?"

"Ahhh, how do I explain this?" he said. "Imagine for a moment your strongest hiccup. Are you doing that?"

"Yes."

"Imagine the one that leaves your lungs and abdominal muscles feeling tired and exhausted?"

"Yes," I said and swung my legs over the side of the bed.

"Now times that by three and have it go on for hours—days even. So forceful that you vomit. Antipsychotics work well for this type of hiccup. We are keeping your father in critical condition as we need to administer his fluids intravenously—he has had a hard time keeping down liquids since the hiccupping started."

"Jeez," I said, "I'm on my way in."

"The hiccups have subsided. You can come in to see him, but a side effect to the meds is that he's going to be sleeping quite a bit. We'll keep him at this dosage for today and then taper it back tomorrow."

I sent Jenny an e-mail saying that I sure hoped she had something planned for our investor's big night, because I now really had no time for his silver spoon.

After visiting my sleeping father in the hospital, I found myself at a local coffee shop. I sat down with my frothing full-fat latte and was soon joined by Detective Shelby.

He brought a cup of what looked like straight-up joe to the table and made an appreciative noise as he sipped it.

"French press. Makes all the difference," I said. "Well, actually it's the type of beans and how they roast them make more of a difference, but you're not here for the coffee, right?"

"Doesn't hurt, though."

I followed his gaze to the windows of the crowded shop. The glass had steamed up, and large droplets were running down the window, giving the world outside a pebbled, hazy look.

"True," I said looking back at him, and dove in. "What do you need from me?"

I felt myself switch to autopilot pretty quickly as Shelby rehashed the questions he'd asked me before. Then he brought up Butch Vellanova. All of the ugly, frightening images and possibilities my dad had laid out for me flooded in, and I felt something close to panic rise from my gut. I focused, pushed it back down. If Dad had made the connection between Butch and his truck, of course the police would. It didn't matter if I never told them a thing; they'd figure it out. So I didn't tell him a thing, but I nodded—yes, that was correct to assume that Butch very well might have taken the Chevy. I asked for only one thing: discretion.

"Well, unless you have any other questions for me, I'll be going," I said, feeling a touch of darkness settle around me. I polished off my latte and stood.

Shelby closed his notepad and tapped the end of his pen on the cover. "What was Nate like when you two were dating?"

I sat down.

"You see, I was there when he was brought in for grand-theft auto and assaulting his arresting officer. You were probably in New York by then, and I'd arrested him a couple times before that, a few bar fights here and there. I tried real hard to keep him off that path of destruction. He'd lived through a lot, physically and emotionally survived a lot, yet I'd always seen—and continued to see, when I visited him in prison—a certain kindness and strength in him. I'm curious, all these years I've been wondering what he must have been like before—"

"Before I made him go nuts? Is that what you're asking?" I asked, feeling my latte gurgle in my stomach.

Shelby thought on it. "Not quite but, yes, let's start there."

"And I'd like to know what this has to do with my father's truck going missing or his father being out. Cross that bridge for me."

Shelby just smiled, a knowing smile. "No reason," he said, standing up and slipping on his coat. "It just seems like he could use a friend right now."

I stood as well. "I realize that. And I've told him as much. As for the rest? It's between him and me."

TWENTY-FIVE

THE CALL FROM JENNY CAME AT SIX THAT NIGHT.

"I need your help."

I had just gotten back from the hospital after sitting with my dad, who slept the whole visit, again.

"Jenny, please tell me you just need help with driving directions or what to wear," I said as I let myself into the house, tossed my keys onto the counter, and flipped through the mail I scooped up off the floor, where it had fallen to from the door slot. There was a bill from Marta's company, and I made a mental note to call her and tell her that dad's hospital stay had gotten extended.

"No, I wish. No," she said, sounding a little weird. "I think I need you there tonight to talk numbers with him."

"Jenny, I thought you said earlier that you had it all planned out with some of the department heads." I tossed the mail on the counter behind the keys and dropped my purse on top of it all and got out the water pitcher from the fridge and poured myself a glass.

"Yeah, I know Eva but...I just realized that he might talk over our heads, and it would be nice if you were there to help out, so it doesn't look like we're a bunch of imbeciles."

"You're not a bunch of imbeciles, and if Ross from accounting is going to be there, you'll have more than enough info to go on—if you are extra nice to Ross, he might draw you some graphs on cocktail napkins."

"Please?"

"Are you begging? I thought this was your big moment: cozy up to the young silver-spoon and end all your work troubles."

"Eva, I'm so not in this guy's league. And after meeting him yesterday when you brought him by the offices, I realized that he's a tad superficial."

I snorted. Yes, *superficial* was the one-word descriptor for Kenneth Wellington III, a dirty-blond who was tanned from extended time outside golfing, playing polo, yachting, and telling the gardener what to do. And the swagger. Lord, the swagger—as if the whole goddamn world owed him, should pay homage to him, lap cream from the palm of his upturned hand.

I sighed long and loud.

"Thank you," Jenny said softly.

"But I didn't agree, Jenny."

"Please?"

"You have to hire the new graphic artist to replace Jessie."

"What? That's what HR does."

"This time you sort all two hundred résumés that come in—it'll be fun. Though you can choose not to if you don't want to. Give and take, Jenny," I said, smiling into my water glass before taking a sip.

"Eva. You know how much I hate our sweaty HR dude. Two hundred résumés means weeks with him. Staring. Breathing heavy. Watching him pretend he's king of the world."

"In his department, Jenny, he is king. And Lord Wellington is as much fun. Choose, Jenny, and give me a call back."

"No, wait!"

"Yes?"

"Fine! Dang it!"

"Where am I going?" I asked.

.   .   .

IT WAS AFTER TEN BY THE TIME I WAS READY TO TAKE ON Wellington and his officious attitude. It was just for a couple of hours, and I debated between the oversized turtleneck and reading glasses with floppy hair and no makeup and the black dress I bought my last day in Manhattan. The latter was black second-skin with a zipper down the entire front separating two inches of gray snakeskin on either side of it. It came up into a mandarin collar and was sleeveless. I'd bought matching snakeskin platforms—the outfit was a showstopper. I'd worn it just once and that was in my room in front of the mirror. It required work to wear, as the zipper stopped low, making the only way to wear it without losing the girls was an old trick I learned from a drag queen that involved duct tape and creative application. The result was magnificent, with breasts that curved and popped like the cover model on *Maxim*.

My dressing like a Manhattanite would be something Wellington would understand. It would convey balls, social class, and an understanding that in media, perception and image were kings. The black dress it was.

An hour later I looked in the mirror one last time. My kohl-edged eyes were very à la Arabian princess, but taking a broader view of myself, I realized that I'd been in Portland too long. I reached under my dress and shimmied out of my undies, instantly erasing the obvious panty line I had been sporting. Even though Festivál was notorious for even more scandalous eveningwear, my heart pounded in my chest. It had been a long time since I'd worn anything so form-fitting, but I loved the feeling that the black dress gave me. The feeling that, for a couple of hours at least, the darkness that had settled on me would be lifted.

I grabbed my clutch and stepped out of the house, the chill night air cooling my skin, my hair waving down my back.

TWENTY-SIX

NATE FLIPPED HIS PHONE SHUT—IT WAS FESTIVÁL FOR TONIGHT. Jenny was a good kid, but that's what she was: a kid. And his reason for helping her out was completely selfish—he knew Eva wouldn't be able to let Jenny handle the exec alone. She would be there tonight, regardless of what Jenny thought. He realized he wanted to see her and maybe, extrapolating, he didn't want her to be alone with the douchebag. A quick online search turned up a press release on the person likely to be this exec. He was from the upper crust of New Englanders, and currently resided in Manhattan, which fit, it was the place Eva loved. The one place that might pull her away from him, again.

He took a quick glance at his reflection in the window: black slacks, navy collared shirt, and black jacket. Fly? Zipped. He headed out, lighting one last cigarette.

The club was packed. Jesus, it was packed.

Nate nodded to the bouncer, then thought better of letting the place continue to swell and walked back. "Joe, no more unless other people leave."

"Right, boss." Joe held up a hand, a signal to his partner to hold the line at the door.

It was body against body on the dance floor, music rumbling in his chest and in the soles of his feet. He pressed through the crowd, an elbow hit here and a breast brush there, to the stairs and up to the VIP balcony.

The escorts Nate had called for were in place, a mix of white, red, and gray minidresses laughing and making sure a preppy guy in the middle of them all was special. The investor was a trust-fund baby if there ever was one. Nate suppressed the urge to pitch him off the balcony.

Peugeot was in the mix of people, along with a couple older guys who looked like they didn't come to places like this often—awkward but loving it. He gave Jenny a wink when she gave him a thumbs-up.

"Where the eff you been, man? Did you see those chicks over there?" Mikey asked. His shirt was offensive.

"What in the hell are you wearing?" Nate said, calmly nodding at Mikey as he picked up a sweating glass of soda water.

"What? What's wrong with it?" Mikey spread his arms wide, looked down at the white shirt embellished with gold.

"Anthony," Nate said, drawing the man into the conversation as he took off his jacket and tossed it over the nearest chair, "talked to Shelby yesterday."

Anthony stepped in closer to hear over the thump and grind of the club music and loud conversation. Mikey looked between the two of them.

"We have to find that truck. Shelby thinks it's in town. Put the word out; keep it quiet," Nate said, cutting his hand low.

Anthony nodded. "Chop shops? Scrapyards?"

"Yeah, start there, then warehouses. If it is," he said and stopped. "If it is him, he'll keep it to leverage what he wants. Right now I don't know what he wants with that thing."

"How much you wanna spend on this?"

"Keep it small for now, just a couple guys. It'll only take a day to check the reputable places, another for the backyard operations."

"What the fuck are you guys yammering on about when there's pussy fresh and waiting right behind you. Hell! Look at them all!" Mikey interrupted, tipping his rum and Coke at someone behind Nate and giving her a wink and an air kiss.

Nate glanced over his shoulder at one of the paid girls making eyes with Mikey. "You touch that ass, my friend, and you owe me a month's salary."

Anthony stepped back, letting out a hoot of laughter. "You owe me, man!" He slapped his hand out to Mikey. "I told you they were on the payroll!"

"Why can't I get a chick who'll give me some ass without me having to pay for it?" He yanked out his wallet and gave Anthony a fifty.

Nate looked at Mikey. "A fifty? You were *that* sure that one of those triplets wanted to suck you off? Mikey, let me give you advice: stick to the chicks who don't come to you—you go to them, and don't wear what you're thinking on your face. And for fuck's sake try seeing them as humans not walking pussies. Remember the other night when I told you to just tell the girl what you make in a year?"

"Yeah."

"What happened?"

"She effin' laughed at me, man, and told me to buy her a drink."

"What then?"

"Well, I did think about what you said, but it seemed your analysis of the situation didn't fit so—"

"You fucking ad-libbed. You ad-libbed didn't you Mikey?"

"I said I'd get her one and anything else she wanted for, um, well, for some action."

"You what—"

"I know now that was the incorrect response, I should have—"

"Oh sh..." Anthony said, looking past both of them.

Nate turned to follow Anthony's gaze down at the crush of

people near the front door. Thinking, his mind still on his disturbing friend, that Mikey's girl in red was rightfully back to start something. The strobes flashed across the bobbing heads, and for an instant lit up the face that Anthony had seen.

Nate's heart went from resting to hammering, and despite his mind telling him it was no big deal, his whole body reacted, in a pleasantly animalistic way, to what Eva Lynn Rodgers walked in wearing.

I love you. The memory of her words, unbidden. He'd never seen her in anything like this before—oh yes, this Eva was different, and he should remember that.

Nate tried to look away, but he was mesmerized as she walked through the crowd, long hair waving and curving around her breasts.

"*Fuck,*" he whispered, his hand in a death grip around the rail.

Mikey was startled. "What, man?" he said and leaned around the people, trying to see what Anthony and Nate saw. "Aw, shit," Mikey said in admiration. "The one in black?"

Anthony gave a chin nod. "You should go talk to her, Mikey."

"Damn, she's effin' hot. Think I got a chance, man?" Mikey said, putting his drink down on the tabletop.

Nate slid his eyes to Mikey and put a hand on his chest. "Touch her, talk to her, you so much as smell the air when she passes," he said, "and I'll break every bone in your body."

Mikey went white, while Anthony laughed and punched him in the arm.

"Ow! You douchebag." Then, as if a light bulb switched on, it dawned on Mikey. "Oh, damn. That's her, isn't it? That's the Eva girl?"

Nate just looked away and watched her as she made her way up the stairs, slipping around people to her group. Watched as Trust Fund dropped the escort girls and descended on her like a bee to the honey pot. Watched as Eva laughed and shook his hand. And kept watching as he kissed her.

The rest of the club faded away—all he saw was Eva, sharp and focused. He couldn't help it; he should just walk out, just leave. He should not step forward, should not adjust his collar, should not roll up his sleeves and make his way through the crowd toward her.

TWENTY-SEVEN

I walked past the line into Festivál, which snaked down the street as though the bouncers were handing out hundred-dollar bills to everyone who'd give them a hello. Earning dirty looks from the line, I told the gatekeepers who I was and why I was there. Jenny had texted me earlier to tell me we were VIP—everything on the house, per the managing partner.

As I crested the stairs to the balcony, I saw our playboy investor with a candy kitten on each arm. Their perfect hair, makeup, and bodies screamed bought-n-paid-for and I made a mental note to make sure Jenny hadn't promised them more than a nice editorial piece in the next issue. At that point I calculated the magazine would be in for a half-years worth of free advertising.

"There's my editor-in-chief!" Kenneth Wellington III said, sloughing off his dates and gripping my outstretched hand.

I smiled, ignoring his use of the possessive pronoun. "Yes, here I am, Mr. Wellington. I hope you are having a good time." I noticed all our department heads were having a good time—they all looked sloshed.

"Oh no, please, not so formal—call me Ken," he said, still gripping my hand from our handshake.

I nearly choked on my laugh, which I hoped he took as just general laughter, but he had to be kidding—all we needed was to call his new lady friends Barbie and we were set. "All the same, Ken. I hope you're enjoying yourself."

"Better than that, especially now that you're here." He kissed my hand.

I politely pulled my hand from his grip. "Well, now isn't that wonderful." I heard the hollowness in my own voice.

Oh, I shouldn't have come, I thought. "We just want to make sure that you remember *Rose City Review* in your future transactions on the IMG board, and we wanted to show you how important it is that we keep up with cutting-edge Portland style, companies, and social issues. We are the only media outlet in the metro area that has provided this on the scale that we do for as long as we have."

One of the serving girls walked past with a tray of drinks; after she doled them out, I put in my request with her for a *double* gin and tonic.

"That was a great speech," Ken said and moved in closer, his eyes glazed. "Now that we have business out of the way, let's get to know each other better...personally." He fingered the zipper pull on my dress. I was instantly glad that the dress had a series of clasps on the inside too.

He was blitzed and I wasn't sure what school of ethics he graduated from, but it sure as heck wasn't the same one I applied to. I grabbed his hand and heard my voice go to sobering ice. "Let's get one thing straight: I'm your editor-in-chief, not your girlfriend. Touch my dress again without my permission and you'll wish you stuck your hand in a bear trap. Got it?"

Ken chuckled and put his hands up. "Ah, look but don't touch, right? Well, I surrender," he said.

"Please continue to have a good time," I said and turned into the group, not waiting for his response.

This is a waste of my time. I thought as I moved through the crowd, smiling and helloing and trying to be a good sport even though it was obvious now that I'd shown up to Drunk Fest an hour late.

I spotted the side of Jenny's head through the crowd and started slipping my way over to her—until something, some*one*, made me halt in my path.

Nate, one hand in his pocket and the other resting on the balcony railing, was talking with Jenny. Suddenly everything fell into place: the club, the comped drinks, the candy kittens—Jenny had help, and she was talking with him now. I thought of Jenny begging me to come and felt a flush of heat. I didn't like being manipulated and I liked it even less with my ex involved. Trying to salvage the rest of my calm, I simply turned and made my way back through the crowd. I was going home before I did something I'd regret. I'd only gotten a few people deep when a wide hand slipped around my middle and lifted me up. I was set down in a corner against the wall a few feet away.

I spun around. "Goddamn you, Nate."

Nate's mood was just as dark as he leaned in. "Goddamn me? I'm the one who trusted you. You *did* need your car fixed because some hotshot exec was coming to town. I just watched him kiss you, and you're saying goddamn *me?*"

"What? I did not—"

"Look around you, none of this shit is free. You think your pretentious ass of an exec would be impressed by anything less? No. I'll tell you what, you know all those comps on your fucking car and house? I'll be sending you the bills."

I went on defense, "Good. I didn't ask for you to give me anything for free. As someone who's self-professed to be rid of me you've done a lot that's in direct opposite of that." I said stabbing a finger toward the Candy Kittens. Nate grabbed my wrist to stop me from pointing. "So what is it, Nate? What is it that you really want from all this? For me to owe you big or do you have something more elaborately sadistic planned?"

My comment hit home. He hissed, "What the fuck is that supposed to mean?"

"You know what it means. You're always angling for something more, so what is it that you want? A Nate-centric editorial in next month's magazine? Free full-page, full-color advertising for life? Stock options?"

I just shook my head. "And here I thought Ken was a breed of his own after meeting him for the *first time* yesterday, but our little conversation here has proved me wrong. There's two of you. You both have a hard time keeping your hands off what doesn't belong to you." I tried twisting my hand out of his grip, using my other to pry his fingers open.

"Elaborately sadistic?" he asked and moved in closer, nearly pressing up against me. "I trusted you when you said you didn't have a boy toy. I believe you when you said you needed your car for your pops, but you lied to my face about knowing this guy. The Eva I knew would have rammed this fuck's nuts up to his throat if he kissed her and didn't want it."

"Yeah, well," I said recognizing the description of the woman Nate once knew, "She would have, but she found some class along with her education and career experience. Two can change, Nate."

"Right." he said looking at me with eyes that said he didn't believe a word I was saying. His voice was low when he continued, "And somehow you still love me too? Eva, I'm just sorting through your bullshit to see if there's anything real left in you."

"Of course you'd throw that back in my face," I said, feeling my insides squirm, "I may love you, but it doesn't mean I trust you, Nate."

I twisted my wrist again in his iron grip.

Nate's eyes were the color of flaming whiskey. "You don't trust *me*? At least I'm not letting my new exec put his hands on me because of some imagined rules for what class looks like."

"Nate," I said, "our new *investor* is one I'd like to take a long walk off a short pier, especially after his hand kissing and suggestions that I get to 'know him better.'" I said using my free hand to air quote. "But I'm not in a position that I can selfishly punch him in the face. He could retaliate and close our rag then I have a hundred plus employees with out a job."

Nate's demeanor cooled slightly as he looked over his shoulder at Ken then back to me. "Fine. I'll do it." he deadpanned.

I laughed, as his comment caught me off guard.

Nate's gaze swept my face before he grinned back at me. "I'll break his knees for you."

"No," I said, "if he's in a wheelchair, he'll just angle for chicks to sit on his lap so he can take them for a ride." I studied his face, the tight smile lines at the corners of his mouth and the glint of mischief in his eyes reminded me that we had been best friends once. "Nate... Can't you and I just be friends? I don't know if I have the stomach to do combat, over whatever it is we're fighting about, right now."

Nate's gaze slid down the front of me and back up.

"Sure. By the way, looking good, Eve," he said, using my old nick-name. I felt the heat that went along with it.

"Thanks, but don't you make eyes on me, either—you might go blind."

He smiled like a wolf. "Blind me right after I memorize every inch of you? It'd be worth it."

I gave a small shake of my head, "Save it for someone who believes that crap, Nate. Now, let me go? I'll get out of your face, since I believe that's what you really want."

"You have no idea what I really want anymore, Eva." He switched subjects as he released me and relaxed his shoulder against the wall. "How's your pops? I didn't get to see him today—he still going home tomorrow?"

Combat aside, we slid back into the familiarity of friends. The club still pulsed on the dance floor below and the VIP room hadn't gotten any less packed; if anything, there were more scandalously clad women fluttering around Lord Wellington.

"He's been better. Doctors say Monday now. Are there even *more* call girls now? Good gosh, Nate, how many do you know?"

"Mmmph."

I looked back at him and laughed. "Are they like chocolates, each one a little different?"

His eyes slowly made their way back to mine. "I don't know, I don't pay for sex, Eva. I've never had that problem."

"Touché." I said, and fully believed him.

"Why is your pops spending another night there? What happened?"

"Side effect to one of his chemotherapy drugs; can't keep food down so they've got him on some neuroinhibitors and keeping him on the IV."

"Damn. Neuroinhibitors? Why don't they give him that antivomiting shit?" he asked.

"Well, he doesn't have a problem with vomiting—he's got hiccups so bad that he's vomiting," I said, thinking that it sounded as weird saying it as it did hearing it.

"Hiccups?"

"I said the same thing to Dr. Zimmerman. He says to imagine your worst hiccups and then triple that; it's like perpetual crunches for days. Makes him unable to eat or keep food down. That, and he's just had heart surgery, you know?"

"Hiccups?" he just asked again.

"Yes."

"Which drug does he have a side effect from? Has he always had hiccups after?" he asked.

"Not sure which one and, no, he just would get really queasy and not be able to eat or drink anything."

Everything just came spilling out—he was like a rock, now that he wasn't trying to get my back up; he was solid and steady. But even rocks were fragile, and this one had a major fracture that I would be smart to stay away from, unless I was prepared to fill it.

But even wise women have moments where they ignore what

they should do and listen to a voice that comes from much deeper inside.

"I'll go by and see him tomorrow," he said.

I smiled. "I'm sure Dad would like that. He could use some friendly companionship in his room," I said thinking about the last time I was there, "I don't think Chuck has been allowed to see him since he's not family. Which reminds me, how is it that you are getting in to see him?"

"Don't forget, babe, that they think I'm your husband."

"Ah, I see."

We lapsed into silence. I watched as women cooed over Lord Wellington, but I was more interested in getting a good look at Nate's club. The entire place was glass, white leather, and polished steel. I thought of Nate when we were kids, elbow deep in a fast car, putting in another turbo kit to make it even faster. The girls who would come to the shop looking for him in their Sunday's best, showing a little cleavage and looking like they wanted more than a good looking at. Before I found that I liked dresses just as much as I liked grease and fast cars, Nate was borderline juvie detention for picking fights; then when I left for New York, he became full-time delinquent and some-how, in the past few years, found the money for all of this.

It spilled out of my mouth before I had a chance to think better of it: "Where'd you get all the money for this?"

Nate looked at me out of the corner of his eye, then back out around us. "I only own a piece of all this, Eva," he said, then added, "What if I did own all of it?"

"What do you mean, a piece?"

"I'm a majority shareholder out of the four investors. But answer the question, Eva, what if I did? Where do you think I got all the money for this place?"

"I'd say lotto."

"Lottery? Why would it have to be from lotto money, Eva?"

"Because if not that, you owe someone a fortune and you'd hate that."

His eyes were hot with anger at my accusation when he looked back at me. "Won it or begged for it? Those are the only two options? How about earned it, Eva—you ever think about that?"

I looked back at him, standing my ground. "Earned? Is that what you call it? What did you do before you were a business owner to earn all this money?"

"So that's what you think of me—still just a thief, only white-collar now? No better than my father, right?" he said, mimicking the words I'd thrown at him in our final fight before I'd headed to New York, his voice like that of a still wind just before a storm.

"No, but the last I heard of you, Nate, you were in prison. Now you own a mechanic's shop and invest in a popular nightclub? What am I supposed to think?"

"I don't give a shit what you think."

"If not illegally, you shouldn't mind telling me how you came by it," I said, then immediately felt petty—he was a man, not a child. "Never mind," I quickly added. "You don't have to tell me—I'm just itching for another fight. I think I'll just call it a night." I spoke with a weak smile, knowing it didn't reach my eyes, I checked to make sure I still had my clutch strapped to my wrist as I prepared to leave.

"My mother."

The club faded in my ears to the silence of a library—I looked back at him. He'd relaxed back against the wall. "Your mom?" I asked, thinking of the bitter woman who could barely keep a job, much less a dime in her pocket.

"She gave me all the money—Jesus, Eva, ask me nicely, and I'll tell you anything you want to know," he said and then amended, "almost anything."

"How did your mom come by that money? Was it her life insurance; were you the beneficiary when she"—I swallowed hard, thinking of the right word—"died?"

Nate took a deep breath. "I don't want to talk about it here."

I looked over at Wellington—he'd have no idea if I left.

"Where do you want to go?"

"Come."

We moved through the *Rose City Review* group and were nearly to the stairs, me working my smile and saying good-bye as I walked, when a hand grasped my arm.

"Ah, there you are!" Ken said, his tie askew and the top two buttons of his shirt undone. "I was looking for you." He was somehow drunker than he had been, his eyes were bloodshot and his skin had taken on a sweaty sheen.

I extracted myself from his grip. "Yes, here I am. And now I'm leaving. I hope you have a nice time. Good-bye," I finished, using up every nice word I had left for him.

I felt a hand at my back and the warmth of Nate as he leaned forward from behind me. "Nathaniel Vellanova," he said, introducing himself to Ken, his voice like vanilla poured straight from the bottle.

"Nate, this is Kenneth Wellington, the third. Kenneth, Nate is the provider of all this generosity." I said and gave Nate a look I hoped conveyed the message: do not start any shit.

"All this?" Ken said, making a looping gesture with his finger in the air. "I always wanted to own a restaurant, but it's too much grunt work. I prefer to just *reap* the *benefits*," he said perversely and winked at Nate as though the two of them were in on a joke.

The old Nate would have gut punched him and tossed him over the balcony. I held my breath.

Ken didn't need any outside shoving—he teetered and then righted himself. "I hope that my associate here..." he trailed off as he gestured with his open palm, nearly brushing my breast. I felt myself sneer just as Nate reached forward, clasping Ken on the shoulder, forcing him to step backward to right himself.

"You all right there, buddy?" Nate asked as if he were giving him a helping hand.

"Woo right, right. I'm fine."

"I think you might be overly intoxicated," Nate said.

"No, don't be ridiculous. It's nothing, just some jet lag. What was I saying? Oh, yes," he said, "I hope my associate has conveyed my thanks. Now, if you don't mind, I'll have to steal her back. I've a few business things to discuss with her." He pulled himself up to his full drunken height, as if he were a king who was not to be denied his request.

Nate nodded thoughtfully and, just as I was about to tell the both of them what stop to get off at, Nate said, "Of course." Hand still on Ken's shoulder, Nate seemed as if he were about to confide something of utmost importance to him. "I need your help first," he said. "You see, your associate has only told me that she's the editor-in-chief of your magazine but not her name—be a sport and help me out," Nate said, a slow smile starting on his face.

It took me just a moment to see where Nate was going with all this. It would be in lieu of chucking him over the railing.

"Well!" Kenneth said and blinked a long, slow, hazy blink.

"I'll need a name so I don't look like a fool asking her again, and you must know her name since she's the chief editor of this magazine."

"Oh, I'd like to be a good sport, but I only give the names of women I don't own and, well, this one I own." He leaned into Nate, throwing a thumb in my direction.

"Own? I assumed you were colleagues, Wellington—"

"Yes, yes, *own*. The word is just a vulgarity of commerce. I own *Rose City Review*, thus I own her. It really is basic business language."

At this, I'd heard enough. I stepped forward and held out my hand to Nate to end the game. "No need to put Ken or yourself on the spot, Mr. Vellanova—it's Ms. Nass. Though, you may call me Ima."

Nate's lips tugged up in a crooked smile as he slipped his hand into mine and gave it a professional shake, which finished with a knowing squeeze. "It was a pleasure to meet you," he said, drawing out the word *pleasure*, putting heat and emphasis on that not-so-simple word.

Kenneth butted in, "My dear, Ima Nass, shall we go?" he said a sloppy grin on his face as he proffered his arm.

"You really are," I said under my breath then louder so that he could hear, "Thank you Mr. Wellington, but I'm afraid that this is where I must say good-bye, as I was just leaving with Mr. Vellanova."

"Oh-ho!" he said, his eyebrows raised in overly dramatic disbelief. "I think not, Ima Nass." He leaned back into the sea of kittens. "This was your one chance to make a favorable impression on me, and you're ruining it by going home with him. It should be my dick you're trying to suck, not his."

I blinked. Hard. Had he just said what I thought he did?

He had.

Anger hot and untainted flushed my skin as I felt my old self barge forward fists clenched. All pretenses were now lost. Emotion that I'd kept bottled up unstoppered, and Wellington, his sneering frat-boy face and silver-spooned attitude, filled my vision.

Nate's too, apparently.

"Hold this," Nate said, handing me the drink he plucked from Ken.

"Hey—" was all Ken got out before Nate's fist hit home in his gut. He slid his other hand across Ken's back and gripped his neck hard. He looked as if he tucked him into an aggressive one-armed embrace.

"Talk to her like that again and I'll bury you. Talk to any woman like that and I'll make sure you spend the rest of your days eating through a silver tube instead of off a silver spoon. Understand?" he said and waited.

Ken made a guttural noise.

"Nod your head if you understand," Nate persisted.

Ken nodded.

"Good," Nate said and walked him backward into the nearest chair, taking his drink from my hand, placing it on the table in front of Ken, and patting him on the knee.

Nate got in my face at the top of the stairs. "Later. Get your piece later."

"No," I said looking around him, feeling the fight in my veins.

"Babe. Kill him here and you'll get blood all over the place, and those white couches aren't fucking cheap. Got it? Let's go. Kill tomorrow, walk now."

I took one more look back at the still-cringing Ken on the couch. Some had noticed he wasn't doing so hot.

I growled before turning and heading down the stairs, Nate right behind me. The crush of people in the club became like nails on a chalkboard. I pushed through them all, not caring how many elbows I threw. I had to get out.

TWENTY-EIGHT

THE NIGHT WAS COOL ON MY SUPERHEATED SKIN. WE WALKED out and down the street a few paces, along a chain-link fence that surrounded the empty lot next to Festival. Seemingly every other available space was taken with cars.

The way Wellington had gestured to himself played again in my mind. His words, basically telling me that on my knees would be the best way to do my job at *Rose City Review*, sounded as clear in my memory as the thump of the music in real time behind Nate and me. The increase in subscribers, the department's higher efficiency, and greater number of advertisers—all of my professional successes were completely overlooked. All because I was a woman. And from women, he was used to getting what he wanted, and what he wanted was for us to be on our knees.

Wait, my ass.

I pivoted on my heel and headed back to the club.

"Eva..." I heard Nate's warning call from behind me and his swift step.

I picked up the pace. Everything had gone blood-red again, the need to have it out with Wellington taking over my mind. I was going to show him what happened when he treated women like he just did me. I was going to be the last woman he did that to. I owed it to my entire sex.

Nate reached me as I got to the front corner of the building, gripped me from behind and, shifting his arm to wrap around my middle, lifted me off the ground. "Leave it for tomorrow. If you're still pissed then, I'll personally drive you to his place so you can punch his lights out. Sleep on it, Eva."

"Shove off." I writhed and shoved against his tightening grip.

Nate turned and walked easily back down the sidewalk with my ass perched on his hip like a sack of potatoes. "Babe, calm the fuck down."

I felt a growl start somewhere in my chest and explode out into the night air; arching back, I put my heel in his knee.

"Goddamnit!" he said and dropped me to my feet, only to grasp me up again, wrapping both arms around me, pinning my own arms under them. "Knock it off," he hissed into my hair.

"No! Now let me go, or I'll do worse damage," I promised from a bent-over position, trying to leverage my full body weight to break his grip on me.

Nate chuckled. "I'm not worried about damages, sweetheart. In fact, keep writhing like that, and we can pick up right where we left off seven years ago."

I pried at Nate's fingers.

Now Nate was whispering: "That's not my cell phone in my pocket, in case you're wondering."

In the moment it took that thought to settle into my brain, I was distracted. Pressed against my backside was definitely *not* his cell phone.

I was quiet as my consciousness tripped over itself, two strong emotions rising up and colliding. The result was utter confusion—something I'd not felt in years. It was as if I were experiencing an awakening: A slumbering beast was yawning and stretching within me, spurred by my own deep need to fight and my old best friend who happened to be a large Italian male pressing against my back. And chuckling under his breath.

"Jerk," I grumbled as he slowly released me, his motions both careful from caution and a desire to linger. I smoothed my dress, down. "Ugh!" I said as I looked up at the dark sky, "I want to punch his lights out. I can't believe he said that to me."

Looking back at the club the urge to do damage to Wellington was still there, but was becoming something else as we moved back down the sidewalk.

Nate's smile at me was genuine—as if he'd gotten away with something extremely naughty and, like all bad boys, was pumped.

"What?"

"It's been a long time since I've gut punched someone who really deserved it."

Nate slipped his hand into his pocket and retrieved his cigarettes. He wasted no time in lighting one and taking a deep drag on it.

I narrowed my eyes at him.

"Don't be jealous, babe."

"Too late. He deserves more than a punch to the gut though. And you look like you're sucking the lifeblood from that thing—you know it's a nasty habit, right?"

Nate regarded me out of the corner of his eye. "I agree, but this is better than what I really want to do, to Wellington. I'm just making the right choices over here, Eva. I expect some thanks."

I choked on my laugh. "Right. How I feel right now makes me want to teach him the finer points of women's softball, starting with the bat against his soft balls."

Nate winced on behalf of male testicles everywhere.

"Never mind," I said taking a deep breath of the cool night air, "I just feel on fire."

I stopped, realizing my ride was in the opposite direction. I motioned. "My car's that way; I'll see you later."

Nate looked to the cigarette in his hand. "You ready to go home?"

I gave a moment's pause. "Not really," I said, thinking about my woebegone gin and tonic and the fight in my veins.

"My place is right there." He nodded up the street.

Before I could answer, Nate's mood sobered swiftly. "Hungry?"

"And thirsty," I encouraged.

We walked some distance toward his place in silence. I convinced myself that dealing with Wellington when he was sober would be best. As in, a sexual harassment lawsuit, threatened to someone sober, would be best.

"So," I said, still feeling like talking about everything that had just happened, "How'd it feel to gut punch him?"

Instead of answering he took a drag and looked askance at me.

"Fine," I said changing the subject, "how'd you finagle Jenny into going to your club?"

He polished off his cigarette and, with a flick of the butt to the sidewalk, exhaled the last of his toxins. "First of all, it was Jenny who accosted me in the elevator that day I came to see you and, two"—he gestured—"I'm insulted that you'd think me low enough to want to worm my way into your life—"

"When you don't ever want to see me again," I finished for him.

"Exactly."

I didn't think that now would be a good time to remind him that he'd invited me back to his place for food and water, which was not something a man not wanting to see someone would do. Generally.

"Well, Jenny is already on my poop list for manipulating me into coming tonight after telling me that she was more than capable of handling Lord Wellington on her own. It's fitting that she accosted you too, so what did she promise for all that extravagance?" I said, feeling the comfort of talking about something as emotionless as business slide around me like a well tailored jacket. "Whatever it is, I'll be sure we do all we can to accommodate."

"You're freaky when you do that."

"Pardon me?"

"That."

"What are you talking about, Nate? I don't understand," I said and truly didn't.

"Jesus, are you having a hard time walking?"

I stopped and looked down at my shoes to make sure they were still all on and in functioning order. "I'm sorry?" I said and felt my eyebrow rise.

Nate stopped as well and looked back at me, his expression serious. "It would seem hard to walk when you have a stick that size up your ass."

And suddenly I was twelve again. "I'm sorry—was I using big words that you couldn't understand? Would I be easier to handle if I giggled and sashayed a little more?"

"Yes. Absolutely."

"Well, I'm not fluent in Giggle so you're going to have to learn to speak Grown-up like the rest of the world."

Nate regarded me for a moment. "And would that require me to put a suit and tie on every time I think business thoughts?"

"What are you saying?"

"Fucking relax."

"Regarding this, I am relaxed. Was," I amended. "All I want to know is what Jenny promised you, because all that extravagance garners financial reciprocity from *Rose City Review* and from what I saw tonight, she did not have prior approval for."

"See, that." He pointed at me.

"Again, what."

"What you just said. I know a couple of asshole clients who drive quarter-million-dollar sports cars and think the world is there to talk down to, just like you're doing. I'm just saying, lighten the fuck up, Eve."

I could feel a snarl starting. "I didn't get to where I am by pussy-footing around, Nate. And yes, I've been called a bitch on more than one occasion, including once by you—"

"Try fifty—"

"That's not the point; the point is: you can have your personal preference on how you want to transact business, Nate, but that doesn't mean I have to acquiesce to it."

I watched as Nate rolled his shoulders and looked up to the evening sky, as if begging the world to answer why he'd gotten stuck with me right then. "Eva, babe—"

"Don't call me—"

"Babe," he said, putting vehemence behind it, "you just want to know what you're giving up in exchange for tonight, not negotiating your own death sentence. Calm. Down." I just looked at him as he continued, "I don't know where the hell you learned to jump into business dealings with an entitled attitude, but you gotta calm down. It makes you seem like you have to prove you're top dog—stop trying. If you're trying to prove yourself worthy, you will always be unworthy. If you are worthy, Eva, you don't have to prove shit."

It was so profound, maybe even prophetic, that I couldn't help but give pause. "I don't do that," I said, a lot softer than I'd intended.

"Maybe I just bring out the bitch in you, but your panties bunch every time you go Business. Calm down."

I felt my eyes narrow. "You know, Nate, you might be right—but I'll repeat, I didn't get to where I am now by schmoozing and high-fiving every advertiser and coworker along the way."

"Where you are now. You mean, without a single friend, without a goddamn man who'd marry your ass, and in charge of a magazine that's one subscription short of going out of business?"

I felt the sting as that missile went right across the bow of my ship. "So in exchange for all the paid women, drinks, and royal Wellington good time, you want to be able to have exclusive Eva harassment rights too? Is that it?"

"No, I don't want shit from you, Eva, and the more you get your back up about this, the more I'm thinking about reneging on that."

From what I could see in the poorly lit section of our sidewalk, his face was expertly blank, despite his tone. He couldn't really believe that he wanted nothing from me. Even I knew that even someone with the most well-meaning intentions wouldn't shovel out that kind of cash for nothing. And suddenly the light dawned on me.

"We don't do IOUs," I said.

"There's not anything I need right now—seems like I should wait until there is," he said, quietly slipping into the negotiations that he'd expertly tried to convince me he wasn't doing.

I crossed my arms tightly under my breasts. "Uh-huh. Again, we don't do IOUs, so I'll just have to talk with Jenny to see what it is she assumed we'd be doing for you."

Nate's gaze was so quick, I'd not have noticed it if I didn't know him as well as I did. It seemed like he found, for an instant, something at my chest level very interesting.

"November's whole issue is on local businesses for everyday needs: dry cleaners that go the extra mile, salons with unique problem-solving products, insurance agents with good track records—and mechanics with loyal customers. We can feature your shop with a one-page editorial spread, plus a leaderboard ad on the website and in the digital edition." I waited.

"Two-page full-color spread in that issue, two-page color ad for a year, and digital ads for a year too."

"Seems a bit ostentatious. How about a half-page color ad in the feature issue, then a quarter-page color ad for six months, with a leader ad in the November digital edition with a rotating leader ad for half a year. I'll even throw in as many updates as you want to either ad."

"You'd do that last part anyway—don't make it sound special, Eve."

"It is special, because we'll do your ad work so you don't need to hire that agency you worked with last time. Cost savings and better graphics, what's not to love?" I felt smug all the way down to my toes.

"Nice job, babe," was all he said, looking anything but pleased.

"Thanks. Do we have a deal?"

"Yes, and I wasn't being nice."

"Excellent! Oh come on, Nate, don't be such a spoilsport," I said, feeling gleeful. "You're still getting a great deal, and I got to one-up you—it's a win-win." Then, in one step, I gave him a quick kiss on the lips. Just a brief touch of skin that felt so natural that Nate didn't pull away but gently kissed me back.

I stepped back just as Nate's hand came up to touch me, and his face had a look of dazed confusion that said he wasn't prepared for that, which made it all the better.

"I assume you're still hungry—for food." He regrouped nicely.

I looked over at him as we walked. His face illuminated in the soft glow of a streetlight, and it was that moment that I realized how little his hunger had to do with food. Despite his objections, he was hungry for something he'd not had from me in the last decade. My own beast, the mirror image to his, stretched languidly under my skin replaying old memories. None of them bad and all of them involved skin to skin contact.

"O-oh," I said, slipping on the *o* and sounding as if I were a lust-addled teen.

Nate's laugh was a deep timbre that warmed my ears and shook within me, taking me back to moments when I'd heard that sound before. That sound was the one of a man who knew his prey had a very good idea of what was on the hunter's mind, yet wasn't running away. Like I should, right back to my car, back to my father's house—and for god's sake *not* into his private apartment where only he and I were accountable for our actions.

"Babe, you look like that, and I'm just going to assume you want what I'm serving."

Partially recovered, I said, "Please—does that line work on all the women you know?"

"No, all I say is, 'Hello, beautiful.'"

I laughed. "Are you serious?"

Nate gave me a smile that said, *Yup.*

I shook my head in disbelief. "Well, it's going to take more than that level of sweet talking and a half-mast member pressed against my backside to get me between your sheets, Nathaniel Vellanova," I said, and felt those words honestly.

"Eva, I wouldn't bait me unless you really want to take that particular trip down memory lane."

"Those were good memories weren't they?"

"Yeah, that right there. Talking like that, let's change the subject. How about we talk about business shit again, like all the comps on your car I'm thinking of having you pony up for."

"Pony up?" I asked, feeling like I was dancing a fine line of good and evil with the devil himself. "What's that? Bending over and letting you give it to me?"

"Oh-ho-ho. I'm warning you."

Crossing the street to the palace of Lucifer himself, I pressed. "Or what, Nate? You'll have your way with me? Remember, you've already got a notch in your bedpost with my name on it."

In one move, Nate had me up against the brick wall of his flour-mill castle. His knees spread mine apart. My dress crept up, and his right arm wrapped around my hips and lifted. My legs, despite my confused mind, knew just what to do: wrapped themselves around him.

"And as I remember, that notch is my favorite." His fingers were at my throat; Nate's breath tickled along my skin as he sampled my flesh from collar bone to earlobe. My earring jingled as he did.

I hoped that it was some other woman who made that groaning sound. Hoped it was coming from an open window where the TV was on, but of course I knew that moan was mine. The sheer power of Nate holding me against the wall, the unevenness of the bricks rough against my backside, combined with the soft, gentle way he heated my neck, breathing me in like I was his own personal brand of cigarette. We were each other's fix, a fix you so desperately want even though you know that if you give yourself over to it fully, it will kill you sooner rather than later. And all I could think was, *More, oh god, give me more.*

I swallowed hard as Nate's finger tips swept off my neck down over the tops of my breasts down to my thigh. I felt my heart hammer anew.

Nate stilled then pressed his temple against mine, his breathing had become rough, "You're not wearing anything under this." He said, the question was a strangled, disbelieving statement. I was well aware of his hand on my naked rear, my dress up at the crease of my hip. The cool night air moved against my bare bottom in direct contrast to the heat of Nate's pelvis pressed against my most sensitive parts.

"Eva. Tell me to stop. Oh god, Eva, tell me to stop this. I can't—you feel—" He choked, "You feel like you want this. *Fuck.*"

My mind swirled. "S-stop?" I managed.

"Like you mean it," he said, and it came out like begging. "Oh-Jesus. Like you mean it, Eva, or I'm going to be eight inches deep in you in about a second...and I don't give a shit who sees."

I swallowed, not knowing what was happening—the monster that had awakened earlier was smiling and stretching out, welcoming the sensations that Nate was causing. "I-I haven't had sex in four years... Be gentle?"

Nate went still. Then, after what seemed like a full lifetime of mortification over what I'd said, I felt his breath whoosh out, tickling my neck. "Four years?" he asked and leaned back, letting go of my thigh, dragging his fingers along my naked legs as he did. Nate slid me down against him, and with gentle fingers he tugged my dress down.

"Yes," I said.

Nate relaxed against me and I put my hands to his hips waiting for the hug I was sure was coming. Only, he moved away and punched the code to the door then pulled it open for me. I, still gathering my wits, walked through it.

"Take my keys—I'll be up in a minute," he said and turned away.

TWENTY-NINE

CLOSE INSPECTION OF NATE'S APARTMENT PANTRY REVEALED club soda and condiments only while his fridge held fruit in various states of decay. I poured myself a soda and tried my damnedest to forget about what had happened downstairs: the ridiculous fact that I'd basically told Nate to go on ahead and dive into me right there at the building entrance. Had anyone else been around?

"Ugh," I said, feeling a fresh wave of mortification sweep over me. I'd lost my mind. And Nate, I was sure, was downstairs smoking the rest of his pack of cigarettes.

I slid open the kitchen drawers and found takeout menus as the elevator rattled up, bringing with it Nate.

I held up Mario's menu. "Flora still deliver at this hour?"

"Yeah," he said soberly and pulled out his phone as he made his way to the kitchen. He took a swig from my glass, looking like he wished it were something mind-altering instead of his innocuous club soda. After greeting his aunt and putting in the order, he hung up and looked at me.

Before I could say anything, he said, "I don't want to talk about it." He tossed the phone down on the bar and turned away toward the bathroom. I watched him as he pulled the hem of his shirt from his slacks and undid the cuffs. He popped the top shirt buttons and, without a hitch in his stride, pulled the shirt over his head, wadded it, and threw it into a corner of the bathroom.

"I gotta change," he said to me and kicked the door shut.

"*Uh-oh,*" I said under my breath at my body's primal reaction to seeing the back side of his half naked body.

Nate emerged a few moments later with just jeans on. Resting low on his hips, they showed the gray band of his briefs as well as his well-toned upper half. The latter drew me in like steel to a high-powered magnet. It was obvious in the years that we were apart he'd matured into a tightly built man. Muscle lines curved and pulled under his skin and the tight V lines at his pelvis with the dark hair below his navel showed the path to righteousness. As he crossed the empty space, he seemed to make a point to luxuriously slip his gray T-shirt over his arms and then slowly pull it over his head, as if allowing me a good long look.

I was going to lose it.

I opened the fridge and leaned in, keenly aware that I was still in stilettos and a minidress with duct tape on my tits, though my mind was just as focused on something else Nate had said. *Eight inches deep?* I thought. *Jeez, did that get bigger too?* Oh, I was sunk.

"You going to set up camp in there, or get what you want?" Nate said from behind me. I glanced over my shoulder to see him leaning against the counter, drinking the rest of my club soda.

"Just getting more club soda, since your ass keeps drinking all mine." I snatched the bottle and poured another glass with a trembling hand. "So," I said, feeling the need to change the subject, quickly, "I'm still envious of that sucker punch you got in on Wellington."

"Just sleep on it, Eva. You'll get yours tomorrow."

"I know, I'm just jealous. You dealt with him with some serious restraint. The old Nate would have pitched him over the balcony for some splash. Where'd you learn how to do that?"

"What? Not pitch him over the balcony?"

"Yes, otherwise known as restraint."

"Mmmph," he said and was quiet as he made his way to the windows and turned sitting down. Our current conversation was ejected out the window the moment his words said, "Why, Eva?"

It took me a millisecond to know what he was asking—deep down in my gut; the moment had arrived. "Why what?" I said, forgetting about club soda. Wellington. The world.

"The way you left me."

"The way *I* left *you*? Please tell me you're kidding."

"Do I look like I'm kidding?"

"Are we really going to keep having the *same exact* fight? Please remember that getting a college education and pursuing a career in that field is not 'Eva breaking up with Nate forever and ever,'" I said with air quotes. "I would think that after all these years you'd recognize that."

Nate looked a way, swiped his palm across his mouth. The old gesture that I now remembered meant he was filtering the words he *really* wanted to say. "For someone who has a guilty conscience, you sure don't act like it."

I felt my jaw tick.

"Let's get it all out in the air, Eva."

I folded my arms across my chest. "Yes, let's. Why were you such an overbearing asshole that you thought my leaving to further my career meant I must hate you —"

"No, Eva, not that. I may have not wanted you to go to New York, but that wasn't the problem. When I needed you—when I walked in on my mother cut to pieces..." he said and stopped. "I stepped in her goddamn blood, Eva. I needed you."

The fight went out of me and I turned against the counter; I couldn't look at him. Instead, I looked down at my hands spread wide on the granite. "Oh boy," I said, feeling the weight of his words, and the chill of the stone under my hands, "I have no excuse."

"None?" he said harshly. "You knew she was murdered, and you called me back and left me a message saying we're over and to grow up, and you have *nothing* to say to that?"

Emotion grew hot in my eyes as I looked up at him. "I had no idea what had happened, Nate. It was years after when my dad told me."

"Cut the shit. Years, Eva? You can't tell me that you didn't know."

"I was in over my head in New York. I ate, slept, and breathed fashion when I was at *Vogue*. If you didn't have anything to do with my next piece, we didn't talk. I spoke to my dad on holidays in the cab or in the elevator between parties. I slowed down for no one and nothing in the two years I spent as an intern because I had to claw for placement as a full-timer. And then, as a staffer, I had to keep clawing for higher placement. I ran hard and fast—not once looking back until I stepped off the plane last year, and all I've been able to do since I've come home is look back," I said. "I'm not sorry for fighting for what I want, but every day I'm sorry that I didn't call you. No words are going to make up for the past—"

"Seven fucking years," Nate cut in. "Seven. In which of those years did you find out that my mother was *murdered* by my father?"

I took a deep breath. "The second."

"That's five years, Eva. Five," he said, holding up his palm, fingers splayed.

I felt the knife twist in my chest. "Tell me now? Where did you find her?"

"On the floor."

"Kitchen?"

"I stepped into her blood before I got both feet into the apartment."

I closed my eyes. "My god, Nate. Why?"

"No one fucking knows. He said she lied to him, had it coming, provoked him. Same shit he always said," he said as I opened my eyes.

"What happened?"

Nate was still as a statue in the window. "He called me, crying—that's a fucking sound, by the way, something I'll never forget—said he needed help, said I had to come help; it was her. So I went. I figured, he tries anything, I'll put him down. I walked in and walked right out after flipping on the light. Cops were right behind me, rolled in as I was puking on the stairs."

"Sounds like he set you up?" I asked.

"Tried, backfired, and they hauled his ass to prison."

"And now he's out."

"Free as a jaybird," he said, working the muscle in his jaw.

The loft was quiet save for the hum of the refrigerator behind me.

"Then," he said, looking me straight in the eye and into my soul, "I called you. I needed you so *badly*, Eva."

I looked down, taking in his words. "*If*," I started, "if you told me, Nate, when you left all those messages, if you told me that your mother had been murdered, I would have been there for you. You just said to call you, and it was only a couple weeks since I'd left and we'd had that fight."

"I thought of that. But I also figured if you really loved me, you'd call."

"I did really love you, Nate. But you didn't ever give me the space to grow. You hated how much college took me away from you, and when I told you about New York, you went ballistic— never once asking me if you could come with. Do you know I went to Portland State to be near you? I didn't even try for any other college because I wanted to be near you. And yet you threw all that in my face that last year. You said that if I really loved you, I would call? I thought that if you really loved me, you'd understand why I didn't."

Nate just shook his head. "I keep forgetting how damn young we were."

I gave him a small smile. "And we can only hope that by now we've grown up."

"Says the chick who's still living with her pops."

I laughed at his sarcasm, "And you, when did you stop acting like a lovesick teenager, obsessing over me, ruining your life, and finally realize that you have to own the things you do?"

"You have no idea how many times I heard you say that to me while I stared at those cement walls."

"I'm sorry."

"Right." He waved it away. "It was halfway through my sentence —six months in, that's when. I spent a lot of time blaming you for where I was, hating that you'd put me on the floor of that prison cell, blaming you for driving me insane. Still do." He gave me a wicked grin. "That day I got your message, telling me to grow up, I'd just come back from my father's sentencing. That day, I didn't cry—and you'd made me cry before, Eva—but I got angry, and it stayed with me. I went far and fast and didn't slow down when the first blue-and-reds came up behind me. My life was fucked: Dad a murderer, mother dead, my best friend just left me for real. I had nothing to lose. I punched out the arresting officer and earned pepper spray in my face and a Taser in the ass." He slid his hands into his pockets. "In the cell that night, your words from our last fight carried me through —I used them like a drug to beat the shit out of anyone who came near me. That's the first time I remember Shelby. Three asshole guards pinned me, taking turns beating the shit out of me. Shelby put a stop to it; he said to me that he didn't know what I was running from but from what he could see, I was going about it all wrong. I flipped him off and spit a mouthful of blood on the floor and didn't think of what he'd said until later." His tongue probed the inside of his mouth as if tasting the blood again.

"Your pops posted my bail that day, but of course I wasn't done, and I was sentenced and sent to Coffee Creek—right behind my own pops. Bastard was lucky he'd been transferred already to the state pen or I'd still be serving time for homicide. Eva, it was bad." He looked hard at me. "Prison was like living with my parents again—watching things go down that you didn't want to be a part of, but you were. Some seriously sick fucks in there," he said and looked away. "Whole months went by that I didn't think of you every moment. I was too busy keeping an eye on my back, everyone wanting a piece of me." He picked up his empty soda glass, then put it down, continuing,

"And then it happened, six months in. And I started thinking about how I was going to get out and set shit straight in my life. That where I sat wasn't where I wanted to be, and that's when I thought of Shelby."

Nate's pause was long. "What happened that day?" I asked.

Nate cut his eyes back to me. "It was rape."

My stomach dropped and everything went blurry with horror.

"Gang rape in the showers."

I could barely breathe; I could feel myself choking on the sick, a vile chill snaked through my body, threatening to make my knees give out. "Nate..."

He just shook his head. "No. Not me. But I was right there, watched every second. I can still feel the water of the showers on my back, remember the smell of the soap. Even though it wasn't me, I'd been standing right next to the guy when he got grabbed. My arm got caught, but I slipped away. They wanted that other asshole—they didn't come after me. Hell if I know why. But thank god, since I collapsed not even out of the showers. I just kept my back against the wall—I was fucking paralyzed watching it. That, Eva, will mess with your head. In one way, it messed with it right. Before, I couldn't see straight; after, everything was 20/20. Get out, who gives a shit what Eva Lynn Rodgers did to me, fuck her, fuck this, get out. After that moment I started to give two cents more about me than about you."

THIRTY

JUST THEN THE FRONT DOOR BUZZER WENT OFF, SIGNALING OUR dinner's arrival. As Nate recounted the rape, ice replaced the blood in my veins freezing me in place. Nate stood and moved toward the elevator.

"Feel free to slip into something more comfortable—I'll just be a sec," he said with the ghost of a smile.

I took a sip of water and a deep breath clearing my head. Nate was back up in a few minutes looking harassed.

"Everything OK?"

"Fucking perfect." Nate said and dropped the take-out bag and a bottle of wine on the counter. I went to work on the wine as Nate lifted box after box of grub out of the bag. "Flora felt she needed to personally come by," he said, tight-lipped.

"So, everything is not OK?"

"Somehow, she learned you're here with me, and now she thinks we're getting back together. Probably planning our goddamn wedding and praying to Saint Gerard that I knock you up."

I laughed feeling our earlier conversation slide to the background. I opened the box he handed me and inhaled the luscious sent of breaded and fried eggplant, sharp parmesan cheese, and homemade marinara sauce. From the heft of the box, I'd guess a one-and-a-half order, my old special request. My empty stomach gave a desperate churn in anticipation. I groaned.

"Glad to hear you react the same way to my aunt's cooking as you do to sex with me," he said, crushing up the paper sack and tossing it into the trash under the sink.

I laughed as an old memory hit me. "You so gave yourself away to her if you ordered this amount of eggplant parmesan *and* fettuccini Alfredo—Flora would have guessed from that alone." I looked from his closed takeout box to his pissed-off face. "Ha-ha," I said, guessing I was right, grabbed the opened wine bottle and the eggplant takeout dish, and settled myself on the cool-to-the-touch leather couch in front of the massive flatscreen. "Bring that fettuccini over here, sweet cheeks," I said cheerfully at his glowering form and took a mighty swig of wine straight from the bottle.

"So, umm, before everything went sideways at the club," I said as he settled next to me, "I asked where you'd gotten the money for all the lavish things you've got." The wine slid and slithered down to swoon in my belly, warming me to my toes. Muscles I'd not realized were constricted loosened, and the eggplant parmesan snuggled in in a match that was pure alchemy. "So I guess the question remains, when did you become a millionaire?"

He nodded, "After I got out of prison. It wasn't until I was released that I got notification that I had received an inheritance from her. I figured it was her last buck fifty, but it wasn't. Well, it was her last buck fifty, plus seven-point-five million more."

"Jesus."

"No, Eva, I got more money than Jesus."

"No kidding. But how? Where did *she* get it all from?"

"Careful."

"I just don't see how..."

He shrugged, a deep, knowing one, as if he'd asked himself that very question a million - seven and a half million - times. "Dunno. It wasn't an insurance payout. It just was there at the time of her death in the account. I remember the guy at the bank was even confused. Anyway, I got more money than I know what to do with, but not enough to sit on a yacht and sip Cristal for the rest of my life. So I figure, fuck it, I'll work how I want, open a shop for high-end cars, invest in a couple nightclubs, bang a new chick every night—"

"That's deep, really deep, Nate. What I hear in all this is that your mother made sure through some crazy scheme that you were taken care of in the event of her death, but—"

"Couldn't give a shit about me when she was alive and breathing."

I was going to finish with something about her living in purposeful abuse despite - it seemed - having the means to escape, but he was more correct. His mother had behaved strangely. "Sorry, but that's just a touch...messed up."

"Yeah, I know. You done with that?" he asked, pointing to my container.

"Ah," I said, my eyebrows raising at him, "no, paws off mister."

"Fine." He said and took the last bite of his fettuccini and got up tossing his container and fork into the sink. Washing his hands, he wiped his mouth, snapped off the water, and dried his hands on his pants and his mouth on the corner of his shirt. As his shirt came up, I looked away.

The small gesture was not lost on him, and he made a small noise that sounded a lot like the combination of a knowing laugh and a grunt. He returned to one of the living space's deep leather chairs with his refilled club soda.

I felt like he was working something as he watched me. His eyes begging me to ask. I raised my eyebrow at him. "What?"

He leaned forward, elbows resting on his thighs, his face all seriousness except for his glittering eyes. "Let's circle back to something else besides my past."

I put a finger up. "Hold, please," I said and took another pull on the wine, then regarded him right back. "I'm ready."

"Tell me about what happened four years ago."

"You mean five years ago when I called my dad from New York and found out you were in prison?"

"No," Nate said, his eyes hooding, "who was the last guy you slept with?"

"I—"

"I've told you a lot of shit, Eva. Only fair."

"I'm not sure —"

"Eve."

"Ugh." I said, sucking my fork clean and leaned back into the couch. But the way his eyes bore down on me—I stood, going to the bank of windows, and cracked one open. "It's a little stuffy."

The collision of two worlds was setting off mini explosions laying waste to all my careful calculating and compartmentalizing. My world that I'd spent years so carefully creating for myself all the way on the other side of this nation, one that denied and dodged all questions as to where I grew up, and who I grew up knowing. The world that held fancy cars, cocktail parties with A-list people, the rolodex of favors I could pull. The world I shared with no one from my past.

"I'm not sure where I should start."

"Let's start with his name."

I turned and sat on the window seat. "Ugh. Names need not be mentioned. I'm not ashamed of the time I spent with him, but I'm still embarrassed at how naïve I was even just a few years ago." I took a deep breath. "I was engaged."

Nate sat forward and put his glass down on the table with more force than was necessary. "What'd you say?"

"You heard me," I said as I looked at my ring finger where my fiancé's ring had shined in all its great-karated glory. I sort of missed the rock, I'd liked the weight it lent my hand, in a purely selfish and materialistic way. The same way I felt looking down from my nosebleed office in downtown Manhattan to the ant people below.

Nate, I realized, was seething. "What?" he repeated.

"That's funny that you're pissed—that makes two of us."

"Who is he?"

"Why? Are you keeping tabs on everyone who's ever seen me naked? How long would your list be, Nate?"

"Fuck it, I don't need to know right now who he is—what'd you do, chew him up and spit him out too?"

I smiled sadly, thinking on that day. "No, I walked in on him and his personal assistant getting to know each other on a level that was a little too personal. I'd left work early to surprise him with lunch, and the news of the promotion to managing editor I'd just gotten."

"He was banging his personal assistant on his lunch break at your place? How goddamn dumb is he?"

I shrugged. "The worst part about it is that I was mostly pissed at him for ruining our lunch plans. I realized then that we were probably not a match made in heaven. Later, I couldn't believe I'd not seen the regularity of our banal sex life as a massive red flag. Tuesdays and Thursdays like clockwork. I just thought it was nice because I could schedule it in, seemed like a good idea for two people in a power relationship. Turns out it was more that he didn't need me Mondays, Wednesdays, Fridays, and most weekends."

Nate ran a hand through his hair and reclined back. "Babe. I know you're running for tight-ass of the year, but I would think that even you would realize you've got a thing for mind-blowing sex."

"Yeah, well," I said very quietly, "I buried a lot of things I *actually* needed in exchange for things I *thought* I did," and looked him straight in the eye, making sure he realized exactly what I meant.

Nate didn't even flinch. He was picking up what I was laying down and knew that he was the only one I'd ever had earth-shattering sex with. I watched as his face darkened, his eyes went golden with a fiery need that had only one outlet. He stood and slowly placed his glass down on the coffee table and looked back up at me. "Four years sounds like a really long time."

"It is." My heart beat; the wine churned lovingly in my stomach, radiating heat that intensified my adrenaline.

Nate's bare feet took him toward me, each step saturated with primal intent. "Eva," he said, infusing my name with heartbreak and need, "I'm going to break your four-year dry spell, right now."

"I—" was the only syllable I could manage before a wide palm at my belly put me back up against a brick wall. This time, inside.

I released a vocal sigh.

I felt Nate smile against my upturned throat. "Don't get too far ahead. I haven't even started yet."

My hands found the hem of his shirt. His belly was hot with the promise of sweat, firm and taut, rippled as I slid my hands over it.

"Oh my god." The connection of our skin held memories of its own. Only now, the power between us wasn't imagined—it was real. Childhood lust had twisted into what we were witnessing now; emotions that had once been pure had become shadowed. They had taken on the complexity of time and were now being served blindly as aching, needful love.

In one move, I slid his shirt up and off, throwing it aside. His strength moved under his skin. His scars, big and small nicks marking his life—like the cigarette burn under my fingers at his shoulder, the ghosts of punches that split the skin. They were tattoos, only they spoke volumes more than ink could ever do. Each one held its own story, each I knew intimately. My lips found them, touching them, connected them all one by one until my fingers rested on his heart. There, I knew, was another wound, inflicted by me.

"I'm sorry," I whispered and kissed where my fingers had been.

Wordlessly, his mouth found mine, and every moment apart, every second of every year detonated between us. My chest squeezed so hard with yearning that I thought I'd only find relief in breathing Nate in; I had needed him to fill the hole in my own heart I'd not realized I had.

Palms at his hips I traced his pelvis's twin creases down to the fly of his button-down jeans, and pulled them open. And then I freed the soft cap of his hardened eight inches.

Nate groaned against my mouth while his tongue slipped in, stirring more memories. His hand slid into my hair and gripped me to him. Years faded away as we tasted each other once more, for each year of absence heat and need built and eddied. All reminding me in sweet hot ripples that this was the foreplay to what was yet to come—it was a promise.

Nate's hands found the latch at the top of my zippered dress and with the finesse of his expert fingers released it allowing the zipper to tear along its track to the bottom. The dress sighed open.

Nate's hand slid across my chest then paused, "What the f—?"

He looked down; confused I too looked down. To my duct-taped breasts.

I cursed. "Hold on—I think I can get this off—water." I fumbled, feeling suddenly foolish, thinking I should head to the bathroom.

"Oh no you don't," he said, pushing me back against the brick, "I'll take care of this."

The strips of tape started at the top of my breasts, curved over them, pushing them in and up, before ending on my belly. Crossing every sensitive part of my upper body.

"Nate—" I said before a lick of pain seared me. Nate, not hesitating, gripped a corner of tape and ripped the first piece off. The silver tape scoured a red mark down my side, feeling like it had taken a piece of me with it. With the pain came something else: a scorching release, cathartic payback.

Nate lowered his mouth, licked where the tape had been, a long cooling trace up the side of my breast from the top of my belly.

"Oh..." I said as the sweet sensations of pain and tenderness muddled my mind.

"That was for coming back into my life," he said hoarsely, his breath warming my shoulder just before his teeth scrapped my skin at my other side as he pulled on the strip of silver tape there. "Nate..." I pleaded.

"Oh no, baby, there's no going back." But he was slow, gentle, over my tenderest parts. Once clear, he ripped. I gasped at the pain and the tingling left behind, welcoming it. I needed this punishment, wanted him to feed me the pain and guilt I deserved.

"That was for making me want you again." Each mark he tasted, kissed, and soothed until only one piece remained. It was the plumping strip that I had placed first, which ran directly over both breasts covering my nipples. With a trembling hand, Nate grasped it, put his mouth to mine and brutally ripped it off. I broke our kiss and cried out. Nate bent and put my breast into his mouth and gently suckled, soothing the throbbing skin.

"That was for leaving me...Eva, there's no turning back now."

Feeling my penance given, I whispered in return, a hint of a smile on my lips, "You promise?" And took up the removal of his jeans once more, showing them no mercy, kicking them and his boxer briefs away. I needed him sweat soaked with ragged breath, and I'd been needing it for seven long years.

I hooked an arm around his neck and with the wall at my back for support arched up, wrapping my legs around his waist and gripped tight. All eight inches slipped in and I nearly expired.

I felt Nate's grip falter. "Jesus fucking Christ, slow down," he said, catching us by pushing me back against the wall, and a firm hand came down on my hip trying to still me. But I was delirious and drunk off his strain for control; that I could do that to him. As he could do to me.

"No," tumbled off my lips as I pushed and pulled with my pelvis. I felt the edge of that blissful cliff and closed my eyes as I approached it with speed. Somewhere far a way I heard cursing, and I was gripped tighter and felt a weightlessness as my head dropped back.

Nate hefted me off the wall. My eyes snapped opened just as I was tossed bodily onto the bed. I rolled across it and, still stilettoed, came up on all fours. A feral smile crossed my lips; Nate's control was shredded.

"Slow down," he said. His body had taken on a sheen of sweat and his penis stood proud like a bold arrow pointing north.

"No," I said scouring his body with my gaze.

"Come here."

"No."

"You won't like it if I have to come for you."

"Oh, no, I think I will, and I think I remember a fun game we used to play: Chase. Can you catch me?"

The glimmer of recognition sparked in his eye and he moved left. I mirrored him and as he came across the bed for me I leaped back.

Only, his arm was longer than I remembered and our game of chase was over as fast as it had begun.

He caught my arm and flipped me backward onto the bed, covering me with his sweat-slicked body. I groaned, and spread my legs, wrapping them around his hips, begging him to slide within me. I closed my eyes and watched him—felt him through my skin. He was over me and struggling to keep his cool. We needed each other like we needed air to breathe. He was the power that ran through me; without him, I was simply one-dimensional, one-sided, and misdirected—on a perpetual search for more. This, what I'd had so many years ago, was what I'd been looking for. Everything else was just that, everything else. With him I felt I could go, do, become, anything.

"I love you," I said as I lifted my hips again, begging.

"Say it again, Eve..."

"I love you, Nathaniel Vellanova," I said as he slipped within me and drove those words back into our dimension, binding us together once more, "I need you, I want you, but *oh god*, I love you." Gripping his taut back as he moved, feeling his damp skin against my tender, ravaged breasts, his sweat the balm to soothe my pain.

My head fell back and a voice that sounded much like mine cried out in blissful pleasure as he relaxed out then pushed in again and again; the rumble of a curse followed it; then the scrape of his teeth along my neck. Our union sucked and pulled all of our darkness, our pain, and twisted it into pleasure, ecstasy, and the first strings of unadulterated happiness. Joy. Together.

My legs slid up, gripping him even tighter; I was wrapped completely and utterly around him. His breath became ragged and he gripped my hip, driving himself in dedicated rhythm. Building us up faster and higher, his tongue dove into my mouth as the first fingers of our orgasm rocked us. My world clenched and pulled, making me cry out his name. Everything slipped sideways. Pleasure and joy exploded as the rolling orgasms pulsed; my legs tightened even further, melding Nate to and into me and sealing our unvoiced vow that nearly a decade would never again pass without this. And with a last blissful cry, we shuddered together, Nate spilling himself fully within me, giving all as I did the same.

HE COULDN'T BELIEVE THAT EVA HAD FALLEN INTO BED NEXT TO him. Couldn't believe how he said "fuck it" to every single one of his rules with her. To be fair though he hadn't put those rules into practice with her until three days ago when her ass showed up at his shop for the first time in nearly a decade. Now, he realized he wasn't ready for this new Eva, the woman who could look at him with those unflinching eyes and verbally strip him to the core. She was hardened by her own ambition and—he hoped—guilt over how she left things with him.

He ran his fingertips up her arm and over her shoulder before letting them swim in the sea of her brown hair. He couldn't resist a single thing about her and before the night was over, he was going to use up every bit of feeling he had left for her.

I WOKE TO NATE UP ON HIS ELBOW NEXT TO ME, HIS OLIVE SKIN darkly contrasting mine. Seeing me awake, he lifted his hand. I followed his fingers as he dragged them lightly from my cheek down over my breasts to the tight crop of black between my legs. There he brushed the back of his hand over it, coaxing my knees to spread and my own hand to caress his arm, grazing over the dives and bumps of musculature to clasp the back of his head and pull his mouth down to mine.

I had years of apologizing to do, and in the dark shadows of his loft, I wanted to spend every waking moment in prayer to his body and soul.

Nate maneuvered over me, his weight on his elbows; our bodies sought connection again. As he lengthened inside of me, he slipped one hand under my shoulder and his other grasped one wrist and then my other. He pinned them together above my head and whispered, "Let's play."

His pelvis pushed and then relaxed back, then did it again.

I breathed him in: sweat, nicotine, and clean sheets. I tugged his earlobe with my teeth before kissing it, before dragging my mouth along his neck, before kissing his Adam's apple. "OK, what are you thinking?"

"Something rougher."

I paused his hips by squeezing my thighs together. "No hitting."

He shook his head. "No hitting. More tape."

I felt my eyebrow rise in question. "Show me."

He kissed my lips, then slipped out of me and then from the bed. I watched his naked backside walk to the elevator and open a tool chest that looked like it was at home in his industrial loft. He was built like the lithe intention of a man who had fought his way to the top and planned to stay there. Round buttocks showed practiced thrusting muscles that I didn't want to know the recent history of. From his wide shoulders down to his broad feet, in another life he could have been a professional athlete, not a man who ran from the law and his past.

He took a roll of silver duct tape from the top drawer and walked back slowly, his fingers teasing out the edge. He found it and ripped a length of the tape.

A delicious chill went down my spine and caught in my breath.

"'George Washington,'" he said as he put a knee on the corner of the bed, "when you want to stop."

I took a shuddering breath. "And not over my mouth."

He looked at me; his eyes were soft. "Of course not."

"Um, maybe no feet too. What are you going to do with it?"

"No questions."

I swallowed and looked to the tape, then to him.

He bent low and kissed my lips. "We don't have to do this."

"I..."

"But there's a part of you that wants to. The real question is, Eve, do you trust me?"

"I..."

"Do you trust me with your body? Do you trust me to bring you pleasure?" he whispered against my ear. The breath of his words echoed down my ear canal and spiked low, igniting arousal. He was asking for full control.

I pushed his chest back so that his face was level with mine. "Yes."

"Give me your hands."

And I did. He wrapped the tape around my wrists, binding them together. My hands went above my head, and he secured them to the headboard. Tape ripped over and over again. The act was methodical, and only twice while he worked did I test the tape's strength. Each time he gave me a grin, a grin that said he was going to be slow and deliberate and push the bounds of my need to control things to the very edge.

He was back at the bedside. "Foot," he said and held his hand out for my right foot.

"But I thought—"

"No questions."

I made to protest again, but he stood and tore a long piece of tape off.

"Every time you break the rules, I'll punish you," he said and lay one end of the tape against one side of my breast before pulling the rest of the piece tight across the nipples of both. "And we both know how much this hurts when this comes off."

I took a deep breath. I wanted to say, "No fucking way," and George-Washington my way out of this stupid game, but he wasn't an amateur when it came to my body and what it wanted, and I did trust him. There was a good chance I was going to love the hell out of what he was about to do if I could get my brain to acquiesce to someone else at the reins.

"I'll need a swig of wine if I'm going to go along with this."

He started to get off the bed when he paused and looked back at me. "No, I want you clearheaded."

"I'm not sure..."

"Just say, 'George Washington,' Eve, and I'll untie you, and we can go back to lying next to each other—pretending we'll sleep for the rest of the night."

I took a stabilizing inhale. "I said no feet."

He ripped another length of tape off and secured it over my abdomen, letting the tail end of it attach to the top of my bikini line. I groaned; that was going to be painful as hell to get ripped off.

I gave over my right leg.

He watched my face as I watched him wrap the silver tape around my ankle and attach it in a long line to the footboard. He moved to the other side and held his hand out, his eyes glittering with joy. I gave over my other foot, and he secured it too. He put the entire roll down with a thud on the side table. There was slack enough for my arms and legs to move a few inches.

He took his time letting my mind trip over itself about what was going to happen next and if I was going to like it or not. He went into the kitchen and looked at me from over the bar. His gaze went straight up between the valley of my knees; he looked as if he were surveying his land, his gaze scouring every inch of me before landing on my own.

He gave me a crooked grin, one that begged me to ask him what he was doing so that he could lay another band of tape on me. He stood there for what felt like hours, long enough to get me to test my restraints. My hands ripped a piece of the tape, and he made his way back and secured it tighter.

I gave the new position a solid impatient yank, and it held.

This time he walked back to the kitchen and took a cube of ice from a tray and came back to me. He started at my thigh and gently pushed the ice cube up over my pelvis to settle between my breasts. Cold droplets slithered over my skin, pooling in my curves and trickling off other places onto the sheet. Nate let his finger follow a trail down to my thigh and between my legs to bring him standing at the end of the bed. He laced his fingers behind his head and regarded me. It was the casual stance of a man enjoying his handiwork and completely unaware that he had become the visual representation of a sex symbol. Nate's bowed arms made his biceps flex and made him into an impressive capital *T*. He was Michelangelo's *David* with his hands behind his head and sex on his mind.

I felt my breath stagger in a fit of expectation as he moved forward. He put his hands down onto the mattress and bent his head.

My eyes closed as my chin lifted. "Sweet Jesus," I cursed as his mouth went directly between my thighs. My knees fell open, welcoming him to taste deeper. His mouth took no time in reestablishing his dominance over my body as my hands fought their restraints to get to him; they wanted to weave their fingers through his thick black head of hair, to grip tight and take control.

I exclaimed with frustrated pleasure. Instead of using my hands, I rocked my hips forward into his adept mouth, begging for more, for him to stop this punishment and yet for him to not stop, to never ever stop. Just as the fingers of climax and the passionate pursuit of an orgasm bloomed between my legs and shot up to my chest, he exhaled a hot breath over me and pushed his nose into my thigh before biting it.

Panting, balanced so close to climax, I looked down at him. Mischief worked the corners of his mouth. He reached up to retrieve the sliver of ice cube that had skittered across my chest and landed in the alcove at the base of my throat. As he reached over his head, I saw he was not immune to what he was doing to me. Red and straining against its own skin was the eight-inch-thick shaft of him. I felt it warm against the inside of my ankle.

Using my toes, I brushed up against him.

His breath caught in his throat, and he paused mid-reach. His eyes went to mine. They were dark and going heavy lidded with suppressed need. Instead of moving away, he seemed paralyzed, and I repeated my movement, bringing his breath harder, and I fought against my restraints again to pull him to me.

With visible effort, he stilled my foot and brought his body up over mine. He took the now fleck of an ice cube and ran it down to the top of my pubic hair and let it melt there, his fingers separating my folds, the ice-cold liquid dripping down between them.

Open-mouthed with the shock of the chill and the erotic slither of liquid over the sensitive skin, I felt my primal brain wake fully.

Then came the first bite of tape.

I cried out as adhesive ripped off of my abdomen and snatched a swatch of hair off my bikini line. Nate watched me as his fingers followed the tape line down and slipped inside of me. Pain and pleasure smashed together within me and made me close my eyes against it. My body writhed around his fingers. Orgasm threatened, making my hips push his fingers deeper, begging for him to end my beautiful suffering.

My mouth was open, and my breath came harder and harder.

Nate wound his leg around mine, pulling it against his shaft; he moved his hips in time with his fingers within me. Climax moved in swiftly, the orgasm shuddering my body over his fingers. Nate moved swiftly, coming over my body as the last of the shudders rocked my body. His pelvis against mine, he slipped into me before connecting our mouths once more. Then, he reached down and ripped. Euphoria shattered and pain moved in, and just as I felt the need to scream in pain, the orgasm bloomed wide to encompass my pain and shoot my body into the stratosphere. Nate's mouth went back to mine, and I kissed him, then bit him. I heard Nate groan as my mouth opened to him. As if in apology, as my pelvis tilted up, meeting his. He pushed faster, making a firm repetitive slap as our bodies physically met and released.

His hand wove up into my hair, gripped a fistful of it, and pulled my head back. Teeth to my neck, he scoured a line down it as his thrusts came quicker. Another peak shuddered through me as his full thickness pressed deep within me driving us into another orgasm.

I cried out with him as we rode it to its very end and collapsed into and on each other.

Nate went up on an elbow. Breathing hard and still within me, yanked directly up, releasing my hands from the headboard. Another reach and he had pulled a blade out from the drawer of his nightstand and flicked it out to carefully cut me loose. He tossed the blade back as I grasped him to me and brought his face to mine. "I love you, you beautiful, beautiful man."

He put his lips against mine, and gently we descended from the heavens.

Sleep was a foolhardy ideal that night. It would come but be interrupted by my body rousing me awake with the awareness of him next to me.

My leg thrown over his hips, I hugged him tight to me. I was fitted to his side like a rider to her stallion. My head nestled in the hollow just below his shoulder. A nest for my cheek. I fit against him perfectly. No awkward elbows or head lolling about looking for a well-muscled hollow to reside in. I breathed him in: sweat from his exertion, sweetness of tobacco, and crisp, clean linens. I felt the balm of those unique Nate smells settle my restless soul. It was as if in a faraway land I held tight to something long forgotten, and the smell of him undid that tight hold. I felt myself relax, drawing that soothing balm over every tight spot until they were all undone and nothing but a quiet mind was left.

Again, sleep came.

And again, quiet sleep slithered away as dawn began to break on the skyline.

Still wrapped against his side, I let my fingers touch the light cluster of hair in the center of his chest before following it up to the superior relief of his collarbone. Perfectly rounded dowels on either side of his throat, his clavicle stood out, making the skin dip down before rising to the tops of his shoulders. I wondered what it would be like to have water pool there so that I could put my lips to it and sip it up. Would it taste like a mountain stream or more like salt spray off an active shore?

"The answer is yes, to whatever it is that you're thinking."

His eyes were a mellow gold, nearly chocolate in color.

I tilted my chin up and reached for a kiss; he met me halfway. Our lips were soft against each other, like a sigh over the memory of what we'd done and the feeling that things were just right in the world.

"I love you," I murmured against his lips.

He pushed my hair off my cheek as I put my hand to his jaw and gently pulled his lips back to mine.

As our lips spoke, I tasked my open palm to remind me what the flat plains of his pectorals felt like. I pushed it lower, toward his navel, before allowing it to follow the dark trail of hair below it even lower. His shaft was at half-staff and firming, but it was the two orbs below it that I had been remiss with during my previous attentions. They too needed love, and with them in my cupped palm, I rolled them softly against my fingers like a set of Chinese meditation balls.

I watched as Nate's eyelids fluttered down and his bicep flexed against my shoulder blades as he gripped me tight.

I gave his nipple a light bite before I slid myself over him. Only he shifted his weight and put me back against the soft sheets and maneuvered himself between my thighs. Welcoming him into my embrace, I wrapped my legs around his middle, pulling him into my center of gravity once more.

Gently, softly, purposefully, our lips touched as our bodies swam together. He pushed in deep and relaxed, then pushed in again as we made love once more.

THIRTY-ONE

You're fired."

I had been thinking of Saturday and Sunday nights, then this Monday morning, as I sat in my HR manager's office. Specifically, I was thinking of how Nate had gotten distant, driving a wedge the size of Texas between us after I'd left his place earlier that morning. It made me feel like I had been just an itch. Nate's itch. He'd scratched, and that was that. How could I have been so unbelievably blind about his intentions? I was so deep in my own thoughts I really didn't hear what my *Rose City Review* HR manager was saying to me.

"What?" I asked with more vehemence than I felt. Mostly because he was interrupting my extremely important inner dialog.

"Eva..." He looked at me pleadingly. "You must have known this would happen when you treated a valuable *Rose City Review* asset as you did—"

"What?" I repeated as if I had gone deaf.

He pleaded, "I'm sorry, but you're fired."

I'd heard him. I let the silence between us soak into the off-white walls covered in motivational posters from the eighties. I watched the way his eyes darted to mine then to the paperwork he had on his desk in front of him. Now, I was mad, but for a different reason. My old days at *Vogue* and the tittle-tattle that I had to deal with there, descended around me like a black cloak of indifference. It undid every relaxing second I'd experienced that weekend and solidified another moment in my dossier that would be wound tight like a noose around the neck of my happiness.

In my indifference I could practically smell the fear and betrayal off the human slouch in front of me demanding my job. If you're going to revoke the editor-in-chief's position you'd better have steel balls.

Or as it turned out, a powerful ally.

He had his hand over a yellow Post-it® and peered at it before saying, "Mr. Wellington has made it abundantly clear that your physical attack at the party suggests that you have anger issues that we cannot condone and as such is requesting your resignation."

I just stared at him. I wasn't sure what I was expecting, probably a disgruntled art department employee that quit the week before, but not Captain Suck My Dick, "Two seconds ago you said I was fired. Now you say that you want my resignation? I'm being let go because I refused to suck off a board member." I ignored HR's horrified expression. "I have a witness to that fact—shall I call him or shall I just call my lawyer?"

"I, well, I don't know what you're talking about, but Mr. Wellington said he is willing to not press charges against, ah, Mr. Nathaniel Vellanova," he said looking under his hand again, "if you'll resign, ah, peacefully."

"Resign peacefully." I said as I tilted my head to the side, "You're my Human Resources Manager, could you decode what 'not press charges means?' Because I feel like that is a threat. A threat that he'll counter sue if I file a sexual harassment lawsuit against him. Again, I ask you, did he tell you that he told me I should be sucking his dick to be in his good graces?

"By your puce expression, I take it, that's a no."

Beads of sweat popped out at his receded hairline, betrayal was unbecoming on him.

"So, you see," I purposefully looked down at his name plate then back to him, "Geoff, you've aligned yourself with a bad man. And why would he press charges against Mr. Vellanova?" I asked.

Again, he looked down at his paper. "Because of his act of violence against Mr. Wellington, from which he has a broken rib."

I was about to respond when he continued, "It is also understood that Mr. Vellanova was at one point imprisoned for assault, and it is Mr. Wellington's wishes for a safe work environment for all his employees. Since you and Mr. Vellanova are...friends...and he has been seen here, it has been deemed safer if you resign. And, and I have to say I a-agree." He blinked rapidly as soon as we made eye contact.

"Please repeat that," I said softly, not sure I heard it properly over the hum in my ears.

"I'm sorry, Ms. Rodgers. Here are your papers and a fine severance package. I-I created your severance package."

I sat in the uncomfortable vinyl chair for five heartbeats, "Thank you. I'll remember that when I sue IMG Media for everything its worth." I stood and looked down at the little man behind his desk, "What'd he promise you, Geoff? A corner office, stock options, your soul?"

Geoff swallowed, "He, I don't know what you're talking about," he said looking quite the opposite.

"What will I find when I hire a private detective to gather evidence for my sexual harassment case, Geoff? Will they find that you accepted a bribe in exchange to fire me? I've worked too hard here, worked tirelessly to make a profit for this company, I'll not be pushed out by an entitled hedonist who's idea of hard work is keeping his smile white while trying to shove everyone beneath him." I said then added with my hand out, "I'll leave now and take that paperwork. I'll be back in when this is all cleared up, try not to miss me."

I left then, trying not to slam the door, grabbed a few things from my office and headed toward the elevators. The main conference room door was closed and it seemed my entire staff were in a simultaneous meeting, which rankled me. This was more coordinated than I'd assumed, as I was sure they were discussing my departure.

The freeways were clear of morning rush hour traffic and back at Dad's house I dropped my things on the dining table. I paced then dug out the paperwork and scanned it. I was to be given a year's salary and a resignation bonus that would wipe out the magazine's annual budget—Wellington was apparently a very helpful investor. I didn't care—it was my life, my career, the thing which got me out of bed in the morning and I'd use every damn dime of mine fighting them in court over it. I tore through the resignation contract and crossed out any and all references to "further legal action" and "absolves IMG of any wrongdoing." I was going sue their asses off.

I called my attorney and made plans for the next steps. Just as I hung up, my phone rang again. I needed time to punch something, but all I'd been able to do so far was wield a pen and talk on the phone.

It was Dr. Zimmerman, with news I had not been expecting of the good variety. I headed to the hospital to collect my father and finally bring him home.

THIRTY-TWO

THE NEXT MORNING I WAS UP AND TO THE STORE BEFORE MY father woke but after Marta had arrived. It was odd, but wonderful, to have Dad home again. We'd been given a new beginning, both of us, in so many ways. I'd taken a shower last night while he slept in the next room, and I'd let loose in there, wiping tears from my face and emotional grime from my body, I washed my past from me too. I forgave myself for all the ridiculous things I'd done and allowed myself to accept them and now to change.

Now, it was also an odd thing to be at the grocery store during a workday. I was surrounded by elderly couples and mothers with babies, all moving very slowly down the middle of the aisles. Finally accomplishing what I'd started out thinking was a simple task, I pushed my cart out the sliding doors.

"Eva."

I turned to find a scruffy man coming toward me, smiling. There was something about his gait, the paunch of his bristled jowls, that spoke of a once savage self-inflicted painful life. My heart tumbled down all the way to my toes taking my blood with it. The man coming toward me was a killer. His hands had wielded a knife and cut his wife to pieces. He had stepped into his namesake - Butch - and worn it like a prophecy.

"Eva..." Butch Vellanova said again, getting close enough to settle a ham-sized hand on the edge of my cart.

I looked at that hand, "Do I know you?" I whispered.

He chuckled, his breath sick and sour; a human pickled in alcohol. His son bore no resemblance to him. "Now, now. You remember me. I can see it in your face." He tried to touch my cheek with thick fingers.

I flinched, the spell of sorts broken. "Don't touch me, and get your hand off my cart."

"Now, now," he said again, "that's not very nice to say to your boyfriend's old man."

"Get away from me," I said loudly. I made eye contact with the store greeter, who had been watching our exchange. He made his way toward us.

Butch looked over his shoulder at the greeter approaching and when he looked back at me, his gaze had gone cold, calculating. "I have a message for Nate."

I tried to give him an equal stare in return. "What do you want with him?"

"Give that little shit a message—"

"Ma'am? Is there a problem here?"

"Yes," I said, looking around Butch to the greeter, "this man is harassing me."

Butch looked like one of the homeless who sometimes begged outside the store. The clerk assumed he was and sided with me without question. "You're going to have to remove yourself from the premises," he said and gestured in the direction of the main road.

Butch turned to look at him. He raised his hands as if in surrender and passed behind me toward the parking lot. But not before he whispered to me, "Daddy's gonna get his piece."

I whirled. Butch was already to the first row of cars in the parking lot and ambling swiftly away; I could say nothing in reply.

"Are you OK, ma'am?" the greeter asked.

I gave him a cursory smile and said, "Yeah, fine, thanks."

Hands unsteady, I loaded the groceries into my car and, once inside myself, hit the lock button and called Shelby. Shelby said that he'd file a harassment report and get the paperwork for a restraining order started. And with that I told him all about my father's encounter with him. I no longer felt any interest in helping my father maintain some fake understanding. Butch was no gentleman—no way was he holding up a gentleman's agreement.

"That's why we need to find that Chevy—if we can pull the prints we can put him back in prison until he'll be too old to move."

"Still nothing?" I asked, resting my forehead on the steering wheel.

"No. And I'm not sure how much Nate has told you, but he is also helping with the search. He's not returning my calls lately, though—if you could find out for me if he's heard anything, I'd be grateful."

"Yeah, I'll see what I can do."

THIRTY-THREE

I RETURNED HOME, SHAKEN BUT SURE I WASN'T FOLLOWED. AND I felt much better once I saw Dad—he seemed to have blossomed overnight and was up sitting at the kitchen table chatting with Marta. I was just about to close the door behind me when I heard a familiar car pull up: Chuck in his seventies Dodge pickup.

"Oh lord," I said.

"Eva!" Chuck said as he bounded up the driveway as if he were a teenager.

"Hi, Chuck," I said and gave him a hug, his shaggy gray hair brushing my cheeks.

"Still got that damn Dodge, I see," Dad said over my shoulder to his friend. "I died and went to heaven and thought I saw it up there!"

"Ha! You weren't in heaven if you saw it! What were you doing in the hospital anyway—getting tired of staying at home?" Chuck asked as they walked into the living room. I looked heavenward and shook my head, "I'll make coffee," I said with a smile.

Marta matched my smile as she continued organizing my dad's medications and refilled her bandage boxes.

"He's obviously doing better," I said to her.

I unloaded the groceries while Marta filled me in on the morning at home. I tried to stay focused on her words but lost them as my mind kept pulling up Butch's face. Tamping down on a little bubble of panic, I switched tasks to filling the coffee maker.

Marta, appeared next to me and interrupted my circular thoughts. "Are you OK?" she asked.

"Yeah, fine."

"You're filling the filter with sugar."

I looked down to the canister in my shaking hand: it was filled with white granules instead of brown.

Marta put her hand on my back. "What happened?"

I just closed my eyes and shook my head.

"OK, but let me do that." She took the canister and the spoon from me.

"Thanks," I said, watching her numbly as she dumped out the sugar and replaced it with grounds. "Excuse me," I said, picking up my purse, and went into my room closing the door behind me.

Sitting on the edge of the bed I pulled out my phone and looked at it. I needed to tell Nate about his father. But the memory of his sendoff after our night together snapped something consequential within me. He had expertly avoided kissing me good-bye by holding my car door open—and between us. I'd gotten a head nod and, "See ya."

Tossing my purse strap over my shoulder, my phone still in my hand, I headed out the front door. "I'll be right back," I called over my shoulder to the house.

European Pro Auto's parking lot came into view quickly. The sun had started to burn off the clouds, and the pavement, damp from the morning rain, was steaming. Mirroring my mood. I pulled the car in faster than necessary perpendicular to the employee parking spots—pulling her into an actual spot at the moment felt like too much work. I yanked the e-brake before she'd stopped, chirping her tires and flipping the engine off I stepped out. All but two of the bay doors were open; as I approached the one Nate was working in, I tucked my keys into my pocket.

Nate took his time stepping out from under the car he was working on. The rest of the shop was busy—I'd seen Anthony talking with a man about his aging Jaguar in the parking lot and a few others paying in the front office.

"Find us a nice quiet spot," I said to Nate, "and I'll make this as undisturbing as possible."

In an equally low voice he answered, "No. You'll leave now, and maybe I'll make time for you after I'm through here."

I folded my arms across my chest. "Last warning."

"I'm not playing, Eva; turn around and leave."

"Funny thing, neither am I." I noticed that Greg the mechanic had completely stopped working and was watching us. I raised my hand and waved at him.

"Eva—" Nate said and got a vise grip on my arm.

"Unless you want your nuts in your throat, get your hand off me."

Nate's eyes narrowed. "I'd like to see you try—"

I brought my knee up.

He knocked my knee aside with his thigh. "Out back," he snapped and pivoted, letting go of my arm, leaving black grease marks on me.

THIRTY-FOUR

THE DOOR HAD BARELY SWUNG SHUT BEHIND US WHEN HE SAID, "What do you want? I thought I told you that I didn't want your ass on my property."

If there were an empty box next to the question of what the weekend had been to Nate, "itch" was just confirmed as yes.

"You. Cannot. Be. Serious."

"As a heart attack," he said, snapping off his gloves.

"I'm pretty sure Saturday night made that statement null and void, Nate," I said, feeling slightly nauseated at his response.

Nate wiped the back of hand over his mouth and looked away.

I felt my heart squeeze and my stomach sink at his denial of our lovemaking.

Nate turned back and got in my face, quietly saying, "You don't get it do you Eva?"

"Get—"

"I'm so goddamn crazy over you, I'd not think twice about putting you back against this wall right now—*Jesus*, Eva. You coming to my shop for the first time was all it took. I even took a girl home that night, that first time you came here, and she spread herself out for me—"

"Nate—"

"Despite that, Eva, I couldn't do it. Had to have her suck me off while I closed my eyes, thinking of you."

"Nate." This wasn't what I came for.

"I can't control myself when I'm with you, and that scares the shit out of me. So when I say don't come to my work, don't get back into my life, I mean it. You don't get to control me here—it's my life now." He quietly added, "I won't lose control again, Eva. I don't give a shit what happened this weekend—you gotta get the fuck out of my life." He enunciated those last four words.

"Except..."

"Except?"

"We both know this weekend meant no going back."

Nate opened his mouth to protest, and I blurted, "I was fired Monday, and I just saw your dad."

Nate's features contorted, trying to process what I'd just said. "Fired and...Jesus fucking Christ."

I felt the fight roll away from him as Nate leaned back against the wall next to me. It seemed like just breathing was difficult.

"You OK?"

I nodded calmly. "Yes, but—"

"Where'd you see him?" he said, pulling out his cell.

"I've already called Shelby."

"Where'd you see him?" he repeated, his tone and gaze going dark.

I told him everything, even down to the type of sneakers he was wearing. "His breath, Nate. He smelled like he'd just popped out of a vat of alcohol. Like a dying pickle."

"Dying pickle?"

I shook my head. "That's not what I meant; I mean—"

"He smells like death," he said, becoming serious.

"Yes. Nate, I'm worried about you."

"Don't be. I'll be ready for him when he comes. Did you at least tell him where to find me so he could deliver his message in person? Like a man?"

"Of course not."

His jaw clenched and he looked beyond me. "Too bad." Then, "If he really wanted to see me, Eva, he would have found me. Be careful —I'm not sure what he's playing at." Taking a deep breath, he looked back at me. "I'm sorry about your pops's truck."

"You think he took it?"

"No doubt he took the truck. What the hell he wants it for I don't know. Got my guys looking for it—it's not at chop shops or scrap places. He's got it hidden in a warehouse somewhere." He mumbled something under his breath that sounded like, "*Fuckingsonofabitch.*"

"Honestly, my dad feels like it's some sort of payment so he leaves you alone."

"That's not how it works. Not how he works. Maybe he'll sell it, maybe he'll drop it off a bridge—but he won't stop until he's got what he wants."

"And what the heck does he want with you?" I asked.

Boxes waiting to be broken down for recycling leaned against the chain-link fence. Nate calmly walked over and put his fist through the top one.

The sound of his bones ripping a hole in the fibers made me flinch.

After thoroughly thrashing the boxes, he calmly folded them and leaned them back against the fence. He stood looking at his boots, his fingers tucked in his armpits. Slowly his eyes rose to meet mine.

"Fired. Wellington?"

"Oh, there's more."

Nate closed his eyes and took a deep breath and then said, "You wanna grab some lunch?"

THIRTY-FIVE

NATE LICKED GARLICKY YOGURT SAUCE OFF HIS FINGERS AS WE sat on a wall along the waterfront. "Cracked rib?"

"Apparently," I said and took another bite of my own gyro.

"He wishes."

"I'm not real fluent on punches, but it looked like you nailed him pretty good, Nate."

"There's no way I cracked his ribs. Remember when you gave your dad CPR? You said you felt his ribs—"

"Give out. Yes." I distinctly remembered that feel in my palms. "It's not something I'll readily forget."

"Yeah, well, I didn't crack his ribs, but I know I bruised the shit out of them."

"Ah, there's my modest Nate. Sweets, you wouldn't necessarily know if you cracked them. A hairline fracture wouldn't crack under your fist."

"I forgot, you're the expert," he said around a mouthful of food.

"Despite all that, you seem pretty calm right now." Thinking about the dilapidated boxes.

"Yup. And I will be, right up until I bring that baseball bat against his knees."

I'd gotten my gyro halfway to my mouth when he said this. "Please tell me you're kidding."

He didn't answer; instead he asked, "Do you know how much stock he owns in the parent company? What's it called again?"

"IMG Media, and no, I wasn't in any mind to find out how much he owned. But I can say that for him to be paraded around like they were doing, I can imagine it's a majority share. I can see the wheels turning over there Nate. What are you thinking?"

"Hmm?"

"What are you thinking?" I repeated.

"Nothing, just keep moving forward with your suit—maybe the intent to sue will get things settled. I'll look into a couple things on my end if it doesn't. You visit your pops?"

I let Nate's cryptic suit comment go. "Yeah, I brought him home Monday."

Nate's mood lightened. "That's great. Shit, that's fast, right?"

"Maybe, but they said that they preferred him to go home since the longer he stayed in the hospital, the greater his risk of infection became."

"I bet Chuck is at your place before the week is out."

I laughed. "He was there when I left."

"See? I should have made a wager."

I polished of my gyro and, relaxing on the wall, I turned my face up toward the glowing orb in the sky like some hippie princess sucking whatever stingy heat my glowing goddess threw out at me. Eyes closed, I listened to the occasional bird and the children in the fountains, the crinkle of wax paper as Nate made progress with his Greek sandwich. The sound of a car with a coffee-can exhaust slowing down along the nearby drag had me opening my eyes. It was a young kid behind the wheel, at that age when all the world is a possibility and scoring chicks is number one on the to-do list.

"Good lord, why in the hell do they do that?"

"What?" Nate asked, pretending not to notice the red hot import with a spoiler the size of Manhattan.

"Stick that crappy after-market exhaust kit on an already pithy-sounding muffler and tailpipe?"

"Makes more power, and sounds awesome."

"Sounds awesome to whom? Noise birds in a rock quarry?"

"Noise birds, are those even a thing?"

"I might have made them up. But really, why?"

Nate shrugged, "With a soldering iron and a coffee can, babe, you too can make your car sound just like that one. You know, to attract noise birds."

I smiled over at him, "And I take it"—I gestured, which in a freak coincidence caught the attention of the boy behind the wheel and he gave a full toothed grin—"that spoiler...Jeez, why does he need that thing to be so huge? And don't tell me it's for all that power."

"OK, I won't then. And be nice and smile back at him. On second thought, stop staring at him—I'd hate to not break his ribs too. You're making me into a barbarian, Eva."

I laughed. "Oh, you do that just fine all by yourself. But really, why's it need to be so *big*?"

"Babe. Do you know what a spoiler is for?"

I just glared at him. Of course I did.

"Keeps the ass end down, tires to the road."

"Yes, but it's an older Honda. Civic," I clarified.

"He could have a turbo kit in there, and you'd not know."

"Sure." I said dubiously. Though, I had seen what Nate and I called "sleeper" cars, cars that looked like little two door putt-putt vehicles that normally would top out at thirty miles an hour, but really had a V8 squished between the engine's firewalls making it both the fastest thing on four wheels and a death trap.

Nate sat up and looked at the car—to the apparent joy of the boy behind the wheel. He'd gotten some alpha attention and revved the engine. The racket the exhaust can made ricocheted off the water-front wall and nearby buildings.

"Maybe."

"He doesn't have the tires for it and hasn't vented the hood."

"Doesn't necessarily need venting."

"OK, that aside, you're basically telling me that thing can do over 130 miles per hour, warranting that gigantic spoiler?"

"Warrant that spoiler? Babe, spoilers keep the ass—"

"End down, I know, but, oh—ha-ha! It's a front-wheel drive. That's awesome. So why would he put one on there that huge?"

Nate chuckled under his breath. "OK, that spoiler is for you. The only ass he's keeping down is the one he's chasing on two legs."

"Ew," I drawled. I noticed the driver was still trying to make eye contact with me. "Doesn't he know the difference between awestruck stares and those of incredulous disbelief and mockery?"

At this, Nate actually did laugh. "Eve, looks are looks. Doesn't matter what kind they are."

"Go break his legs for me," I whispered to him, laughing.

"You started that staring contest, you gotta finish it. Just give him your number and get it over with." He gave me a nudge.

I leaned in and kissed him instead, softly lingering, letting the laughter bond us. Nate's hand landed softly on my knee as he leaned into me, and then he slid it up my leg and around. His kiss deepened as his other hand dove into my ponytail at the nape of my neck.

I brought the tips of my fingers to his face, memorizing the bump of his cheek bone and the strong angle of his jaw. Both his wide hands came up and gently cradled my face as he pulled back.

His thumbs swiped across my cheeks. We reluctantly broke eye contact and looked over toward where the loud muffler sounds had been. The boy and his car were gone.

"Nice job, babe."

"Mmmm, no. That was all you."

He took in my face, his gaze traveling from my lips to my eyes. "Wanna go for a drive?"

THIRTY-SIX

NATE CALLED WORK, LEAVING THE AFTERNOON IN THE CAPABLE hands of his crew, and we walked back to the car along the waterfront. As we approached the black coupe from the rear, I once again felt my heart swoon at the sight of the raised wing insignia and DBS inscribed on the corner of the trunk.

I looked back at Nate's grinning face. "Please?" I asked as we got in.

"If you have $140K, I'm sure the dealer will let you drive it anywhere you want."

"I'm a little short on spending cash these days."

"It's been a long time for you and me, babe, but I haven't forgotten what a maniac behind the wheel you are."

"Really? Because I remember it was *you* who liked to take corners a little too fast, and what was your motto? Oh yes, 'If you're not slidin', you're not drivin'.'"

Nate grinned as he shifted into reverse, maneuvering us from the spot into traffic and the freeway. "We'll head out toward the coast; I've got a couple good runs I want to show you. And we'll see if you still feel that way."

"I'd feel better if you let me show you a few things too," I said, baiting him.

"You're still not driving it."

"Too bad. You'd be surprised what I can do with a paddle...shifter."

We took the freeway to the foothills of the coast range, where Nate exited onto a rural road empty and well paved, gracefully climbing higher and higher into the trees, leaving everything else that went with it. It was now just him and me.

"Hold on." He downshifted into the power zone and hammered it. The wide-bodied black sports car ate up the asphalt like a shark through a school of fish.

"Oh yeah," I whispered. Nate handled the car like an extension of himself, the leather bucket seats cradling us like lovers.

The road was new to me, and I found myself trying to memorize the corners and straightaways, the thickness of the trees on either side and, on a few stretches, the bits of rock that pebbled the surface. A million years ago, Nate and I would do this. His father would get rough, and we'd escape. I'd thought being an adrenaline junkie was something that I'd simply outgrown. Now, as the scenery rocketed past the windows, I yearned to feel the wheel under my own palms. To press the pedals and have the car—no questions asked—do my bidding.

We sailed around another corner, my hair that I'd loosened from my ponytail swinging out gracefully as we careened through the apex and gunned it out the backside. The trees, broad-leaved and towering, became denser. I started to recognize the corners and straight bits; I knew there would be an overlook soon.

"Is this...?"

"Yeah, I found it again"—he broke off as he transitioned around a corner—"a couple years back."

There was a particular place that this road always led to for us. Always.

As if reading my mind, he said, "I came alone." The road twisted back on itself under the green shade of the trees lining the road, and then Nate slowed the car and pulled off the road onto the wide gravel overlook.

Nate rested his dark eyes on me. "Know where you are?"

"Yeah...?"

As he slid out of the car, he said, "Don't put her in a ditch."

I watched him round the front as joy surged through me. "Oh! Yes!"

German-built like my BMW, the Aston Martin was also a fine machine; as in, blow-your-mind-to-pieces fine. The interior may have been leather luxury but under the hood were enough ponies to take you into time warp, as in, five hundred and ten ponies. It was like outfitting a fly with a jet pack.

In the driver's seat and unfamiliar with the clutch catch and how much power to give her, I burnt out of the gravel overlook with rocks pinging the undercarriage. Nate looked over, silent, but his glare was clear: *Don't make me sorry.*

"Just like riding a bicycle."

And oh the power, lord, the *power*.

I pushed the accelerator on the straight bits, feeling as the car swallowed gasoline and bulleted, hugged the corners like a lover, responding to my every command with blind obedience. No thought of mine as the driver was too small for her to notice, and she executed them all with engineered finesse. A slight left into the shady corner and power through the curve—both were done with a, *yes, ma'am.*

Thankfully the road's corners came up from my memory faster than we approached them, because I wasn't going speeds to polish my nails. I remembered each of them. How tight they were and how long they lasted. And I drove through each of them like that was my last day on earth.

The rest of the world fell away. It was just her and me, the pavement and the yellow line. My hair swung out again and again at the apexes; the corners elicited a small curse from the passenger seat. But under it all was joy. Sheer, unadulterated, adrenaline-driven joy filled the cabin.

"Oh god, this is fun."

"Know where you're going?"

"Ye-up."

The road continued to climb; in several miles, a flat stretch with a drive off to the left, an old logging road.

"It was a little overgrown," Nate said about the logging road a few minutes later. "Shit! On your left!"

"Uh-oh," I said and slammed on the brakes and shoved the clutch to the floor downshifting. The antilock brakes went to town, and the tires screamed, but still we slid. "Going to have to pass—"

"No. Turn it, I gotcha," Nate said calmly as the tires screamed.

"OK."

Nate braced one hand against his door and grabbed the e-brake with his other hand, yanking as I turned the wheel sharply.

The entire car turned back the way we'd just come in a fiery plume of smoke and rubber. We slid sideways for a moment on asphalt. The wheel bucked and vibrated under my grip as I fought the claim physics had on the car. Just as the nose of the car came around, Nate dropped the brake and I let up the clutch, putting power back to the rear wheels. Tires caught the gravel at the entrance to the logging road and sprayed rocks out behind us. Fishtailing up the logging road, and the traction control flashing angrily, the DBS tore up the steep rutted incline.

Taller weeds snapped and pinged the undercarriage. I felt it fully then, the small trickle of insanity mixed with adrenaline that says you're alive. If you're just one second off, if you're not totally, one hundred percent in tune with yourself, the road, and the car, you'll be upside down in a ditch or wrapped around a tree. That synchronized tightrope walk that Nate and I had just taken was exhilarating, an addicting adrenaline rush with one distinct outlet.

The clearing at the top of the dirt and gravel road came fast. The pasture, bordered by thick pines and oaks, created a private oasis that overlooked the valley we'd travelled through; the city anchored the vista in the distance.

I hit the brakes hard, sliding us to a stop, putting up a plume of dust as I turned the car off. My palms were sweaty, and I wiped them on my pants.

"That was fun," I said and grinned over at what was now an empty seat and dust—the door slamming shut.

I undid my seat belt as my door was wrenched open, dust floating in. Nate, silent and aggressive, wrapped his hand around my upper arm and pulled me from the car.

"What the—" I managed as he slammed me back against the warm car and silently fed our other need.

Saturday was no itch.

"You're gonna be the death of me," he said against my ear.

His lips moved down my neck as his hand moved over my hip, dipping in at my waist. Nate's palm scoured my side, coming to rest under my arm, and with his thumb, he caressed my nipple. My reaction was instantaneous and erotic as goose bumps broke out over my body, tightening the flesh of my breasts and bringing my nipples to attention.

"Nate..."

"Yes?" he asked, kissing along my jaw then down my neck as his other thumb found its breast.

His back muscles jumped as I worked my hands over them. The dip of his spine accentuated as he lifted me, parting my legs and planting himself between them.

"Your pants are going to be a problem," he said as I toed my shoes off. They landed with a thump in the grass behind him.

"I was thinking," I said as I kissed and teased his lower lip, "that same thing about your clothes. Take them off."

I heard him growl as he set me back down and, breaking our kiss, ripped open the fly of my jeans and yanked the pants to my knees before I kicked them off the rest of the way. In the same moment I pushed his jacket off to the grass and, a woman wild with need, grabbed the collar of his shirt and pulled. Nate ducked out of the shirt, came up against me again, and hefted me back against the gentle slope of the car.

"Now, where was I?" he said against my neck. "Oh, yeah, fuck this." He pulled the tie on my wrap shirt and pushed it open to reveal my lace-lined breasts.

I barely heard his voice as he brushed the tops of my breasts with his lips. "Will I ever get enough of you?"

I worked my hands over his shoulders, absorbing the strength there as I headed to the snap of his pants. "Nate...I need you."

I felt him shudder as his face came up, dark and shadowed, pained and lust driven. I watched as the last of his emotions lingered, the one that was the strongest, acquiescence. His voice was hoarse. "That makes two of us."

I slipped his fly open as he made quick work of my bra's clasp. Just as quick, he slipped my breast into his mouth, tugging softly with his teeth, making me gasp.

In the fading afternoon sun, a breeze kissed along my skin, giving me relief and adrenaline-fueled freedom. The speed-induced adrenaline and the heady feel of Nate against my body doing things he was so expertly good at all set my mind and body alight.

I slipped my hand into the front of his pants and pulled him free.

His breath caught as I stroked him gently; then I licked my thumb, placed it against his tip. The circular motion captured Nate, held him breathless.

Goading the devil would have been a wiser move.

The only sound he made was a simple growl before his hand grabbed a fist of my hair and sunk himself into me. His mouth, teeth bared, came down on my breast again. My mind went completely blank. Pain mingled with pleasure as his thick erection made quick strokes in my slick confines. The only sound was the repetitive smack of my buttocks against the Aston's side panel.

"Oh god, Nate," I gasped.

His breathing became heavy as he whispered my name, as if pleading for me to give him the release he so desperately sought.

A hot fire expanded with the repetitive friction; my heels pressed against his buttocks, driving him even deeper still. I had to have him farther in me, had to have us become a single being. Sweat trickled down between my breasts. Nate brought his mouth to mine, his tongue in my mouth mimicking our lovemaking.

Pleasure built until it ignited, pulling from me a blissful cry of release. Nate's breathing hitched as he groaned in release, warmth filled my insides and, with a last cry, we slid to the ground in each other's arms.

THIRTY-SEVEN

STRADDLING NATE, I LAUGHED AS WE FELL BACK INTO THE pasture. Blue sky stretched out over us, dotted with perfect cumulus clouds that made cotton balls and whipped meringue seem like copycats.

"I'm remembering why I liked you so fucking much," Nate said.

"I love you too," I said, even though he hadn't really said he loved me. *Liked*, not *loved*. Well, he might not have said it with his voice, but I heard it loud and clear from his body. "You know...it's been a long time since I've driven a car that fast or fed my need for you so often. I missed all of that. What the hell was I thinking going to New York to be a fashion princess when I had *this* the whole time?" I said, letting my innermost thoughts slide out of me.

He put his hand behind his head, "Nah, you remember. It wasn't how it is now. I'll be honest—I was a real prick back then. I might still be, but I've learned to turn it down and find other outlets for it."

"Like fast cars and women?"

"Careful. You sound jealous. And for the record, it's money and fast cars."

I looked over at him. His hair was trashed—he looked as if he had let some woman run her greedy hands through it—but his face was bright and clear. Any darkness he'd held that day was gone.

The afternoon sun kissed his skin, both brightening the plains of his body and making the brown tones darker as its angle threw the hollows of his cheeks and collarbone into relief. Sweat was drying on his skin, and his whiskey-colored eyes glittered with happiness.

I'd forgotten what I was saying and what he was saying and let the mental peace breathe in and out before I touched his face, saying again, "I love you."

"I know," he said, his voice quiet under the sound of the cicadas in the distant trees. "It feels so good to hear you say it. I don't want to admit it, but I'm feeling the same about you. I don't want to...I don't want to be powerless again if you leave. But now, today, I don't care. I'll take what you give me, Eve, and I'll deal with the rest later."

I gave him a quiet smile. "If it's any help, I don't feel like leaving. It's like I had something to prove, and I've done it, and now I want to come home. It's selfish to want you, to expect you to feel the same, especially after not being here for you when you needed me the most. I want to be here with you, forever. And ever, and ever, and ever..."

He shifted, pulling me against his naked, sun-warmed body as he curled against my back. He smoothed my hair from my face. "I'm going to hold you to that."

We were quiet, absorbing the last of the sun, luxuriating in the feel of each other's touch and keeping the outside world just that: out.

The black car stood watch over us, and looking over its dusty chassis, I said, "I loved driving that thing..."

"Mmmm, I could tell, babe."

"I love that you are passionate about cars, too."

"I feel like you're leading me somewhere."

I was quiet at first but decided it was better to be out with it. "With everything that's going on, I feel stupid focusing on this one thing but—"

"Spit it out."

"Please stop seeing other women? I feel like that might turn me into a wraith, and I'll snatch their souls if they sleep with, touch, or kiss you."

He gave a low laugh and buried his face into my hair before coming back up and resting his cheek on his fist. "I would like to drag this out as long as possible, teasing you about being jealous, but I'm buck-ass naked, and you're a good shot with hitting my nuts, so let me just say that, yes. I agree. And same goes for you. I'd also like to promise that you won't have to schedule sex with me. Just ask, if for some reason I'm being stingy. I'll listen to you and try hard to make this work."

I held up my pinkie. "Pinkie swear?"

He grabbed it with his own little finger. "Pinkie swear."

I settled back deeper into him as if the micro-distance that had come between us had been a cavern.

Laughter was in his voice when he added, "And I promise to not hold it against you that you don't have a job and are still living at home with your pops."

I laughed; the absurdity of it all was that it was absolutely true. "Careful what you promise, I'm feeling like sweatpants and temper tantrums are right around the corner for me."

"I'm not afraid, babe. I'll take it all," he said and was quiet, but something he was thinking was making him laugh inside, I could tell.

"What?"

"I was just thinking about temper tantrums being something punishable. Then I was thinking about punishing you..."

A shiver ran over my spine all the way down to between my legs.

"Did you just shiver?"

In the warm air dotted with tiny insects floating in the late sunlight, I said, "No. Maybe?"

He kissed my shoulder. "I'm sorry I went cold on you after all we did. I thought I could get you out of my system." He gently traced my brow with the side of his thumb. "I can't."

"Apology accepted," I said and tilted my head up for a kiss to seal it with. He met my mouth and pressed his own against mine, softly apologizing. "So, what kind of punishment am I looking at for future temper tantrums?"

"Mmmm," he said and, sliding his hand over my abdomen up to my breast before cupping it, added, "I'm developing a fetish for tape since my girl just showed me what can be done with her body."

"Oh, man, I think I need to show you some things I learned from a Manhattan dominatrix I interviewed. She uses soft rope."

He made a groaning sound and sunk his teeth into my shoulder.

"But this time, I do the tying."

While his brain was fat with ideas, I pushed him onto his back. He pulled me with him, putting me on top. As I slid him into me, I closed my eyes, feeling the warmth of the sun's heat on my naked breasts and belly. A gentle breeze moseyed over the tops of the pasture grass and caressed against my skin as I brought myself forward and back on Nate's thickness.

Our lovemaking was slow and deliberate, the kind that comes with patience, time, and love. I was savoring the drive of it, the love of him being within me, and the closeness of having our souls intertwined that made nothing else matter. Our fingers intertwined and gripped each other hard like hands on a steering wheel. Our climax was soft and thundered roughly in the distance before sliding away and leaving us both ticklish and laughing. Nothing else in the world mattered right then. We were together.

THIRTY-EIGHT

AFTER NATE AND I MADE LOVE IN THE PASTURE AND THEN meandered lazily back to town, I went home and showered. Marta was still there; Chuck had gone home with the excuse that he was working on a grand gift for my dad's birthday. Dad, still in a jovial mood, entertained Marta and me with his narration of what Chuck looked like the time he tried to change a spare tire without a jack, using just 2 x 4s and a tire iron. I felt for the first time in a long while that things were going to be all right.

The televised baseball game was going in the background as Marta made her way to the door.

"See you tomorr—"

Her voice was cut off by the sound of snow on the television. I looked past her to my dad, who picked up the remote and started clicking.

"Dad," I said, "mute it."

"Dang it, I was just watching the game! Bases were loaded—all the stations are out," he said, clicking incessantly. "Eva, call the cable company; this is ridiculous."

"Dad, give it a moment—"

"No! Bases were loaded!"

"It's just a game—"

"Fine! I'll do it."

"Dad," I said, giving Marta an exasperated look. "Fine, I'll call them right now. Thank you again, Marta; we'll see you tomorrow."

"I'll keep your dad company while you call," Marta said; then, to my dad, "Martin, be nice to your daughter while I'm gone."

I picked up the cordless in the kitchen and clicked it on—no dial tone. Clicking it off then on again, I listened and waited for the tone but heard only the silence of an empty line. Batteries full. I peeked around the corner at my father, whom Marta was trying to distract.

"Dad, pick up that phone next to you—do you get a dial tone?"

"Nothing. Is your phone out too?" He was working himself into a fit that would no doubt end with his tirade about corporations taking over the government.

Just as I opened my mouth to tell him to relax, the sound of branches snapping outside the curtained windows reverberated through the momentarily silent room.

Marta tilted her head to listen better.

Steps sounded, crushing and loud outside the front windows, then the unmistakable sound of a man laughing.

Chills rippled up my arms, and the back of my neck tingled as the footsteps quieted. Then, my name came like a whisper.

"Eva." Butch Vellanova's voice was unmistakable.

Just then the front door handle jiggled.

The air seemed to suck right out of the room, I could see his face again, hear his voice from earlier in the day. The sick smell of his breath close enough to mingling with my own. My knees nearly gave out, but I lunged for the door to twist the deadbolt. My hand bent back as the door crashed open—the edge of it struck me in the face, sending me recoiling back. Butch came into focus. He held a gun in his hand and pointed it first at Marta and then at my father.

"Surprise."

THIRTY-NINE

Nate, pulling a long night to make up for his afternoon off, leaned against the garage door. The elongating days that eventually turned into summer in the Northwest had just started to show themselves; the sky was still a dusky purple. Nate pulled the grease off his fingers with a thin hand towel. It was peaceful. He took in the giant fir trees along the property line. It was as if there were no road beyond. A street lamp flickered on down the road as he thought of Eva.

He thought of her against the car, of her under him, of how good it felt to be with her. They'd made plans for him to head over to her pops's place. Maybe make a couple phone calls, see if there were any places they could check together for her pops's truck. He wasn't kidding himself: His mind was crystal clear because she was a drug to his senses. When he was with her, he wanted to be closer; when he wasn't with her, he was looking for reasons to be. Despite everything he'd done to keep her from him, he'd failed. Her voice came to him; her words played over and over again: *I love you.*

Shelby drove into the lot then, his cruiser's headlights sweeping over the parked cars and Nate. He watched as the older man parked and slowly made his way out of his vehicle, as if he had something heavy on his mind.

"Shelby." Nate nodded as he approached. Nate's insides clenched and he reached for his cigarettes in his back pocket. But remembered he'd had the last one that morning.

"Nate," he said in greeting.

"You find him yet?"

"No," he said, situating himself on a metal stool at the garage entrance across from Nate, "and how'd you know we were having difficulty locating him?"

"Didn't, you just confirmed it. How long he's been off leash?"

"Less than twenty-four hours. He checked in with his post-prison supervisor at two p.m. yesterday, and we have folks stationed at his place. Most likely he'll be back within the hour, and we'll take him in for questioning. We have a motive now," he said, then very seriously asked, "Did you speak with Eva today?"

"Yes," he said, looking the older man in the eye. "You'd better find him before I do..." He let the statement's implications stain the air.

"Careful."

"I am, very," Nate said. "What do you always say—I do better facing my problems head-on? I agree."

"If you find him before we do, call me, Nate—do not take him on. We have no conclusive proof that he's done anything but harass Eva. We need to question him clean. Once we get the Chevy, we can lift his prints and put him back in prison for the rest of his sentence."

Nate was quiet before responding. "I'm not convinced that was long enough or hard enough for him. How long do I have to wait for you guys to find him? How long do I have to wait to get another fucking phone call from him? Every time my phone rings, I think, *This it?* And the first thing he does is track down Eva? Why not me? I'll tell you why—I would have rearranged his fucking face and had you pick him up in a goddamn body bag, that's why." Nate stopped, feeling the old fury in his veins seep out. He closed his eyes and took a deep breath.

"All right," Shelby said, standing, "I know you might take this the wrong way, but it's probably best for you to keep Eva Rodgers close until we find him."

Nate stepped out into the night with Shelby and closed the garage door behind them. "That's my plan. Headed there now."

Shelby nodded as he opened his driver's door. "We'll find him."

Nate was about to retort when Shelby's radio squawked to life. Nate squinted as dispatch relayed shots fired, a request for all available units, including paramedic, to an address that made Nate's knees give out.

He looked to Shelby in question: Had he heard right? But Shelby was already picking up the two-way to respond. Nate ran back into the shop, into his office, and in there Nate swung his office door shut and opened the wall safe behind it and took out the 9mm he kept loaded there.

Tucked it into the back of his jeans, lifted his jacket over it, closed the safe, locked the office, and strode to the black car waiting for him in the parking lot.

"Nate!" Shelby shouted, sounding as if he'd called him more than once.

"What?" he said, opening his driver's side door.

"Stay out of the way when you get there. If they see you armed, they'll shoot you."

FORTY

My face slammed into the television, cracking the display. My entire skull rang. Pain, sharp and ruthless, shot through my face and was mirrored at the back of my head, where Butch's grip twisted painfully in my hair.

"Shut your fucking hole," he said over Marta's voice, "or I'll give you something to scream about, cunt."

"Go to hell," I said, wincing through the spit and blood I could now taste on my lip.

"Stop! Stop it!" Marta pleaded; out of the corner of my eye, I saw her get up.

"I told you not to move, bitch." He spun, pulling the trigger.

Marta had frozen in place, but it was too late. Her body folded as if someone punched her hard in the gut. The entire scene was surreal. As much as part of my mind was failing to process what was currently happening, another part—the one that recognized and associated gunshots with the temporary death of my father—freaked out.

I slammed Butch into the corner of the wall behind us and shoved my elbow into his gut.

I saw my father as he struggled forward, his cane far away from him on the ground. He crawled to Marta, his mouth moving as if shouting but no sounds came out.

Marta.

The blood—so much blood.

FORTY-ONE

SEEING THE STRETCHER, COVERED IN A WHITE SHEET, COME OUT of Martin's house, Nate's insides went cold, icy fingers that clenched his gut and slithered out through his limbs. He angled close: Martin's nurse, an oxygen mask over her nose and mouth. Nate's breath returned, and the world became a flurry of action once more. His feet carried him up the stairs into the house where he heard the shouts and pleas for someone to do something. Martin was being restrained by a female cop who had her hand on his shoulder to keep him seated. Martin's eyes, filled with tears, reached for him. Nate moved aside the cops with his body as he squatted in front of Martin; his hand grasped his.

"Where is she?"

"He's got her, he's got her." Martin sobbed. "And these idiots! Aren't doing a damn thing!" he said, gesturing to the cops.

"Sir, we're trying to get more information so that we can locate her. Do you remember exactly what it was that Mr. Vellanova said?"

Nate bristled at the sound of his last name being used in conjunction with this madness. Looking over his shoulder at the female cop— short brown hair in a no-nonsense bob and a grizzled expression on her face—he said, "Her BMW 5 Series isn't in the driveway, so we can assume it's the one he used to take her." She took notes while he relayed year and color, and another cop passed this info into his two-way. Then, back to Martin, Nate said, "Tell me what happened." And Nate listened, registering that this was his ultimate horror coming vividly to life.

"I couldn't get her—" Martin said, breaking off into a sob. "Couldn't, couldn't reach her, Marta was bleeding, her blood..." He looked down at his hands as if there would be blood, and Nate realized that he indeed had some in the crevices of his hands.

Shelby walked in then and put a hand to Nate's shoulder. Standing, Nate looked into the detective's face. Looking for something, anything. "What'd you find?"

"Eastbound on Sandy a half hour ago. It's all I've got." Shelby sat down next to Martin, his voice going inaudible to Nate.

Nate stood there. He was helpless, waiting. Waiting for the phone call that would have his father on the other line sobbing for Nate to come home—his mother had an accident. Only this time, it'd be Eva.

Nate made his way to Eva's room. Her smell engulfed him as he pushed open the door, nearly bringing him to his knees. Nate took another breath and saw that her purse was on the bed, slouched open. Making quick work of it, Nate found the one thing that gave him hope. Or rather, he didn't find it. Her cell phone was missing.

Nate wasted no time in calling it and when it went straight to voicemail, he dialed Mikey.

"Yoyoyo, big dawg! Whassup?!" Mikey answered on the first ring.

"Mikey cut the shit. I have a job for you. Quarter mil if you attempt it, another quarter if you complete it." Nate said and waited.

"That's a lot of money, bro. What's up?"

"I need you to track a cellphone."

"Sure, there's a bunch of apps you can use—"

"I don't have time for that shit, I just need to locate it, now. Ready for the number?"

There was a long pause on the other side of the phone, Nate heard him walking through his house then the squeak of a desk chair, "Man you sound panicked, um, maybe tell me a little on what's going on before I break privacy laws for you?"

Nate pulled the phone from his ear and slammed his fist against the wall. Taking a deep breath, he put the phone back to his ear. How the fuck could he explain any of this?

"It's Eva."

"Man if you guys are having some domestic issues—"

"Mikey, I'm in a house filled with cops. It's her pop's house, she's gone and his nurse just got carted away in an ambulance, she was shot in the fucking stomach. You don't know where I come from but believe me when I say that Eva's life is in danger, she's been taken by a man and the only evidence the cops have is that the car she has was seen going eastbound on Sandy Boulevard over a half an hour ago."

"OK, no problem I can run a trace just as good as the cops can. As soon as she makes a call they can trace it using the cell towers. Get me the detective I can walk them through it."

"Mikey, fuck that. She's not calling anyone. And if her cell is off, you're the only one I know who could possibly track it."

There was silence.

Nate lost it, "Seven years ago my father cut my mother to pieces and laid her body out on our kitchen floor like a gift to me. I still remember the smell and the way my boot slipped as I walked in on it. He wanted me in prison, he tried to make me into him using her and now," Nate choked, "Now he has Eva."

Nate heard Mikey rub his face then blew out a breath into the phone, "Hold on." Nate heard the phone click over then the sound of keys. "What's her number and her carrier, just in case."

Nate rattled them off.

Mikey's fingers clacked over his keys, "And for the record I can't just randomly turn her phone on, there's a bunch of background work that needs to be done, like send her firmware to get her phone to pretend to sleep so I can turn it on whenever I like. So, we need to pray her phone is on, this will be a whole lot more simple if it is, and more legal if she calls."

"Trust me she's not thinking of her privacy right now."

"Right. Well...got her. OK," Mikey said with more typing.

"You found her?" Nate said in disbelief.

"No, dude, still making my way through the network. I got her number, pinging the phone now. Gonna take me a sec."

Nate was about to respond when his phone lit up with an incoming call. "It's her."

FORTY-TWO

WHAT DO YOU WANT WITH ME?" I ASKED TO THE ROOM. I
pulled on my arms and legs only to find them restrained behind me to
an old metal kitchen chair. Blinking through the fog of pain, I realized
I was tied up in the kitchen of the apartment that Nate used to call
home.

"Shut the fuck up," Butch said, looking through drawers.

The apartment was eerily the same. It was one of those small,
low-rent places in which the furniture fit in only one configuration.
The fixtures looked like they were updated last in the late sixties and
had been used heavily since.

Beneath the surface ugliness, there was something more. There
was something in the air; I could taste it on my tongue when I
breathed. The smell of raw meat left out and forgotten. The unmistakable smell of fleshy decay.

I winced as the ties, which felt like nylon ropes, refused to budge
under my attempts to twist myself loose. Deep down, I knew exactly
what Butch was looking for. And I prayed I had enough moxie to
figure out a way out of my bindings before it could be found.

He stopped rummaging then and slowly pulled something from

the drawer in front of him. It made a thin metal pinging sound in the suddenly deathly quiet space. I forced myself not to gag on the panic that rose up into my throat.

He turned slowly, breathing labored breaths. "I'm going to rip you apart—and lay you right here." He gestured with a wide, rusted butchering knife. "Everything has been taken from me, but today I'm gonna take it all back. All of it, and you're gonna fucking help me."

Butch approached, a slight limp in his step. Keeping ahold of the knife, he untied one of my hands and handed me my cell phone, which he'd pulled out of his pants pocket.

His pants hung three sizes too large, and the coat he had on was well worn and stained. He would be pathetic, a sick, aging criminal with ashen skin and bloodshot eyes were it not for his one power: sending a shiver down my spine every time he looked at me.

"Call him," he said.

I wrapped my hand around the phone but dropped it. My hand was numb from its loss of circulation. I bent forward to pick the phone up, only to have the knife at my throat.

"Don't fucking try anything."

"I'm—I'm not," I said. I'd not even seen him move. With my shaking hand, I picked up the phone and held it out.

"I'll watch," he said and tipped the top of the phone down with the knife so he could see the screen.

I fumbled with the screen lock and managed to get the contact list up just as Butch's open hand collided with my face.

I felt my head snap to the side and black flitted across my vision.

I came to screaming as I was lifted off the floor by my hair.

He dropped me back in my seat as I broke out into a cold sweat. Damp shivering heat flowed from the pain in my head through my back. Focus was slippery at best.

Butch gave me the phone again. "No fucking around. I wanna see you dial that thing."

I felt my head nod back, and all went black again. I came to with Butch in my face, saying something: "—cking dial."

I looked at the phone in my hand, unsure of what to do with it. *Call Nate*, I remembered. Then, as if my thumb knew more than my mind did, it slowly pressed the buttons on the screen and then pushed the green button at the bottom, send.

I kept the phone in my lap, and my thumb brushed the speaker button, making it ring in the small space of the dank kitchen.

Only one ring sounded before Nate's voice filled the room. "Where are you?"

"Nate."

"Where are you?" I heard him ask again, the pain obvious in his voice. I felt my heart clench and my eyes fill with tears. Adrenaline seeped into the fog in my head.

Butch pointed his knife at me and mouthed, *Tell him*.

I breathed open-mouthed, looking from Butch to the phone where the man I loved was waiting for me to tell him where I was. I'd been Butch's puppet, and it was going to stop. "I love you," I said and hurled the cell into Butch's face.

"*Raaaaa!!*" Butch hollered.

I pulled free my other hand, which I'd been working loose. Seeing Butch moving in my limited peripheral, I got one foot free and slid to the floor as he swung.

He missed and fell, off-balance, to one knee but leaned in again to punch me. With my one leg still attached to the chair, I dodged to the side, dragging the chair with me, and he hit the carpet.

Grunting with exertion, he stood and grabbed the chair, lifting it as my fingers worked frantically. He slammed it back down as my ankle came lose. The chair crashed into the linoleum a second after I rolled out of the kitchen and into the side of the living room couch. On my knees, I lurched toward the far end of the sofa. That end formed the start of the short hallway, which led to the master bedroom, where the fire escape once was. Before I made it off my knees, Butch lunged for me and captured the back of my pants.

I turned, connecting my fist with his face. I hammered the side of his face until I fell loose.

My knees barely hit the carpet before I lurched forward again and, this time, up.

"Fucking stupid cunt." He hissed from behind as I became an all-star track athlete down the hall. Past the bathroom, the shower curtain was ripped and gone—the window, miniature, there'd be no escape there. I raced past Nate's old room, closing in on the end of the hall where the master bedroom door was ajar. I burst into the room and as the air puffed out, I reflexively gagged. My feet refused to go further. The old woman who used to live in the apartment was rolled up in the shower curtain on the dilapidated bed. The grotesque contrast between her gray features and the curtain's colorful butterfly print was obscene. Instinctively, my feet moved me away, back out the door, only to come up against another horror.

"What the fuck, *WHATTHEFUCK?*" Nate whispered as the phone went dead and Mikey clicked back on. "Mikey, please tell me you've got something." The finality of Eva's voice telling him she loved him before the line went dead had him falling to his knees. "Mikey."

"Stand by, dude. *Damn*, come on, come to papa." Nate heard the fiery clacking of typing over the open line, the only thing keeping him from going completely insane. "Got it: 1232 NE Flag Lot Street, dead ends. Looks like an—"

"Apartment building—holy shit." Nate left the house, moving like a wraith to the last place he'd thought he'd ever go again.

Metal ratcheted against metal, echoing in the tight confines of the hallway. A handful of my hair was wrapped around Butch's fist, and his rusted knife was at my throat, where - it seemed - we struggled there for an eternity.

Turning to face the sound, Butch pressed my back against his putrid, sweating front. Nate, dark in shadow at the end of the hallway but unmistakable to me, pointed the black muzzle of a pistol directly at us.

"Pops."

This Nate was not a man I recognized. His attitude toward me when I'd first come back was friendly in comparison to that of the man who stood in front of us. This man was a black hole. As if the very last vestiges of good were sucked from him and what was left was the archangel of death sent to take his last assignment to the grave.

Butch laughed hollowly, phlegm rattling in his chest. "Well, glad you could join us, little shit. Got here a whole lot faster than I expected. I was hoping to have a little surprise for you."

Nate's response was to cock back the hammer on the pistol. "I'm not here for the family reunion. We both know what needs to happen here. But you've always been one brick short of a full load, so let me explain: let Eva go."

"You got your cunt of a mother's smart mouth, boy," he said and moved us closer to Nate; at least one brick short. "See your girl? Smell her blood? Remind you of someone?"

The blade broke skin.

I hissed, going up on my toes, trying to get away from the rusty edge, but maintaining the downward death grip I had on his slippery arm.

And I watched Nate, watched as the blood drained from his face. Watched as he pulled the trigger.

The explosion made me wince, and as I opened my eyes, Nate's pistol fist slammed home next to me.

Butch's nose crunched on impact. Nate's other hand wrapped around Butch's blade wrist, twisting it away from my neck.

I simply slid to the floor; my knees had gone completely liquid. Nate stepped over me and brought his knee up, striking his pinned father in the kidneys. I heard the knife clank to the ground as I slid out of the way, crab walking backward down the hall.

Butch yowled, a sound that seemed almost deliriously gleeful. He threw himself backward against Nate, slamming him into the opposite wall.

Butch landed a well-aimed ham fist, and Nate's gun came loose, sliding down the hall at me. Reaching forward with hands sticky with my own blood, I picked up and aimed.

My shot was clear, then obscured, then clear again as they tangled for the upper hand. I gripped the gun tight in my shaking hands and waited—if Nate moved for long enough, I'd not hesitate to be Butch's grim reaper.

Nate grunted as a punch landed in his midsection, doubling him over. Butch pinned him against the wall in a choke hold. They were body on body and, in a practiced motion, Butch struck Nate in the face.

Butch only landed one.

Nate bellowed and bulldozed his father into the far wall. Leaned back cracked his elbow across his father's jaw, then grabbed fistfuls of his father's ratty shirt front and stepped back.

Sounds of ripping fabric filled the hallway as Nate lifted him clean off the floor. I scrabbled back into the dank bathroom as Butch crashed to the floor in front of me. Nate fell to his knees onto his father's outer arm and shoulder, slamming his fist into Butch's throat as he descended. Nate was ready when his father's free fist swung around at him. Grabbing it, Nate twisted. Butch's fingers uncurled under the pressure Nate caused by rotating his palm back on itself. At the end of the twist, bent it back. Nate used his other fist to draw more blood from Butch's face.

"Had enough, old man, or should I keep going?"

Butch responded with bloody spit. Nate calmly wiped it off his face with his shoulder.

"Gonna finish what you started, little shit?"

The muscle in Nate's cheek twitched.

"Wanna see me squirm, is that it? Wanna make me scream?"

"You deserve it."

I could feel the seething blackness coming off Nate.

"Then *do* it."

"Burying you would be satisfying, after all those years. It could be you crying—begging me to stop. I could tie you to the stove too, and smash your face onto a hot burner just to see you cry. But you'd like that, wouldn't you—"

"Shoot me. I don't wanna listen to your shit."

Nate talked over him: "It'd be a real goddamn moment for you, wouldn't it?"

"You don't got guts enough to fucking kill me. You don't got the guts to treat me like a real goddamn man."

I watched in horror as Butch played out his mind game on his son. It was a vicious reminder of what life had been for Nate. Every day of his life until he left.

A sinister smile crossed Nate's lips and for just a moment, I thought he'd actually do it.

"No, Pops, just a strong hand, right?" and struck Butch in the face once more.

This made Butch cackle nasally. "Ha-ha! Maybe your cunt of a mother had you wrong! You are my son. Down to the fucking blood and bone." He accentuated the *f*, letting bloody spittle fly into Nate's face.

"What?"

Butch's eyes got wide, mocking. "What?" he said, his voice going high. Butch got vicious and tried to knock Nate off him, which made Nate tighten up on Butch's twisted wrist. Twisting it until it cracked.

Butch's toes pointed as his eyes screwed up.

"Do it again. I fucking loved it." His voice screeching, eyes gleaming with something that was becoming close to feral.

"What. Are you. Talking about." Nate's quiet, measured voice shot chills down my spine.

"Your mother was a whore. A fucking cunt whore who married

me with your bastard ass already in her. Her old man would've put a bullet in her if he knew. She fucking used me. Used me! Over twenty fucking years, gets fucking millions from that cocksucker for you, and thinks she's done? She can walk away? And you? You knew, didn't you? Made me eat shit for twenty years in prison. Well, it's your fucking turn." He roared as he brought his knees up in a move I didn't think was possible for him, knocking Nate forward. He pulled his arm free and nailed Nate's gut, slipping his other hand free.

In the next second, Butch was on me, his sweaty arms grabbing at me. He wanted the gun. I fell back into the bathroom, his body weight pinning me to the floor.

"No!" I hollered and lifted the gun over my head.

Butch reached for it as I cranked off round after round into the bathroom shower, no longer caring about using it as a weapon against him, just trying to unload it before it could be used against me. Tile splintered around us. Just as he was lifted off me, his hand grasped the hot gun barrel.

"He's got the gun!" I said as Butch caught his footing and swung his elbow back just missing Nate's face. The gun came around again, and Nate slapped it to the side as I leaped up onto Butch's back and snaked my arm around his neck.

Butch roared and grabbed my wrist and slammed my spine against the corner of the door jam.

As he fought me, he tried to bring the gun back, setting it off, shattering a window.

"You'll never get away with thi—" I said as he slammed me backward again.

Nate brought his fist in with force, snapping his father's head to the side. Butch lurched down the hall, throwing me off his back. He shot wildly back in our direction the gun just *click-click-clicking* as he escaped into the back bedroom. The bedroom door slammed shut with the lock clicking as Nate hit the door.

"Goddammit!" he said and reared back, struck the door with his booted foot.

It took two more tries before the door simply gave up and ripped off its hinges. In a fray of wood splinters, Nate waited a beat next to the door, looked into the room slowly, and then stepped in and rushed to the window and swore.

"Out the front!" he said and grabbed my arm as he passed, which was good, because my knees gave out at the couch.

Nate squatted next to me. "Babe, we gotta go—"

I was already up, pushing off his shoulder, and was at the front door as he opened it. We descended the stairs as my BMW tore out of the lot, clipping the back of the Aston.

We ran across the gravel lot and into the dented car; I had barely hit the leather passenger seat before its motor roared to life. Making quick work of the driveway, Nate reached under his seat as we merged onto Sandy Boulevard. He pulled out a pistol and handed it to me.

"Nate—How many guns do you have?" I said, feeling a numbing tightness beginning in my face.

"Two." He shifted through the gears, plowing past traffic toward a light where the silver of my BMW glimmered, hung a left, and dived into the industrial district. "Bullets in the glove compartment."

We came up on the next light as it turned red, not in our favor. The cars slammed on their brakes and horns as we tore through it and into the corner business's parking lot and out the other side.

"Put on your seat belt," I told him as I checked the safety on the pistol.

Up ahead on the twisting road were the brake lights of the BMW as it turned right.

We hit pothole after water-filled pothole until we came to a major intersection north of my father's place. The intersection teemed with traffic coming off the freeways and out of the strip malls lining the boulevard. We watched the BMW take the entrance ramp to the I-84 westbound.

"*Sonofabitch*," Nate spat as one word and looked over at me. "Do you trust me?"

"Yes," I said and looked to my right. "Two-second gap, first lane."

Nate hammered on it, and diving through the intersection, we ignited another flurry of horns.

"Red car, then go. All clear next two lanes, two-second gap. Go!"

Blowing through the first lane, we entered the second around the red car and shot into the third, bulleting onto the freeway.

A light rain began to fall, beading up and off the windshield as we tore through it.

The BMW and the Aston, both made for the autobahn, easily made it past one hundred miles per hour, but with a V-12 under the hood, we closed the distance. Still, it seemed like an eternity.

"Why are there so many goddamn people out right now?" Nate asked as he politely put on his blinker as he winged around a gray minivan.

In the far right lane we could see through the first sweeping bend of the freeway. Ahead, a steady stream of cars was puttering onto the freeway, heedless of our excessive speeds. In seconds, we'd be plowing into the back of the first one.

I wrenched around in my seat and looked out the tiny rear and side windows. Headlights sparkled off the streaming droplets. "First lane clear, second clear after the dark...blue?...SUV. One-second gap."

Nate was already moving under my command. Butch, however, was not a seasoned driver and had no assist. He plowed between lanes, causing cars to swerve away from him and others to fishtail as they braked on the wet pavement.

Nate cursed and hit the brakes.

I was on it. "One second, left, now." Nate shoved us between the cars as I whipped back to my side window like Goose in *Top Gun* looking for the bogeys. "Right lane clear, now." One more glance back. "Left, clear. Bullet, baby."

Nate swerved us through the stopping cars and put the hammer down once more. The motor roared before Nate gave her the next gear, keeping the torque high and the speed like Mach 1. We had a five-second clear shot to Butch. I put the window down; rain pelted into the car like tiny meteors, stinging my face, as I leaned out the car to look down the barrel of the pistol and line up my rear tires over the aiming post.

"Aim higher and tighter into the curve than you think."

I did, held my breath and flicked off the safety.

The first bullet exploded out of the chamber as Butch swerved erratically.

Nate put room between us. "Squeeze, babe! Empty that fucking clip."

Two-handed now, I pulled and pulled and pulled. The movies made it seem like hitting a car on the freeway at one hundred miles an hour was easy. Tires should explode, gas tanks incinerate, but the worst that was happening was rain hitting my sore face like mini bullets.

I growled under my breath. I had just two more shots; then the window would close as we'd catch up with the other cars.

I aimed, compensating for the turn. I pulled the trigger. The rear window exploded. Once more, and miraculously the front windshield spiderwebbed.

Nate shouted next to me, "Nice fucking shot!"

I slipped back in. "Yes! But it's not slowing him down."

Traffic clustered as the 84 freeway began to morph with the I-5 and the towering freeway bridges over the Willamette River. Three exits loomed as Nate downshifted and mind-read what his father would do: ride the emergency shoulder off the freeway.

I looked to my right. "Clear." My head was still turned when Nate shouted.

"Fuck!"

He slammed on the brakes.

But we were two seconds behind Butch's maneuver. And slid with the race tires on the wet asphalt.

I got my arms up just as Butch used the BMW like a battering ram into the passenger side.

Metal crunched and tires screeched as we slipped sideways. Our momentum spun us like a dryer. Nate muttered a steady stream of epithets as he fought then released the wheel then grasped it again. His feet were a dance on the pedals, pulling and pushing, giving and cutting power to the rear wheels. The scream of the tires in the spin quieted as we hydroplaned sideways into the far cement barrier in the fast lane.

My hair, body, pistol, everything flew on impact. Nate's window shattered as our seat belts locked, keeping our butts firmly in the leather bucket seats.

Three heartbeats passed before our brains stopped sloshing in our skulls, and with a scream of metal tearing along cement, Nate put us back into traffic.

"Fucking faulty side airbags," he muttered, then: "Sight line?"

Giving my head a shake to clear it, I was back at my window. "Hold. They're coming too fast, Nate."

"Eve! No opinions, directions!"

I swallowed. "Half second. Red car, two-second gap after. Second lane stacked."

The DBS lost traction as the red car passed and suddenly gripped, putting us into the two-second gap. The next lane was the same. The drivers made last-minute decisions about which lane they needed to be in to go north or south over the bridges. Traffic slowed with indecision.

"Two seconds, then a blue truck. Next lane, five-second gap after the tan Civic in front of the semi."

Nate slithered the coupe through the traffic to the emergency shoulder where we assumed Butch had gone.

Horns blared at our recklessness. Once in the emergency lane, Nate popped on the hazards. In case our psychotic driving wasn't a deterrent enough for the other cars.

I squinted through the wipers, looking for the silver glow of my car as we blew by the stacked traffic.

"Did he go north or south?" I asked Nate over the rush of wind at his open window.

Nate shook his head and passed another semi. The north exit was coming up.

"Shit!"

Headlights lit up the cabin like daylight before we were struck from behind.

We were forced off onto the right exit going to I-5 north and toward the perpetual construction zone of the Fremont Bridge.

Nate cursed as I braced myself; the cement barrier now on my side of the off-ramp slammed up against us. Only this time we were going twice as fast. Nate took his foot off the accelerator to slow us. The headlights came around and smashed into us. The rest of the Aston's windows popped and shattered as we ping-ponged off the steel-framed BMW and the barrier. Arms over my face. The car grated itself against the cement barrier, shredding its aluminum paneling. Nate hit the brakes.

"Goddammit," he swore and downshifted the abused sports coupe. Power slammed to the back tires, throwing us forward in an angry flare, the car fishtailing on the damp pavement before catching traction.

A siren wailed in the distance as water pelted us with small bits of glass from the shattered windows.

The Aston cut through the rain and closed in again on the BMW's bumper, creeping up to its side. Just one tap to the side of the rear bumper, and it would spin out—or we would. Butch yanked the wheel instead, taking the BMW wide and away from us, and then he slammed his brakes and yanked the wheel back, preparing to plow us sideways again.

"Shit. E-brake."

I yanked the lever as Nate whipped the nose around, turning into Butch.

The front impact jettisoned us back; my hand ripped from the e-brake as my airbag went off. My head snapped back, and I heard the

Aston's engine rev as we shoved against the BMW. The aggressive power play made the rear tires scream as they each fought for traction, and the smell of burning rubber filled the drafting cabin.

I heard and felt the reverberation of what sounded like scaffolding breaking apart and falling to the ground. Pushing at the airbags, I tried to see around them. Nate had no airbag, so he had 100 percent visibility. He shifted to reverse, popped the clutch with the accelerator to the floor. The coupe roared, plowing again into Butch. Nate hit the brakes as the last remnants of the shattered windshield buckled in, and right behind that, a *pop*, then *whiz*, as bullets tore into the cabin.

"He has another gun. Get down—" Nate didn't finish as his face contorted in pain. His palm slipped off the wheel.

The DBS came to a stop, but my BMW disappeared from view in a clattering smash.

"Nate?" I asked, reaching for him. "Nate?" I repeated when he didn't answer. I ripped off my seat belt. "Nate," I said, careless of bullets, and pulled off his seat belt. "Where?" I asked, my voice cracking in panic.

He shook his head, his hand gripping his side. "Get out. Get out."

"No," I said. "No, no, no, you're coming with me. Move over. I'll drive."

His eyes were heavy lidded as he looked at me, the focus glazing with obvious pain; his arm was still caught in his safety belt. "No, we've lost power," he uttered, demonstrating with his foot on the gas. We didn't move, but the motor sounded like it was tearing itself apart. "Get—ou…"

"Nate? Nate." I pulled on him, but his eyes had closed against the pain. I turned to my door, which wouldn't budge—it'd been smashed in—then back to Nate. I felt his pulse: slow and weak, but it was there. It was then I saw the bloom of blood on his shirt.

My world dove into that blood bloom, making everything I saw red.

I looked for his cell phone or mine and found neither. I cleared the remnants of my side window from the frame and pulled myself out, needing to find help.

Traffic stacked in the distance as police sirens wailed toward us. The closed construction site we'd bombed into was empty of workers, thanks to the five o'clock whistle. Plastic sheeting protecting the workers against the weather flapped and slapped in the wind against the metal construction scaffolding attached to the side of the bridge. The cement barricade to the construction zone was sideways. Silver paint off my sedan ran along its front as evidence of its impact against it. My shirt billowed as I staggered to the place my BMW had gone off. In the scaffolding, off the side of the bridge, was the sedan. It was seesawing on its roof, like a teeter-totter on a high wire. Over the Grand Canyon.

It was there at my distance that I watched Butch, blood dripping from a gash on his temple, punch out the remains of the splintered passenger window.

Anger gripped my guts.

How was he still moving?

I stalked toward him, my fingers dragging along the long silver scar on the concrete barrier. Chunks of it littered the ground along with the first twenty feet of metal piping used in the scaffolding. I stepped carefully and made my way through the debris field toward the car. Pain throbbed through my eye, as boats and the flashing lights of the Coast Guard worked toward the bridge on river in the distance.

The BMW was still settling from its fall. The nose of it tipped down toward the water and stopped with a *clink*. A single upright pipe, loose in its hold, kept the nose from descending. Gently, almost methodically, it tipped back toward its trunk.

I stopped at the rough edge of the bridge. Construction during the day was widening it for pedestrians. Behind me was sidewalk; in front of me was nothingness save for open air, scaffolding, and a teetering car.

I looked at my car and the demon birthing out its side and picked up the biggest pipe I could get my hand around. I dragged it the edge. It rang its hollow, metallic song across the hard surface like a useless metal leg behind me. The car descended once more to its nose.

Seeing only Butch, I stepped out onto the crushed scaffolding. Wind blew my hair back. Two hundred feet below, the muddy river rushed by. I took the pipe in hand like a bat and swung at the loose metal pipe beneath the car's nose. My swing missed. Off-balance and at the edge, I let go of the pipe. It banged off the side as the river rushed up to me. My arms windmilled, and I stumbled back.

Heart pounding hard in my ears, I took a steadying breath.

The BMW was slowing in its forward rock. Over the rush of the wind and the dull white noise of the river below, I heard Butch grunting with effort over the broken shards of the window. There was only one more chance to strike before the car pitched back toward its trunk, and away from the drop, and stayed there. I retrieved another pipe, hauled back and chucked it.

End over end, it cartwheeled through the air. It banged like aluminum bat against a fastball. The pipe and the loose piece of scaffolding fell, swooping end over end down to the river below.

I stumbled back, and Butch, having worked his belly through the window, lunged for me, grabbing a fistful of my pant leg. "We have a score to settle, bitch," he spat.

The BMW's hood made a metallic ripping racket as it slid. I kicked at his hand. "Let go of me!" I screamed, panic bubbling up into my throat.

The car picked up momentum off the iron scaffolding.

"No!" Butch screamed. I kept twisting, reaching for anything that I could hold on to as the car slipped off the edge.

Butch's grip ripped loose, pulling me forward. I looked down off the scaffold at the river that seemed miles below me. My arms swung back, but that feel of lightness that comes right before a jump sunk into me. I had two options, neither of which guaranteed survival: dive or cannonball. Just as the resignation to fly like a bird off my perch settled into my mind, an arm snaked around my middle and yanked. I felt ripped in half as the front part of my body was already falling. I was thrown down backward. My head slammed into something hard.

Before everything went black, I heard a distant, crashing splash.

Nate's face swam into my vision. "Holy shit."

I wanted to touch him, but my arms felt heavy, and a tiredness had sunk into my bones. Happy to not be diving off the Fremont, I closed my eyes.

FORTY-THREE

An incessant beeping sound and a heavy warmth on my lap brought me to. A dim light in the hallway illuminated my white, sterile-looking room. The smell of the hospital lifted more grogginess from my mind as I looked down.

Everything was blurry. My mouth was dry and the first full fledged thought that came to my mind was the memory of Nate and the bullet wound in him. I struggled to get up, "Nate?" I asked the room.

There was a rustling on my lap and I blinked to clear my vision. The warmth on my lap had been his head. He winced as he looked up, "You're awake."

My body sagged with relief into the starched white linens of my narrow bed.

His wince turned to a smile as he stood gingerly and then sat again. He wore jeans and a T-shirt; his upper arm was wrapped with white gauze. "Hi."

"Hi, back." I said.

Our fingers found each other and wove together. I looked down at our linked fingers as my mind probed its last haunted memories. And with it I got the eerie suspicion that I'd missed some time.

"Have I missed some time? I feel like I've slept for days."

He brought his free hand up to my face, "That would be about right."

"Oh," I said, unsure how to process that information.

He brushed my cheek with his thumb. "I love you. Don't ever leave me again, OK?" I felt the heaviness of his words in my chest.

"I love you too. And you have a deal," I croaked and then added, "If I remember correctly, it wasn't me that left—it was you. I thought you'd died with that gunshot wound."

"It went through the fleshy bit here." He pointed to his side. "My —he—Butch," Nate fumbled, "hit you," he said and stopped again as he struggled with something deep within himself, his eyes becoming haunted with the memory. "He struck you so hard that day - the head doc said your skull must have been slammed into something like glass or a mirror because of the head wound you sustained. So, when I saw the flatscreen at your pop's place . . ."

I thought back to when Butch had come in, when he'd shot Marta, and I'd lost my marbles and attacked, "Oh yeah."

"Fuck," he said looking pained, "I was hoping you'd say 'no,' that it was something else." Nate tightened his grip on our linked fingers. "The docs say it was that hit that made your last fall against that chunk of concrete too much . . . they had to induce a coma or you'd have die—" He choked then and took a deep breath. "Died."

"I'm here," I whispered, covering Nate's hand with mine as he gently laid his forehead down on our clasped hands.

"I'm so fucking happy about that, Eve, I really am. I love you so much it hurts." He kissed the back of my hand gently.

I leaned down to him and rested my bruised face against the side of his. Nate sighed as he looked up, the crystal dew of unshed tears brightened his eyes and tugged at my heart. I kissed his lips then, a soundless nod to his emotions, I felt those emotions too and needed him as much as he needed me.

The door opened then. "Aww, cut it out, you two—can't a father come to see his daughter in the hospital without having to see a bunch of kids sucking face?"

Nate leaned back as my dad approached, smiling.

"Hi, Dad," I said. "And the answer is no."

My dad dragged a chair next to my bed and sat. "Scared the peewahs out of us, kid." He gestured to Nate. "This one's been sitting in your room since he was out of surgery—hasn't eaten, hasn't slept, and I don't think he will until you run a marathon to prove you're fine."

"Even then . . ." Nate said.

Dad patted my hand. "You know, it's kind of strange, you in that bed and me sitting here."

I laughed but stopped quickly, as my face hurt. I gingerly touched it. "Why does my face hurt? And can I get some water?"

Nate reached behind him and held the jug for me as I sipped from the Big Gulp sized hospital water container. As he put the container back on the table, Dad said, "Fractured cheek bone and skull. You also have four bruised ribs, a bruised pelvis, and a seat belt laceration. But other than that, you're fine."

Heavy-lidded, I said, and meant it, "I feel fine too."

"Morphine."

"Ah." Then remembered: "Marta?"

Dad nodded and took a deep breath. "She's out of ICU and in critical care. The bullet hit her lung, collapsing it. Unlike Nate, who got off easy with a nick to his, hers went clear through."

I looked at Nate. "Just a flesh wound?"

He just shrugged and winced.

"What do the doctors say?"

"It'll be another week before she's released, but she's making progress. Her whole family is there—downstairs. They've been by to see you too," Dad said, looking behind him.

In the dim light from the hall, I noticed the room's far wall for the first time. Or rather, didn't notice the wall, as balloons and flowers and cards obscured it. My heart lightened at the kindness.

"Wow."

We were silent for some time. I looked at Nate, but before I could ask, he confirmed, "He's dead."

I nodded.

"Your car went to the scrapyard, and his body was identified—he was downstream...I don't know how much you want to know. Ask Flora if you want all the details—she didn't believe it at first and from her descriptions, it sounds like she grilled Shelby for the details just to make sure he was really gone. She's been celebrating ever since."

I was quiet, absorbing that fact. "I remember something, something happened that was important you had punched him, at the apartment. Something about your mom, he knew about the money your mom had."

Nate nodded.

"Your mom married him but was already pregnant?"

Nate nodded, and smiled. "Motherfucker wasn't my pops."

"Language." Dad said.

"Sorry. He wasn't my biological father. I don't know the full story —Flora and the lawyer who dispensed the funds I inherited they were able to give me enough to put pieces together. We know now that the funds came from my biological father's estate. Flora remembers my mom talking about working with her mother cleaning houses in Italy when she was a kid. She used to talk about how handsome this one guy was whose house they cleaned. Flora thinks he had a penchant for young things and, well, yeah, you get the point."

"But how'd the money come to you and not his kids? His other kids, the ones he acknowledged?"

"Or knew about. Dunno, maybe my mother contacted him and he was willing to give her support, or maybe he didn't have any other kids?"

"Wow," I said and smiled at him. "So that explains a lot, huh?"

"Yeah, now I know where the money came fr—"

"No," I said. "About you, chasing chicks, having an affinity for fine things."

"Ha. Just *one* fine chick." He leaned in, and my father cleared his throat. Nate stopped and smiled. "Later, babe."

Jenny came in the next day to give me the lowdown on the magazine. My replacement had been flown in from a sister magazine in L.A., but he was suffering since Portland had had close to zero sunny days since he'd arrived. Some of the staff were stirring up talk of a walkout until I was reinstated or the board relieved Wellington of his duties. I learned that my lawyers had filed the intent to sue IMG and have Wellington removed. Instead of feeling relieved, I felt instead like taking up knitting like Jenny. It seemed a whole lot nicer, quieter, peaceful even.

Shelby came by to check on me and tell Nate that he'd closed up his father's case. My father's case, however, was still pending, and now that the prime suspect was dead, getting the Chevy back was looking like a lost cause.

"I was thinking," Nate said the afternoon before my release, "that I want to see more of you when you get out."

"Oh?"

"Yeah."

I waited.

"And?"

"And what?"

"Nothing more? Just, you want to see more of me?"

Nate stood and went to the window and peeked out through the miniblinds, then turned back to me, obviously wrestling with something. "I—" he said and stopped, then blew out a breath. "I don't want you over at your pops's place anymore; I want you living with me. But I know that'll seem like old times, and you thought that was suffocating and ran away. I don't want you to run away, but I want to spend more time with you."

"Yeah."

"Yeah what?"

"Yeah, I'll move in with you—if that's what you're asking." I smiled. "I'm not eighteen anymore; the thought of moving in with you seems nice. Very nice."

Nate's whole body relaxed. He whispered, "I was hoping you'd say that."

FORTY-FOUR

I SPENT THE DAYS IMMEDIATELY FOLLOWING MY RELEASE FROM the hospital unpacking at Nate's loft. It was nice, recovering slowly; the only thing planned in my future was my dad's birthday that weekend. Flora volunteered to cater it—we all needed an excuse to celebrate.

The day arrived and carafes of Flora's good wine filled wine glasses, and chafing dishes chock-full of marinara, alfredo, and pastas lined my father's kitchen counters. Chuck was to be there, of course, and though Marta was still in the hospital, she called that morning to wish Dad a happy birthday. To round out the celebration, Nate and I had invited some of our friends and Dad's extended network. We were setting Jenny up with Anthony—unbeknownst to her—as only slight payback for her tricking me into going to Wellington's party. Donny joined Lou and Flora to represent Nate's family, and those four people alone talked loud enough and gestured wide enough to drown out a rock concert.

As I set a couple of dirty plates in the sink, I saw through the window Chuck outside pointing.

My father's newly painted '57 Chevy sat on a flatbed trailer backing into Dad's driveway.

"Holy mother of god."

Lou and Flora stopped talking about the optimal temperature for melted cheese. "What? What is it?" Flora asked.

In the living room, I heard Nate curse then say, "Martin. That your truck?"

"What the..." Using his cane, Dad made his way out the front door with everyone trailing him.

I just stood in the kitchen staring. When I found the ability to do it, I walked outside and down the steps toward the group.

"Ha-ha!" I heard Chuck say to Dad. "You like it, Martin? I thought with your cancer and all, I'd help you out with that bucket list of yours—always said how much fun you thought stealing a car would be."

"Gosh, well," I heard my father respond as I walked closer. The flatbed that held Dad's car now had been the one that'd taken it away that night. That night he died, and was brought back to life. And Chuck had known all along.

All.

Along.

"I did want to do that," Dad was saying, "but I guess I wanted to be the one doing the car-stealing part, you know."

"Are you kidding?! This was better." Chuck slapped him on the back. "You got to shoot off your pistol, chase down hooligans, ride in an ambulance after you fainted, and your truck has that better paint job you've always wanted."

"Fainted?" I asked.

Jenny stepped back, so I could see Chuck.

"Fainted?" I repeated. "You mean, had a heart attack?"

"Now, Eva," Dad interjected, "it wasn't all that bad."

I ignored him and took a step closer to Chuck. "You do realize we have a police investigation going?"

"Well, now, I did, and, Eva, darlin', you have to understand that when you get to our age, sometimes you can't fake life experience, and this one sure as shootin' couldn't be faked."

My mouth gaped as I looked at the pair of them. "You two are insane."

"Eva," Dad said, "what's done is done, and, Chuck, I'm glad you did it—best present I ever had."

"Anything else on that bucket list of yours I should know about—like skydiving without a parachute? Playing Russian roulette? Or maybe just a fun game of tag in light traffic?"

Our exchange was like a tennis match to those around us. Surprised expressions moved back and forth between us.

My dad went on the defensive. "No harm done, and I'm better off for it. Now, why don't you simmer down, Eva Lynn?"

I felt my eyebrows practically graze my hairline. "Simmer down," I repeated. I poked his chest.

"Ouch."

"Oh, sorry, is that still sore from where I administered CPR to your corpse?"

"Got it," I heard Nate say as his arm wound about my middle and hoisted.

"I'm not done with you two!" I called as Nate hauled my butt back into the house.

Nate set me down in my old room, closed the door, and leaned against it.

"Chuck" was all he said and shook his head.

"This whole damn time! He knew and didn't say a word—I'm gonna kill him."

"The whole. Damn. Time," he repeated slowly before pinching the bridge of his nose, laughter and disbelief coloring his expression. He looked back at me, a smile threatening to grow.

I put my hands on my hips. "I don't know whether to smack Chuck or my dad for making light of it or for the two of them having a bucket list like that! Who does that?"

Nate gave me a knowing smile. "Best friends do."

And just like that I was thinking of him and me again. "Yeah, they do, don't they?"

He held his arms out, and I walked into them. I wrapped my arms around him in a hug as I leaned against him.

"They do," he confirmed and tucked an errant hair behind my ear with his free hand before giving me a soft kiss.

"Nothing on our bucket list is like that, though."

"Right. I think that's because we've done it all. My bucket list looks more like a nursing-home activity calendar now."

I laughed, giving him another kiss. "Knitting at ten, listening to soft guitar music at noon, nap—"

"With a hot naked chick named Eve," he said, deepening the kiss before breaking off. "Let's go for a drive," he whispered against my lips.

"Lead the way."

Nate took my hand and led me out the side door and to his car.

The Aston Martin had been fun, but he'd lost his shirt over it, specifically $140,000 worth of shirts over it. Nate had been disappointed that the dealership hadn't asked what had happened—he'd been wanting to tell them a high-speed car chase—but instead they just handed him an invoice. As if loaner cars to rich men often came back looking like that.

Now, he had his two-door 3 Series that he'd loaned me. The drive to the pasture was different in her, scarier almost. All cars can be fast—twenty-mile-an-hour corners at forty feel fast. But when a vehicle was driven to the edge of its capabilities, there was something scary—and satisfying—about it. That afternoon there was less "yes, ma'am" and more "oh god, today I die" as it ripped through the corners. The rear tire lifted, swinging the ass end out, threatening to take the car—and us—over the yellow and off the other side of the road.

I braced myself, laughter bubbling up at the psychotic way we took each corner. As if we were still in the Aston.

The tack redlined, Nate shifted and bulleted us out the back end of the turn. This time as we headed to our pasture overlook we approached from the opposite direction. Ahead in the mottled light through the trees was an obvious dip in the center of black circular tire marks from when we were there last.

"Is that a—?"

"Yup."

"Are you going to—?"

Nate shifted in answer.

I sent up a prayer to the gods of car chassis that ours would stay in one piece when we landed on the other side. My hand shot up to the roof and the other to the center console for moral support.

The greenery bolted by us; the nose of our car pointed dead center of the small hump in the road.

A small hump—that hit at this speed would toss your head into the ceiling if your seat belt was slack.

Nate kept the tack redlined. We hit and were airborne.

"Holy...shit!"

The car landed on the gravel of the logging road with a teeth-rattling slam. The undercarriage bottomed out, and gravel flung out the back with the spinning wheels.

We fishtailed before the traction caught and bolted us up the road to our overlook.

Nate slowed at the top and meandered over to the edge before putting her in park.

I was laughing so hard in the passenger seat that I had to wipe my eyes to see him. "Nate, baby, I think you broke something."

He undid his seat belt, a grin wide and white lighting up his face. "I just might have. Shit, that was fun."

Laughing, I kissed him as he put his seat back.

"Oof," I said, falling onto him as he reclined.

"Catching air isn't the only thing I like about this car," he said, pulling me onto his lap. "Miles of driver space is the other."

I settled my knees on either side of his lap and put my lips to his. "Oh, you don't say."

"I do."

"I don't know. I think we should test that 'miles of space' theory."

"Agreed."

Our clothes seemed to slip off of their own accord, exposing naked skin to naked skin. Hands caressed and memorized curves and contours as Nate and I connected once more. His voice was rough with his emotion as he told me he loved me, as I rocked my hips, pushing and pulling his thick pride within me.

I rocked us to blissful ecstasy as his hand gripped the back of my head, crushing my mouth to his before he cried out and his warmth matched my own shuddering release.

NATE WAS ON THE HOOD OF THE CAR AS I FINISHED SETTING MY clothes right and grabbed his hoodie off the back seat and slipped it on, wrapping it tight around me. As I approached him, he pulled me in against him, each of us looking out over the little rolling hills and the city in the distance.

"Feeling better?" he asked and kissed my neck.

Leaning back against his chest as his arms tightened around me, I said, "Yeah, remind me what was I worked up over again?"

"I'm not going to remind you."

"Wise, I think," I said and tilted my head back, begging for a kiss.

He smiled and gave me a soft press of one against my lips.

"Maybe," he said against my neck. "Eve?"

"Yeah?"

"Can I ask you something?"

"Always. And let the record show that you asking means it must be serious and the defendant is now nervous."

I heard a soft chuckle rumble in his chest. "I'm having a problem with a new investment and need some advice."

I waited a beat. "Sure."

"Is it ethical to be banging the head of an investment that you own?"

"I'm not the head of any investment you own, so I'm not sure you'll need that answer."

"I need you to take that chief editor position again with your old company."

I turned to look at him. "What?"

He took a deep breath. "I garnered a deal with the board of directors to have you drop the suit if Wellington would take his money and go—"

"What? No, I'm in the middle of that suit—"

"I'm not finished," he said, glaring at me. "But as we figured—"

"We?"

"Seriously, Eve—you want to hear what I got to say or what?"

"Yes, but who's 'we'?"

He kissed the end of my nose. "You're going business mode on me, babe. Quiet. It's just me, my lawyer, and agent. Happy?"

"I bid you continue."

"Turns out the IMG board was unhappy with the transition of Wellington's father's position on the board to him. Among the actions he took in his father's place that made them unhappy was your firing. They'd been content with *Rose City Review*'s revenue growth and with the new chief dude—"

"Editor in chief."

"Right, it's only been three months, but Wellington's RCR replacement has already shown a massive revenue loss—he's pissing money down the drain on personal shit—and with that in addition to your sexual harassment suit, they unanimously voted him off the board. Additionally, they requested he relinquish his shares in IMG at quarter cost or be barred from the industry. I think there's some bad blood that goes back farther than us, if I read between the lines of what I was told. With Wellington fired, you'll need to personally sue him for sexual harassment and omit IMG from the suit. He's easily worth fifty mil."

"Wow," I said, impressed. "I can do that. I'll call my attorney tomorrow." I added, "So, I take it you're the person he had to relinquish his shares to at a quarter of the cost?"

"Something like that. I pitched in some money, and the rest were scooped up by other shareholders."

"How in the world did you finagle all that?"

"Agents, attorneys, shit like that. And one of the board members brings in his aging Porsche once a month to my place. So, luck, really."

"Luck, right. Nathaniel Vellanova, you're the smartest man I've ever met."

"You should get out more, babe."

I just smiled at him. "So, you've gotten saddled with a magazine, and you need someone you trust and look up to to run it? Someone with genius and vision?"

He smiled. "Basically."

"I accept. Did you really have your attorney and an agent work it out for you? Not a baseball bat and your temper?"

"Ha."

"I just want to know so I can imagine it—in detail."

"Nope, I didn't see or talk with him."

I sighed. "Too bad. I'll definitely have to get my peace in court."

We were quiet for a while, listening to the birds in the trees in the distance and the echo of a plane miles away. Sideways between his legs, I gripped him tight in a hug.

He smiled down at me and whispered, "Are you happy?"

I tilted my chin up to him and, kissing him softly on the lips, said, "Blissfully."

ACKNOWLEDGMENTS

The first people I'd like to thank for making this book possible are the fans of my first work, *The Legend of Lady MacLaoch*. Thank you for the immense positive feedback and exuberant encouragement to write more.

I could not have accomplished *Forged* without the generous feedback of my loyal peer reviewers: Annie, Ayn, Heather L., and Joelle. Annie, I want to especially thank you for all the advance readings, bloggings, textings, last-minute feedback, and questions you offered me with this book. Knowing that you're just a call, text, or email away for positive encouragement and honest feedback is priceless to me.

Thank you to Geneva, whose experience in high-end clubs along the West Coast helped to shape Festivál, and for great one-liners that became infused in Nathaniel's vocab. You, my dear, put the double *o* in cool.

Also to my writing group, Adam, Chris, Jennifer—you were instrumental once again in helping me flesh out the ending, and gave me great feedback on the early drafts of the novel. And Jennifer, I'm sorry about the truck, I really am. Thanks again to the pro's behind my prose: Kristin Thiel and team—I wouldn't look nearly as smart without you all!

To my Aunty Elaine Massotti, thank you for floating around with me in the pool last summer telling me stories of your grandmother and all her plastic-covered furniture. I wish I could have put in the tidbit about chocolate in the underwear drawer, but I'm not quite sure where I could have fit it...other than here in the acknowledgement section.

Thank you to all the random people I bounced ideas off of, like my ever-patient insurance agent and my BMW mechanic. Also, thanks goes to my father-in-law, with whom I argued at length about what constitutes a '57 Chevy. And it's here that I acknowledge you—yes, the idyllic '57 Chevy is a car, but Martin owns the '57 Chevy *truck*. Yes, *truck*.

Most importantly I'd like to acknowledge several girlfriends—without naming you—for sharing with me about first loves. It was the question that has been repeated on so many occasions with dreamy eyes and a glass of wine in your hand: *Where is he now?* It's that question that resonated within me while I wrote *Forged*. I hope this comes close to what you were dreaming of.

I'd also like to thank my parents for my automotive-love genes. My mother gave me the need for speed and my father was my first mechanic and teacher. Though it was with my friends and sibling that I learned to drive stick, do burnouts, and safely exceed the speed limits through corners. It was the culmination of those building blocks that set me up for the ultimate partner, my husband. It is to him that I'd like to thank for all of his applicable and encyclopedic knowledge of vehicles, both with two and four wheels. He is my first love, and it is to him that I quietly but purposefully dedicate this novel.

AUTHOR BIO

Becky Banks is a bestselling and award-winning indie author from an old Hawai'i family, who currently lives in Portland, Oregon, with her husband and two children. Becky likes to craft dark romances that stem from her past and require love to see her characters through. When she's not crafting love stories, she's packing lunches for her little ones and breaking up *Minecraft* fights.

Visit Becky Banks online at beckybanksbooks.com and follow her on social media for updates on new releases and more.

facebook.com/beckybanksbooks

instagram.com/authorbeckybanks

amazon.com/author/beckybanks

goodreads.com/beckybanks

bookbub.com/profile/becky-banks

ALSO BY BECKY BANKS

Clan MacLaoch Curse Series

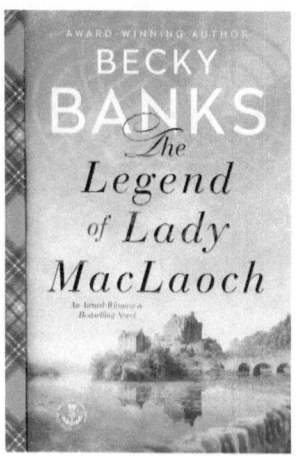

The Legend of Lady MacLaoch. *Book 1 of the Clan MacLaoch Curse Series.*

Centuries ago a vengeful curse buried itself deep into the history of the MacLaoch clan and became a legendary tale told by all those not cursed by its words.

In present-day Scotland, the laird and chief of the MacLaoch clan is an ex-Royal Air Force fighter pilot who has been past the gates of hell and returned a changed man. Rowan MacLaoch does battle with wartime memories and a family curse that threaten to consume him—unaware that his life and that of the history of the clan will be changed forever by the arrival of an American woman.

Cole Baker, a feisty recent graduate of a master's program, stumbles upon the ancient curse while researching her bloodlines. Moved by the history of the MacLaoch clan and the mystery of its chief, she digs into the legend that had been anything but quiet for centuries.

On their quest for answers, Cole and Rowan travel to places they have never before been and become witnesses to things they have never before fathomed. The legend—one started with blood—will end with more shed as its creator finally exacts her justice.

Book 2 of the Clan MacLaoch curse series, The Legend of the Viking.

In this second book of the Clan MacLaoch Curse series, we see our favorite characters, Rowan and Cole, return in their most passionate selves yet. Coming off the loss of the Gathering and the thought-to-be-extinguished MacLaoch curse, Rowan finally has a chance at his happily ever after. That is, until everything that he loves is put at risk, sparking events, that once set in motion, will not be stopped—except by love.

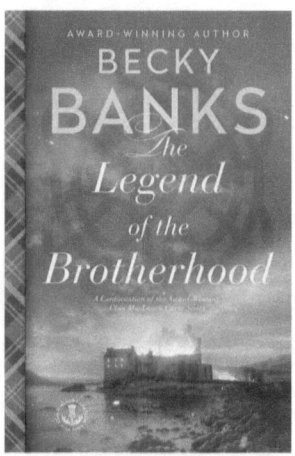

Coming soon. Book 3 of the Clan MacLaoch curse series, The
Legend of the Brotherhood.

In this third book of the clan MacLaoch curse series, Cole's two worlds
collide when her brother TJ stops by Castle Laoch for a surprise visit. His
presence upsets more than the status quo at Castle Laoch; Rowan struggles
to find a solution to the bankruptcy proceedings, which are starting to look
like the end for the MacLaoch clan. Cole and Rowan - fresh off the battle
on the cairn knoll - are bonded even more profoundly as they move to save
the castle from bankruptcy and a villainous bankman set on a generation's
old revenge. While Cole and Rowan's love is secure for eternity, the struggle
for the ancestral MacLaoch home hangs in the balance. Can Rowan's
determination, the Baker kids' ingenuity, and residual Viking power from
Ormr Minorisson save the castle and clan from ruin?

Romantic Suspense Titles

Flux. *Can one notorious hacker protect the women she's saved before her dark past finds her?*

Vega Flux, a notorious hacker whose single mission in life is to protect the weak from online trolls, crashes up against an impenetrable powerhouse of a man who wants nothing more than to slip the dark shroud off her persona and protect her from her torments.

In this smoldering high-stakes game of defense and one-upmanship, Vega takes a bet she knows she shouldn't and starts the largest hack she's ever attempted, against the only worthy opponent she's ever known, tech billionaire and ex-NFL tight end, Hoyt Kahoʻokalakupua. Master of his domain, Hoyt, welcomes the chance to flex his power in a true challenge. With the stakes dangerously high, and his heart on the line, he enters a game with a woman he wants it all from. There's only one fatal flaw: Hoyt and Vega are following different instructions to the same game. He's a law-abiding billionaire, and the world Vega lives in breaks every rule.

Dark passions ignite in this fast-paced thrill ride from award-winning indie author and Maui girl, Becky Healani Banks. As the torments of Vegaʻs past breach her defenses, she reaches for the one man who is uniquely capable of providing the shelter she seeks. And in that process, she touches a power she's never known, real-life love.

Forged. *First loves, dark pasts, and fast cars collide in this high-octane thrill ride.*

Managing editor of a Manhattan fashion rag, Eva Rodgers, couldn't believe she would ever step back into her old life, but the day her father called with his diagnosis, she had little choice. Returning home, and to the past she left behind, Eva signs up as editor-in-chief of the struggling Portland magazine, *Rose City Review*. There in the drizzling Portland metro Eva still holds firm to the New York city values that defined her time there: compromise on nothing. When her European auto, one luxury she missed in the walking and hired car world of Manhattan, needs fixing, she doesn't compromise. Even when the best European auto mechanic her assistant finds turns out to be an ex with a vendetta, Eva doesn't flinch.

Nathaniel Vellanova can't believe what the fuck just showed up at his garage. He'd gotten his life together, buried his dark past, and definitely put Eva Rogers in his rearview mirror. Right?

But fuck him if she wasn't standing right there in the pouring rain needing his help. He'd do it—help her out—just this once then forget all about her. Again.

In this dark and suspenseful story of broken first loves, readers will ride the smoldering heat of high-octane fast cars, glitzy club fashion, and tainted love and ask themselves, are first loves the only love?

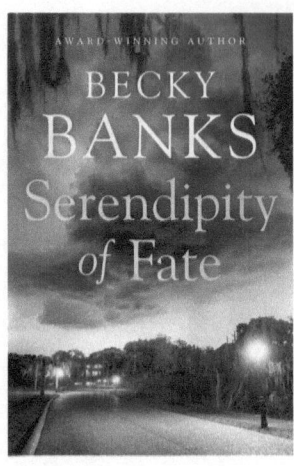

Serendipity of Fate. *Enemies to lovers romance. One war, one blood promise, and the love to save it all.*

It has been two years since Cason McPherson watched his best friend, Ryan Sparling, die in his arms. Now, with a blood promise tied to his heart, shrapnel in his hip, and a war behind him, he's focused on building a useful civilian life in his hometown of New Orleans. Living with Ryan's mother, a widow and retired nurse, he gives back the protection and care his best friend wanted. Only Ryan's sister, a woman whose well-worn picture got him through the darkest parts of the war, does not see it that way.

Savannah Sparling has spent the last five years building her career and life to the exacting expectations needed to achieve partner at Knight Interiors. And nothing could derail them except for the one person from her past who returned home a changed man. Cason McPherson and her brother Ryan had been her entire world once, but now she no longer recognizes him with his caustic attitude and effort to turn every conversation into a verbal sparring match. When a potential client, one large enough to secure her place as partner, requests her as lead designer, Savannah sets a plan for her final career move and Cason's eviction.

In a series of unstoppable events, Savannah's carefully laid plans backfire, and an unfathomable truth is revealed. In the aftermath, Cason and Savannah find that the only people strong enough to save them from themselves are each other. But will either one of them accept the help—and the love—that is offered?

Future Series

Coming soon.

Set one-hundred years into a dystopian future, this socio-political romantic thriller takes place in the sprawling catacombs of The Peoples Republic of Portland. In a world that has been punished by the misdeeds of mankind, one writer sets out to answer one simple question: What would happen if everyone had hope again? Absorbed onto a misfit team of ex-war machine operators, junior journalist Wendy Wilson, moves quickly to adapt or die while trying to save the city she loves and maybe, just maybe, change the hearts and minds of even the most blood-thirsty among them.

PREVIEW: FLUX

He's untouchable. She's a notorious hacker. It's a million-dollar cash prize. The challenge? Break him. If you can.

Vega Flux, a notorious hacker whose single mission in life is to protect the weak from online trolls, crashes up against an impenetrable powerhouse of a man who wants nothing more than to slip the dark shroud off her persona and protect her from her torments.

In this smoldering high-stakes game of defense and one-upmanship, Vega takes a bet she knows she shouldn't and starts the largest hack she's ever attempted, against the only worthy opponent she's ever known, tech billionaire and ex-NFL tight end, Hoyt Kahoʻokalakupua. Master of his domain, Hoyt, welcomes the chance to flex his power in a true challenge. With the stakes dangerously high, and his heart on the line, he enters a game with a woman he wants it all from. There's only one fatal flaw: Hoyt and Vega are following different instructions to the same game. He's a law-abiding billionaire, and the world Vega lives in breaks every rule.

Dark passions ignite in this fast-paced thrill ride from award-winning indie author and Maui girl, Becky Healani Banks. As the torments of Vegaʻs past breach her defenses, she reaches for the one man who is uniquely capable of providing the shelter she seeks. And in that process, she touches a power she's never known, real-life love.

Turn the page to start reading a sample of Hoyt and Vega's story in _Flux_.

FLUX: CHAPTER 1

Rain struck the kitchen window of the sprawling home nestled deep in the forest of the West Hills, the pot on the stove mimicking the plunk of rain as the popcorn kernels hit its sides.

"You're kidding, right?" Lei asked her older brother as they sat at the long wood-topped kitchen island.

"Not kidding," Hoyt replied. He had hoped it could be a nice, peaceful night in, but his younger sister was out to prove a point as they tossed back handfuls of popcorn their father was making in batches at the stove.

"Ho'o," she pressed, using the nickname he had gotten his first year playing college football over fifteen years ago. "This time last year you were loving single life and being on that *Forbes* tech billionaires list, and that local one—what's it called?"

He didn't want to answer, but unanswered questions gave him heartburn. "*Rose City*—"

"Yes! *Rose City Review*'s top ten bachelors list. Now, you're all grump-tastic, saying, 'It's time for me to settle down,' and, 'Marriage is serious.' What you and Londyn have is none of that—"

"It is." He hoped his curtness would get his sister to drop it. But she was too much like him—and not just in their shared black hair, hers long and always in a top knot, brown skin, and weird eyes that didn't know if they were brown or hazel and usually ended up looking a disarming gold—to let him off the hook. He may have even known she was right about the woman he had asked to marry him a month ago.

Londyn was the third in a string of bad time-investments and from an elite marriage broker who had promised him results. Instead, she'd said he was difficult and particularly discerning. But the thought of spending the rest of his life with someone should mean he could ask for the best. He shouldn't have to settle for mediocrity. Then again, he wasn't sure exactly what he was looking for. Just that he'd know her when he saw her. Thinking of Londyn now, however, made his stomach ache, as if he'd had ahi poke that had been left out for a few days.

"Admit it, Londyn isn't your type. Even Amy could see it in your face the other day, and if she can see it over a video call, that's not good. The marriage broker was wrong. Again. She pushed Londyn on you because her daddy is a shipping magnate who paid tons of money for the match. And she was the perfect angel when you two were under contract. Now? She's a party girl, booze and Ecstasy at the clubs. She's like a younger version of you—"

"I never did Ecstasy."

"Right, like, that is my point. Let's face it—she's a different person. You and the matchmaker got hustled." When he said nothing, she repeated, "Admit it."

"Not doing that." He reached for the fresh bowl their father had just set down, wondering if HR would allow him to fire Lei as his director of engineering at Hoyt Securities. It was *his* company after all.

"Fine, then, I will. Londyn 2.0 isn't the one. Let me tell your marriage broker what you really need. You totally have a soft spot for antiheroes. And Londyn is so far from being an antihero she's an actual hero. Hero of social media selfies to make young girls feel inadequate."

Their father chimed in from the stove. "Lei, that was unkind." Curtis was a tall, soft-spoken man whose hair had gone gray at the temples. His tan skin was the deep color of his plain morning coffee, evidence that he spent his days fishing, and now that he and his wife, Ginny, were both retired, golfing. Ginny would say she would never retire, as she continued to manage the Kahoʻokalakupua Estate and Trust. Curtis pressed his youngest child, "Londyn is going to be family. She's ʻohana—treat her with more respect."

"Fine."

"Come, Hoyt, bring her around more. So we can stop this nonsense, ya?" He pointedly glanced at Lei to tell her to quit her Londyn bashing.

Hoyt mumbled, "Yeah, sure." Thinking the opposite was what he was going to do.

"Or," Lei said, tossing her father's advice to the side, "you can forget this matchmaker business and bring someone you actually like. Someone like the antiheroes from your comics you worshipped when we were kids."

Their father tsked from the stove.

"I'm too old for comics, Lei. And Londyn and I are fine." He heard the lie in his voice, his monotone as dry as his unbuttered popcorn.

Their father shook the large stainless-steel pot as the oily pings of the kernels struck the sides.

"I can hear that Marvel show, *Jennifer Jones*—"

"*Jessica*—"

"On your phone while you poop."

"I don't do that here."

"Why does it take you an hour in there? Are you hiding?"

He threw his arm out at her. "And you wonder why? What's with the interrogation?"

The pot on the stove gained steam once more until the covered pot sounded like it contained firecrackers. The mini explosions mimicked the rapidity of the thoughts in Hoyt's brain.

Lei shrugged. "Tomorrow you go to Festivál for Zane's thing at the club, and I'm just saying, maybe you should let loose. Find someone new and have a good time. I'm giving you permission to let her go. Why you proposed, I dunno. Are you desperate? You got a three-for-one: the first two sucked, but if you marry the third, the match cost is free?"

"That's insulting and makes no sense." He was definitely firing his sister.

"Lei," came from their father, "mai hana kuli."

"Sorry, Dad, I know. I'll be quiet. It's just that, Hoyt, you just don't seem happy, and you're here all the time, and I'm guessing it's because you don't like being at your place. And I wanna help."

"Lei..." Curtis pressed. "Leave him be."

"Yeah, leave me alone," he grumbled, standing.

"I'm just saying that a month is long enough. No more marriage broker. You should be honest about what you really want, not what you think you need. Having a wife should be more like what Amy and I have, a partnership, not whatever it is that you told the marriage broker. You have two eyes, and you need to trust your gut. And take down that wall you have around your heart. I swear you built Titan's Wall then made a second one around your emotions."

"I'll meet you in the movie room." Standing, Hoyt ended the conversation with finality. As he left, he caught a glimpse of his father giving Lei a stern look.

Hoyt didn't need the haranguing from his sister about his choice of fiancée—he was doing enough of that all by himself. Had he noticed he rarely went home these days? Yeah. Had he noticed that Londyn was happy in her wing of the penthouse and gave him only an air kiss if their paths did cross? Yeah. Had he noticed that she didn't want to talk with him since moving in? Had he noticed that since the ring hit her finger, they had zero intimacy?

He could use a hug.

And he definitely didn't want one from Londyn. He was convinced Londyn didn't want one from him either. She'd already made it clear that the things that defined him she wanted removed. The talisman around his neck she wanted put in a drawer, and the ink on his body she wanted covered, and then one morning, she didn't want him all together.

It didn't take a rocket scientist to see his marriage choice was a bad one. Their relationship, despite what he'd thought when he put a ring on her finger, was barely social, much less civil. Somehow Londyn had skated through the matchmaking with promise, and the marriage broker's notes matched Hoyt's own: Londyn was engaging and interesting. She had him convinced that she was a sure bet. It turned out he was her sure bet. He needed to make the call to end it and start another round of dating, and he would. The only problem was that he was tired. This was his third serious attempt at finding a life companion, and it felt like doomsday. And if he made the call, ended things, and started over, the engagement announcement the broker had already sent and the social media posts that congratulated him would make everyone think they had permission to ask questions. Questions he could give a shit about, but they were exhausting. He had an international, high-level-security company to run. And this was the pilikia he'd hired a marriage broker to avoid. Now he had to find another broker. Or say fuck it to the whole thing. The only silver lining was that while he figured out what to do, he would enjoy the quiet. Date requests from others had all but vanished now that he was thought to have a fiancée, and that, he thought, was close to priceless.

Lei followed her brother only a few minutes later. The movie room was on the house's lowest level, where it tucked into the hillside. The décor mimicked the underground atmosphere with walls and furnishings in deep earth tones that absorbed light. The plush, velvety couches made a large U-shape that blended into the shadows and invited a person to snuggle into the pillows and luxurious throws. Hoyt was already stretched out on the far leg of the *U*, making his side of the couch seem small under his six-foot-plus frame.

Lei plopped down next to him, wedging between them a large bowl of popcorn now sprinkled with dark flakes of furikake seaweed and toasted amber nuggets of mochi crunch to make it island style.

"Look," she said, taking off right where he'd physically left, "I want you to be happy, and I think you need to find your Jessica Jones or Selina Kyle or—"

"Those were fantasies of an adolescent, Lei. I'm running a multi-billion-dollar company with thousands of people dependent on me." He fed her the excuse he told himself: "I need someone who has her own life, so when I'm not around, she's not heartbroken. I need someone who won't be corrupted by all the money either. It's a lot."

"And you think that matchmaker was right—Londyn is the one?"

"It's a marriage broker, and sure. Londyn comes from money, Lei—"

"But she spends it like she's never had a dollar in her whole life."

"Lei..."

"Look, I'm just saying, I want to see you happy or at least pursuing more of that proclaimed bachelor life you wanted until a year ago until you woke up and decided forty was coming up on you fast and you wanted a bride on your arm before then."

"Lei, fuck off."

"Fine," she said. "You guys settle on a wedding date yet?"

"What movie are we watching?"

"Dunno, something Dad will like."

"Superhero then." He picked up the remote and got things started.

"Londyn would have a date locked down— Oh."

"What do you think of this one?"

Lei looked at the screen where the hero stood in a solid stance, ten rings on his arm, then to her brother. "Hoʻo...I'm sorry. You *are* thinking of breaking up with her?"

"It's a new idea. I don't want to talk about it."

"I know how much you hate quitting things." For a minute, his sister sounded thoughtful before she snapped back to her original purpose: "But think of it as another game that didn't go well: learn from it and move on—"

He pointed the remote at her. "Lei...just because Amy, your perfect wife, is stationed overseas so you have extra time to dive into other people's shit doesn't mean I want you in mine."

Lei grabbed the remote from him and switched streaming services. "Here, let's watch your girlfriend, vigilante and all-around—"

"Alcoholic."

"Badass."

"Fine," he said giving in. He tossed a blanket over his legs and tucked his hands under his crossed arms. His personal life was shit, but he could dream.

It was ridiculous to crave a fantasy superhero type, but he definitely wanted a woman with powerful confidence who wouldn't shy away from him. He wanted someone to look at him and see *him*. Not his career stats or titles: MVP and legendary tight end for the Seattle Seahawks. Nor his second-career stats as tech-security billionaire.

His dad caught up with them then, coming into the room with a tray of fruit punch for himself and Lei and a glass of ice water for Hoyt.

He passed them out before settling in his movie-watching seat. "Oh, good, this show. That's the one we were just talking about. Let's do it."

Lei grinned at Hoyt and got it started.

Their father added, pointing at the raven-haired woman on the screen, "It's a good thing she doesn't exist, or Hoyt would follow her everywhere she went."

"Not true," Hoyt mumbled. But he couldn't hide the smile that broke out inside. It was completely true. He wouldn't mind getting obsessed with someone as strong as him, someone who didn't want to ride his money train and didn't feed him false narratives she thought he wanted to hear. And yeah, she had to have that save-the-underdog thing going.

He sighed at his own reality, watching the stomping combat boots and snarling red lips of the actor who played the dark vigilante on screen. He was going to be alone for the rest of his fucking life.

FLUX: CHAPTER 2

"Vega, Vega, Veg-ASS!!!" A second before the chanting started, the door to Vega Flux's apartment had burst open, shocking her fingers up off her keyboard. Into her low-lit space swept her childhood friends Cindy and Peace like models showcasing the latest in glittering nightclub attire. They were still shouting her name as they kicked her door shut.

"Ugh!" Vega feigned disgust, rolling back in her chair and taking in her beautiful friends. "What are you guys wearing? Are those tube tops supposed to be dresses? And no! I don't want whatever you're up to," she hollered, although she already knew why her gazelles were there.

Vega smothered her grin as they lit up her dark industrial apartment that was as classy as a second-story defunct-scrapyard office space could get. Once a maze of cubicles, it was now one cavernous room. Brick walls and single-paned windows were nods to its Prohibition-era construction, when the view to the river was decent. Now she had to look around the concrete footings of the I-84/I-5 interchange.

"Aw! Come on, Vega!" Peace Scott trained her cornflower-blue eyes on Vega. Her fine blond hair was pulled into a braid that danced down her back. She turned toward Cindy, who was already elbow deep in Vega's snack pantry. The cabinet had once held parts that made bombs during the WWII. Now it just held sugar bombs.

Cindy tossed back a mini chocolate chip cookie before saying, "Come on, you have to come to this one! It's literally two blocks away." Giacintha Merino-Perez went by Cindy off the clock and liked rum, chocolate, and chocolate-drenched rum parties. And handcuffs. On and off the clock. On the clock, she was Special Agent Merino-Perez. A job both Peace, who was a corporate attorney, and Vega, a haxor, found useful in their passion project, Project Valkyrie.

Cindy dropped the cookie bag on the counter and bent to see in Vega's antiquated fridge, exposing the lower curve of her bum as she dug through like a big sister inspecting how her little sis lived. "You know, one day these leftovers will kill you." Vega heard the clang of the kitchen trash lid pop open and objects dumped into it.

"I'm busy!" Vega said before sliding even lower behind her wall of monitors. She popped back up for a moment to holler at Cindy, who had more takeout boxes in hand at the garbage bin. "And those weren't that old!"

As Cindy looked over her shoulder at Vega, her bossy black curls slid out of the way of her glare. "You're busy? With what? We closed all the Project Valkyrie cases for this week. Or are you breaking the rules and fucking someone up?"

Vega slid low again. Being good for a year sucked, and it made her want to shout at happy people. "For the record, no, I'm not breaking the rules. And, two, I *could* be busy with something else!"

Peace sauntered over, her unfastened breasts lightly bouncing under the thin fuchsia fabric of her dress. She and Cindy were glittering spotlights among Vega's dark and brooding things, from the dark stain of the linseed-oiled old timber floors to the black desk and the dimmed semicircle of monitors that made up Vega's command center.

Peace's voice was soft and soothing. "Are you, though? Busy?"

"Yeah. I totally am."

Peace scrunched her nose and watched Vega pick at the corner of her thumbnail. She squeezed her shoulders up in a shrug as if she really wanted to believe Vega, but it was a stretch even for her, and she had the tenderest heart of them all.

"Peace," Vega said, "I'm pretty sure I just saw your vag. Don't shrug while you're wearing that sparkle-bandana."

"It's a dress."

"Exactly. And I don't wear tube tops that pretend to be dresses."

Peace's countenance warmed as she knew that arguing was just stage one of getting Vega ready to party.

"Yeah, you only wear knee-high combat boots, a hoodie in scathing black, and pants that look like they've been through razor wire, twice."

Vega poked at her skin peeking out from between the frayed threads at her knees. "Yup." She winked at Peace. "And that means I'm not going wherever you are going."

"You might change your mind..."

"We're meeting some guys—"

Vega's scoff interrupted Peace. "Oh, some *guys?* Then even harder pass."

"You haven't heard who they are. Their portfolios and physiques are to be admired, Vee. Be open-minded."

"They're next-level hot," Cindy decoded.

"And one in particular has a profile that we think you especially will appreciate. Appreciate so much you'll leave your computers behind."

"No one's worth leaving my command center for. And a woman needs a man—"

"Like a fish needs a bicycle, we know. But this one's different."

"Yes, Cin and I are in agreement—this is someone you could actually get distracted with," Peace encouraged.

Vega felt her lip curl at her friend's implication that someone in a group of "hot" guys was anywhere near what she considered distraction-worthy. In Vega's experience, stereotypically hot men were a couple bricks short of a full load. It wasn't their fault—she assumed that happened when people cooed at your face your whole life—but she didn't need someone in her life who never had to apply themselves.

"For being my best friends, you sure—"

Cindy held up a hand. "Your *only* friends, but yes, do go on."

"That's even worse—my only friends have no idea what motivates me. Hot guys are fun for a nanosecond; then they open their mouths, and dumb shit falls out. Do you remember the last time you said I had to meet a hot guy?"

They collectively groaned. "That was once, Vee." Cindy held up a finger. "One time."

"All it takes is once."

"This is different."

"Different? I'm not flying wingman, then?"

"Technically..." Peace started.

"And if he asks me if all bitches are feminists?"

"I believe we remember vividly, Vee. That *one* time."

"And the lawsuit that I had to help you dodge," Peace added.

Cindy dogpiled: "And the relocation we all helped with."

"There was that." She beamed her charming I-couldn't-have-done-it-without-you smile. "I appreciated the help. I know you were worried that he would expose our operations, but he had no idea it was me..." Her grin changed into a grimace. "Until I asked what he thought of feminists now, and told him who I was, and what I could do to him. That was a false move, I see that now. But seriously, before that was fun." Her grin was back.

"You're an adrenaline junkie," Cindy chastised. "And need to start going to Gamblers Anonymous meetings again."

"Sure, I'll get around to it. One day. Look," Vega said, back to Mr. One Time, "he gave me a come-on I couldn't refuse. 'One night I'd never forget.' And he was right—I've never forgotten it."

"And neither has he," Peace said.

Cindy was as unimpressed by the memory as she had been by her friend's actions in the moment and now folded her arms under her ample bosom. "So, instead of excusing yourself, you took a bet you shouldn't have with money that wasn't yours and slipped a bot in his phone...all before getting banned for life from the casino for counting cards."

"When you put it like that..." Vega stretched out on her black rolling chair that looked as if it could double as a Formula 1 driver's seat. "Remember, I was just giving him what he wanted—he got to fuck me earlier that night, and in return, I got to fuck him. A win-win, and let's be real—he got to witness one of my finer products after I lost his life savings at blackjack. He got a good little Bunny bot that was just having some fun until we saw who Hot Guy really was when the chips were down: a suddenly broke bro who—surprise, surprise—downloaded free porn like it was water in a wasteland and fat-shamed women online."

Cindy and Peace let out a collective sigh. That had been the moment they knew they'd lost the fight to get Vega's bot off his phone. When his actions put him squarely into the Project Valkyrie zone of noncompliance. Their silence at the time had been their unspoken agreement that it was OK to remove Vega's limitations and let her do what she did best. Up until that point, she'd just been having fun, like a cat with a mouse, but then the mouse turned out to be a feminist-phobic prick with a god complex.

"That was fun. Or at least it was until he got freaked out and got the cops involved."

"Making you have to move yet again." Cindy raised her brows to drive home her point.

"Which—silver lining—brought me home to Scout." She thought of her little sister then added with a sad face at her frowning friends. "Just out of curiosity, why do you keep asking me to these things? *No one* is 100 percent aboveboard."

"Because you work too hard, and you need to have time to focus on yourself and let go. It keeps the darkness away."

"You spiral when you work too hard, and that makes you reckless."

They knew why Vega punished herself to achieve the things she did for other women online. If she could protect one, she would. Only, right behind that one, was another, and behind her was just one more. Every one was important, and every one she identified with. And because of that, she'd gladly lose herself in trying to protect them all.

"One night," Cindy reiterated. She glanced at Peace. "This one is different."

Peace, glee coloring her tone, launched into the details. "It's a launch party. I was invited by the CEO, and he's got a friend..." Incredibly, from inside her tiny dress, Peace pulled out a playing card–sized invite and handed it to Vega.

Vega analyzed the body-warmed cardstock and its gold-embossed text. "Printed invites. I hate them already." She picked up one of the six phones sitting on her desk and using the camera pulled the invite data into her main terminal's search bar. The party sponsor's website came up on her monitor, and then there were the executives.

Cindy and Peace, giddy with something they both seemed to think was exciting, vibrated, waiting for her to see it too. Vega looked at the group of twelve men and women standing like dopes in front of the fresh-faced façade of a place called Big Friends Bigger Hearts in downtown and did not think, *Hell yes! Let's party!* The one labeled Zane Winters, CEO of Big Friends Bigger Hearts looked like an actual athlete. "What is he, like, a pro football player or something? Why is his jaw so wide? Why is he so hot?"

Peace was humble. "His heart is a magnificent thing to behold. I really like him. And yes, he's retired from the NFL for a few years now, and he is friends with—"

"Are. You. *Fucking*. Kidding me?!" Vega had been giving Peace a mental high-five on her new guy friend while using her facial recognition overlay to review the names and data dumps for every other person in the photo. "Your date, Peace, is friends with the man known as Ho'o Kaho'okalakupua?" Hoyt "Ho'o" Kaho'okalakupua. Tech billionaire. Founder of Hoyt Security. And egotistical maniac.

Peace clapped, her expression simultaneously hopeful and optimistic. Wringing her hands as if squeezing her excess excitement out of them, she said, "He's a major investor and close friend of Zane's from their football days. They, the two of them, go all the way back to college."

Vega breathed out and looked back to the screen. Hoyt was built like he could step back onto the field at a moment's notice. The sharp cut of his open-collared white shirt beneath a gray linen suit jacket, the kind that financiers preferred, would have left an average white tech nerd looking simultaneously wan and sickly and trying too hard, but the broad-chested, 253-pound former All-American tight end from Maui, so said the stats that were still rolling by on her monitor, still looked like a champ. Tan, proud, and smart as fuck, Hoyt had earned a reputation for creating an unhackable security system, which he kept unhackable with the double team of tech brainiacs he employed. One team to break it in-house, another to fix it.

Their constant stress testing had proved out its name: Titan's Wall.

The tech security community knew that Titan's Wall cost a mint to even attempt a breach. As in, enough money to buy an army of bots, a team of university experts, and somewhere to store the million-dollar cash prize that that egotistical maniac put on any person who could hack it. Hence why that amber-eyed towering giant had a billion dollars of net worth. Add that to his reputation as a powerhouse on the NFL field, and he was handshaking every pharma and energy bro from here to Brussels.

"Fuck," Vega whispered, taking in his gaze that said he was amused, even though his mouth wasn't smiling. He seemed genuinely happy in the photo, but she'd bet her tech that when it was game on, that gaze went sharp and calculating. She shouldn't bet; she was trying not to do that anymore.

Cindy brought her back to the apartment. "So, will you come?"

Vega had the itch to have a go at it. Titan's never came up as a wall she had to scale—her clients weren't that high up. The prospect of going up against him... Vega knew it would be delicious. In person? It could be mind-bending. So many technology bros graduated with a BS, sometimes figuratively too, in business finance. They may, *may*, know the ins and outs of revenue and sustained growth on a spreadsheet, but they left the in-the-trenches engineering to their top dogs. They knew fuck-all about the minutia of their own tech. Or the ones who had been young-pup developers too often got sloppy as the years passed. Sure, this football god looked like he was better at the fifty-yard dash than C++, but his work was supposedly legit. That he kept his code as tight as Peace's dress by still having a steady hand in the game. Vega wanted to find out more about those rumors and those hands. Did he keep his skills as a developer as tight as he obviously did his body?

"I tell you what," Vega said to her friends, "if I can't hack into just one of his personal devices, I'll go. If I can, he's just another pretty face." Vega knew Titan's Wall would have all business phones locked down tight. But the odds that his personal cell did? His first cell? Hell yes. Second? Maybe, but new phones required updates to Titan's Wall to be compatible with the new firmware, and she was sure by phone five, he had said fuck it trying to make his kit compatible. Titan's Wall was geared for corporate data centers, and he had better things to do.

"No, wait, Vee, that sounds like a bet." Cindy called her out.

"Think of it more like a litmus test."

She started three of her homemade programs to find his devices: Hunter, Seek n Find, and Sing. Hunter was as it was titled, a hunting application that combed through social media and communications from the IP address of Hoyt Securities. Seek n Find was the program she used to get stats on the board of directors, and Sing was the app baby Vega was most proud of. Another stellar program that used the cell phone tower data of every smart device in use to triangulate where someone in particular was located using voice recognition.

She'd track him using voice prints taken off his voicemail and YouTube TED Talks.

From next to her, Peace asked, "Is any of what you're doing legal, Vee?"

"Legal in what sense?" Vega asked absently as her heart rate kicked up at the potential of engaging a man like Hoyt Kahoʻokalakupua. For the first time in a year she began to feel genuine excitement glow deep inside.

Cindy looked worried at the green code flying up on the three programing windows Vega had open. "Instead of walking up to him digitally, come with us and talk to him in person. Let's keep it light, Vee. Don't go deep."

Vega swatted at Cindy's hands as they tried to grab her arm, a bit of a trick in her overlarge hoodie. "Nope, if he's a dunce, I don't wanna go. It's too much work to get pissed off over nothing."

"But what if you have fun anyway? You'll have a good conversation with someone, some dancing, with us at least, and maybe even some anonymous make-out session—then back to work tomorrow all refreshed."

"I just want to know if he's gone soft— Got him," she said, and both women leaned in.

"Where? There's only all that coding stuff."

"He's at Festivál already, which, let's face it, I probably didn't need Hunter and Seek n Find for that. Now, let's watch what happens when you get to be a billionaire: you lose focus on the little things." From within that glow that had begun, Vega hoped she was wrong.

Cindy, voice low in agent mode and full of confidence, said, "How about I hit your closet and get you something to wear."

Vega didn't hear her as she plowed through the three app's results. She found his personal device and its firewall, like any good tech, but this one wasn't strictly Titan's Wall. It was, and it wasn't. It was dynamic, not just an impenetrable surface like classic Titan's Wall, but rather, fail to guess the riddles three, the application's programming interface protection key triggered a defense she'd never seen before. It went on the offensive, collecting user data.

"Shit," Vega muttered as she started a slew of her own defenses, allowing her to stay at his wall anonymously. Then under the barrage of thousands of bot-bees, she fired up a basic hack of coming at the firewall in an attempt to force his device to route her to a denial-of-service error path. Then she hoped the engineers were lazy and didn't lock the error path door, leaving her uninhibited access to his device. Only, it wasn't some random device; this was Hoyt of Hoyt Security, and her defense programs were logging data hitting *her* firewall. They were holding; he'd have no idea who attempted the breach as long as she could hold him off long enough for her secondary systems to boot. She swallowed a tickle of apprehension at the out-of-the-gate aggression. Then smiled. "He's good."

Cindy was back in front of her, something glittering in her hands. "Excellent. Time to get dressed."

✻✻✻

Continue reading *Flux* in ebook or paperback at Amazon.com.

www.ingramcontent.com/pod-product-compliance
Lightning Source LLC
Chambersburg PA
CBHW020913130726
47904CB00006BA/1900